KIM O'BRIEN

secrets can be deadly and the truth can cut...

BONE
DEEP

Spencer Hill Contemporary

This book is a work of fiction. Names, characters, places, and incidents are products of the author's imagination or are used fictitiously. Any resemblance to actual events, locales, or persons, living or dead, is entirely coincidental.

Contact: Spencer Hill Contemporary, an imprint of Spencer Hill Press
27 West 20th Street, Suite 1102
New York, NY 10011, USA

Please visit our website at www.spencerhillcontemporary.com

First Edition: May 2015
Kim O'Brien
Bone Deep/by Kim O'Brien—1st ed.
p. cm.

Summary: When a teen girl must visit her father for the summer, things look up when she meets two hot young men, but take a turn for the worse when her best friend vanishes.

The author acknowledges the copyrighted or trademarked status and trademark owners of the following wordmarks mentioned in this fiction: Amazon, AP/Advanced Placement, Barbie, Bing, Cheerios, CNN, Coke, Columbia University, Diet Coke, Domino's, Doritos, Dr. Pepper, Dr. Seuss, Expedition, Google, Harvard, Home Depot, Honey Nut Cheerios, Igloo, Indiana Jones, Ivy League, Jack in the Box, Jeep, JELL-O, Jimmy Eat World, Kool-Aid, Life Flight, Listerine, Marriott, Neosporin, Nike, Pendleton, Popsicle, Pottery Barn, Princeton University, Prius, PSAT, Red Sox, Rutgers, SAT, Scope, Skittles, Snow White, Starbucks, Stouffer's, Tide, Timex, Tropicana, Urban Outfitters, Velcro, Vera Bradley, Vick's VapoRub, Victoria's Secret, Walmart, Weber, Wrangler, Yamaha (keyboard), Yankees

Cover design by Christa Holland (Paper & Sage Design)
Interior layout by Errick A. Nunnally

978-1-63392-002-6 (paperback)
978-1-63392-003-3 (e-book)

Printed in the United States of America

BONE DEEP

KIM O'BRIEN

For my family—near and far—I love you all.
We may march to a different beat, but I know
we will always be there for each other.

ONE

Paige

When I was a little girl, I loved playing hide-and-seek in the earthy hollows of pit houses and dark crannies of the rock caves where ancient American Indians once lived. I knew my father was fascinated with these places and that he liked finding things. I liked him finding me.

Later, I wanted to be like him. I spent hours beneath a blazing desert sun carefully excavating my Barbies from their shallow graves in the dry, clay earth. I even dismembered a few to make their plastic limbs more like bones that could be painstakingly cleaned and pieced together.

I believed the stories my father told in the light of the campfire, about the people whose ruins he restored. I remember the smell of smoke in the night as he talked about the existence of multiple worlds and how people traveled through them and became transformed along the journey. Somehow, I always imagined these worlds separated by a curtain as thick and black as the ones on our elementary school stage. The ones actors used to exit the stage, but sometimes couldn't find the overlap and spent long seconds desperately groping the material before they finally managed to vanish.

A year ago, the curtains in my life parted a little, and I saw into a world that existed between my parents—a world defined by whispers as sharp as broken glass and the doors that slammed like shouts. I learned what a marriage looked like when two people hated each other enough to methodically shatter their world—and me in the process.

I had thought it was always better to know the truth.

I was wrong.

"She's something, isn't she?" My father mops his face with a bandanna. The armpits of his green, official park shirt are ringed with sweat.

We are standing at the base of the ruins of an ancient Native American dwelling built into a limestone cliff. It has taken us about a half-hour to climb the ladders to get up here, and both of us are soaked with sweat and slightly out of breath. There's not even a puff of wind, and the sun on my shoulders feels hotter than the lasers we created with magnifying glasses in Mr. Zimmerman's pre-AP physics class.

"She?" I lift my brows and ignore the deeper lines around his eyes that weren't there six months ago. He's thinner now, and more deeply tanned than I have ever seen him.

"If a ship can be feminine, so can these ruins." He adjusts a battered Indiana Jones-style hat on his sweat-stained head. "So what do you think, honey? Was it worth the climb?"

"Sure, Dad."

He tries to read my face to see if I'm being sarcastic, but my sunglasses hide my eyes. After a moment, his gaze returns to the cracked plaster walls. The custody arrangement says I have to spend the summer in Arizona with him. It doesn't say I have to like it.

"This is where it happened, Paige." My father walks toward the ruins. They remind me of a giant sandcastle, which are doomed things to begin with. This one, with its thick masonry walls and empty, blackened windows, is no exception.

"Hundreds of prehistoric American Indians—an entire civilization—disappeared. They left so suddenly that there was still food on the table. To this day, no one knows what happened."

His voice lowers, and he gestures to the ruins. "Think about it. The people here invested hundreds of years in this place, building these homes, learning how to farm the desert, and then, overnight, they vanished."

The irony of what he's just said makes me laugh. I mean, it's so exactly what he did to me and Mom. He pretty much disappeared.

He frowns. "What's so funny?"

My father—the famous archaeologist—doesn't see it, just doesn't get it. And so I let my face go blank and say, "Nothing."

He takes a swig of water from a canteen, wipes his mouth with the back of his hand, and then shakes his head as if I am impossible to understand.

The truth is that he could make the connection if he tried. But that's the problem. He wants to pretend that everything between us is okay. To admit something is wrong might mean he'd have to do something about it.

"Come on," he says, "I'll show you around."

He leads me into the ruins through a T-shaped entranceway so narrow he has to turn sideways to get inside. Small bits of sticks and mud poke out of the plaster walls like plants desperately trying to grow in bad soil.

The chamber inside is much smaller, darker than I imagined. The walls are blackened like the inside of a chimney, and they smell smoky.

"Careful, Paige," my father warns, pointing out a hole in the floor the size of a manhole. When I peer into the dark opening, I see the pale stubs of a ladder reaching up like a pair of hands.

"What's down there?"

"Another chamber. I'll show it to you another time."

He gestures me forward to the ladder leaning at a sharp angle against the blackened wall and then pauses to show me traces of fingerprints. They look fragile, like smudges of breath on a bathroom mirror. As I move closer to inspect them, my father places a hand on my shoulder.

"Careful. The oils from your skin…"

"…could damage them. I know." I twist out of his touch.

Part of me wants to remind him that I could read a petroglyph before I could read Dr. Seuss's *The Cat in the Hat*. He's forgotten this, however, and I don't know which is worse. That he doesn't remember who I was or that he has no idea of who I am.

The third level is as dark and gloomy as the second. We enter through a hole in the floor about two feet deep and weave our way through a narrow, stone corridor with a wooden plank floor and a rusted handrail bolted to the limestone wall.

The handrails, my father explains, were installed in the first half of the twentieth century when the ruins were open to the public. He strokes the blackened railing. "We're going to take all those out and restore this girl to her original glory."

His face has a dreamy expression, as if he's imagining what these soot-blackened rooms will look like when he's finished. I want to tell him that these dark, abandoned ruins will always be empty. And no matter what traces of the present he removes, it won't change that the people who lived here are gone and he can't bring them back.

My father prompts me forward, and we retreat into the shadows of small, low-ceilinged rooms filled with odd assortments of crude stone tables and broken pieces of pottery scattered about like rejects at a tag sale.

We climb higher, through another dark hole scabby with stones and even narrower than the others. The fourth level of the dwelling is a cavernous room that extends well back into the deepening shadows. The high ceiling is as sharp and jagged as coral. The side walls are scraped smooth.

Voices drift toward us. In the soft glow of lantern light, I see people clustered along the back wall. There are two distinct groups. One consists of Native Americans dressed in beat-up, baggy jeans and plaster-splattered T-shirts; the other group wears tan shorts and green park polos like my father's.

The voices and work stop as my father and I get closer. "Hey, everyone," he says, and then puts his arm around me. "I want you to meet my daughter, Paige."

All eyes turn to me. My muscles go tight as he squeezes my shoulder as if he cares about me. As if today is not the first time I've seen him in six months. As if everything between us is okay. I want to shrug off his arm, but I don't. I guess it's okay to hate your father but not want to embarrass him.

"Your father has told us so much about you," a tall, massively built man with long black hair and a face that looks chiseled from stone extends his hand.

"This is my foreman, John Yazzi," my father says and releases me so I can shake hands.

The next person I meet is a short, muscular man with a broken front tooth and an impossibly thin braid that hangs to the middle of his back. His deeply calloused palms make his skin feel like leather. "Welcome. I am Jacob Begay." His voice carries a Southwestern cadence.

"And this is Jalen," my father continues. "John's son."

He's tall, not quite as tall as his father, but enough so that my head comes only to his shoulder. He's about my age, with deep-set black eyes, light-brown skin, and shiny black hair tied in a ponytail. His cheekbones are high, his nose straight, and his lips so full and perfect it's hard not to stare, but my father already has gone on with the introductions. I shake the hand of another dark-haired boy without ever hearing his name.

My father continues introducing me, but their names slip past me. I steal another glimpse of Jalen and feel the sudden heat in my face when he catches me.

"And this is someone who doesn't need an introduction," my father says. Even without seeing his face, I hear the triumph in his voice.

My heart stops as a tall, deeply tanned blonde wearing a sage-green Arizona SciTech tank and a pair of black Nike shorts steps forward.

"Hi, Paige," she says, smiling.

A rush of joy shoots through me, followed by a stab of something else. She is part of every happy childhood memory I have and some that I've worked hard to forget. For a moment all I can do is stand there staring. And then, as the silence turns awkward, I say, "Emily?"

TWO

Paige

Emily steps forward and hugs me hard. "I know," she says, "isn't this crazy?"

We look at each other. She's much taller than me now, and the small gap between her front teeth is gone. Her thick blonde braid, and those green eyes with the gold speckles, are exactly the same. She's curvy now, and it feels weird to hug her.

"I can't believe you're here. Why didn't you guys tell me?"

Emily exchanges a sideways glance with my father. "We wanted to surprise you."

"I almost blew it when you asked about her last night," my father admits.

"You said I might run into her, but..." I shake my head, trying to decide if I am happy or angry that they've blindsided me. I clench my hands into fists and will my face to go blank.

Emily sees me struggle, and her face softens. "Oh, Paige," she murmurs. "I'm so happy to see you, too."

My father chuckles. "I thought you'd be pleased." He turns to Emily. "Why don't you take a break? I'm sure you and Paige have a lot of catching up to do."

"Thanks, Dr. Duke." Emily pushes a strand of hair behind her ear. "Let's go before he changes his mind." She slants a grin at my dad. "He's a total slave driver."

My dad rolls his eyes as Emily grabs my hand, urging me to hurry. I follow her down the ladder and through the dark passages to a small recess in the wall in one of the chambers on the third floor. The nook is so cleverly designed that it blends perfectly, almost invisible. At one time, I suppose it was a sleeping chamber.

"We can talk here." Emily presses herself deep into the crevice. It's small and barely fits the two of us. "So you were surprised. I wasn't sure your dad was going to be able to keep it secret. He's been really excited about you coming."

I lean back against the wall, remembering how he'd tried to hug me back at the airport and the conversations I've shut down. I know he's trying, but it doesn't make up for what he did.

"I was surprised," I admit. "You're, like, a foot taller."

She laughs. "My parents were beginning to wonder if I was ever going to stop growing. Fortunately, five-foot-ten was the magic number."

It gives her four inches of height over me, making her somehow seem older, although she's seventeen, the same age as me.

"So you're interning for my father?"

Emily nods. A pleased, slightly shy smile crosses her face. "I'm blogging for the park website. I'm so excited about it—and it's all because of your dad. Technically I'm underage, but your dad talked Dr. Shum into making an exception."

Oh. So that's why she's here. It makes sense. My father and Emily's are best friends. Dr. Linton works for Arizona SciTech, and he pretty much got my father this job—a fact that makes my mother hate him and his name unspeakable in our house. To thank Dr. Linton, my dad probably pulled some strings for Emily. I wonder if Emily knows, and if she does, if it matters to her.

I realize I've been silent too long. "So, you blog. You were always a good writer."

"But you've always had the better imagination."

I wrinkle my nose and try not to think just where my great imagination led us. "Not really," I tell her.

She smiles, draws her knees closer to her chest. "Well, fortunately I don't have to make anything up. I basically interview people and then blog about it. As long as it makes the park look good, I can write anything." Her face lights up. "The ruins are so cool—you'll like it here, Paige. I know it."

"I don't know. I'm still at the 'Paige-don't-touch-anything' stage."

She laughs. "He'll soften—I know he will. And then he'll probably assign you to one of the research projects. The grad students are studying everything from the DNA in bat guano to…" She pauses to use her fingers like quotation marks. "A palynological interpretation of plant utilization."

"Wow," I say in a tone of voice that means the exact opposite. "I can hardly wait."

Emily studies my face. "I know your parents' divorce totally sucked. I'm sorry. I was going to email you, but I didn't know what to say. It'd been so long. And then, when I knew you were coming here, I was afraid I'd give away the surprise. You *are* happy to see me, aren't you?"

A note of doubt creeps into her voice, and I realize that I don't want to put her in the middle of the war between me and my father. Besides, under the jet lag, the fatigue, and the stress of being around him, I *am* happy to see her.

"Of course I'm happy." I give her a smile, my first real one since I arrived. "I just don't want to talk about the divorce." But inside, I can't help but wonder what my father told her. If, in his version, he's the hero, and my mother was the villain who was always complaining about his hours at Rutgers, the family dinners he missed, the female students who always clustered after hours in his office.

"You don't have to talk about it, but if you ever want to, I'll listen."

"Thanks."

She leans forward a little so our shoulders touch. "Tell me everything. Tell me about New Jersey."

I'm telling her about the Round Rock Crusaders, my high school soccer team (which lost every game last season), when my father and another man step into view. They don't even glance in our direction; we're probably lost in the shadows. Emily and I look at each other and wordlessly press ourselves deeper into the crevice.

"The 3-D images from Chamber 17 are amazing," the other man says. He's lean, muscular, about my father's age, and wearing the same green polo shirt and tan shorts. "Duke, you can see right into the wall…"

"Who is that?" I whisper.

"Dr. Raymund Shum," Emily says so softly I can barely hear her. "Your father's boss and the head of this whole thing."

"I'd love to see them, Ray," my father says. "Do you have all the pictures you need before we start removing the railing?"

Dr. Shum nods. "Yes, and Julia's coming along on the backdrops for the exhibit. One thing—when you expose the plaster, make sure you take samples from the holes. Better yet, I want to be there. We may even be able to bore a little more deeply into the limestone."

The conversation turns geological, something that I once might have found interesting, but now couldn't care less about. More important is the opportunity to study my father without him knowing it.

There's something different about him, more than the weight he's lost or the dark tan. There's a looseness about his body posture, an easy way he's standing as if he's more comfortable in these broken ruins than he ever was in our house. He laughs at something Dr. Shum says, and I realize it's been a long time since I heard that sound.

I turn to ask Emily what was so funny and catch her watching the two men. Her eyes have an intent, almost hungry expression. When she realizes I'm staring at her, the look in her eyes vanishes so completely that I wonder if I've imagined it.

THREE

Paige

My father lives in a small, one-story stucco house with the same flat, red roofline as every other house on his street. Two giant, spiky cactus plants grow out of a bed of pebbles in the front yard, and two empty terra-cotta planters flank the wood-and-glass front door.

"You hungry?" he asks as we step into the air-conditioning. He drops his keys next to a pile of mail stacked on a table that consists of three unopened moving boxes.

"I need to shower first."

What I need most is to avoid my father.

"Sure." He sets his hat on a hook on the back of the front door. "I'll start dinner. You want hotdogs or frozen pizza?"

For a moment I think he's joking and then realize he isn't. My mother always did the cooking. With a sudden pang of longing, I think of her marinated chicken and pasta dish. Suddenly I understand my dad's new, leaner look. "Pizza."

There's no lock on my bedroom door, but I shut it with a definite *click*. The room is like walking into the pages of a Pottery Barn catalog. My dad basically went for it, and although I'd never tell him, I've always wanted a room like this.

On the back wall, there's a white vanity flanked between two towers that have hooks and cubbies for every kind of accessory. A brightly colored quilt covers the twin bed, which has hot pink sheets and pillows in four different shapes.

My room is the only fully decorated one in the house. Apparently guilt, especially divorce guilt, has a price tag.

Kicking my sneakers off, I head into the bathroom. I peel back the straps of my tank top and catch a glimpse in the mirror of a fairly good sunburn on my shoulders. For some reason, it makes me happy, as if finally the outside of me is as painful as the inside.

Dinner is awkward. My father doesn't have a kitchen table, so we eat in the living room on the smelly green velveteen couch that used to be in our basement. After a feeble attempt to discuss the great surprise of Emily and a long monologue on Dr. Shum's exciting 3-D computer model of the ruins, he abandons the conversation effort and turns on CNN. Occasionally, he asks my opinion, and I reply in monosyllables. I think we're both relieved when I retreat to my room.

Settling myself on top of the quilt, which according to the Pottery Barn website is ironically called "Peace Patchwork" and costs nearly two hundred dollars, I log onto Connections. The first thing I see is a connect request from Emily Linton. I accept it and then check out her page. Her status says, "So excited my BF is finally here!"

I scroll through a few of her conversations. Most are from friends I've never heard of, and it makes me feel sad that we've fallen so out of touch. I spend a lot of time looking at Emily's photos. Most have been taken at the park, and the ruins, miniaturized by the massive cliffs, show in the background.

In one shot, Emily has her arm around my father and a wide smile on her face. I study this shot the longest. Both of them are tanned and blond and wearing green park shirts. I think Emily looks more like his daughter than I do.

By the time I log off, it's late and the house is totally quiet. I think about calling my mom, but can't bring myself to do it. The conversation will turn to how much she misses me, and I'll end up comforting her instead of the other way around.

I love her, but I'm also mad at her.

Last fall, she could have fought harder for me. She could have given up the Yamaha piano and set of sterling flatware and maybe gotten more of me. Instead, she gave my summers to him, even though it wasn't what I wanted. When I tried to talk to her, she simply said, "Please, Paige, you're just making things harder."

Slipping out of the room, I feel my way silently down the dark hallway, avoiding the edges of the framed artwork, still wrapped in brown moving paper, which lean against wall. The lights in my father's bedroom door are off, but a small beacon shines from the kitchen.

I open the refrigerator and peer in. There's a gallon of skim milk, a carton of orange juice, jars of some random condiments, a package of hotdogs, and several takeout containers.

I systematically go through every drawer and every cabinet. I'm careful not to clang the silverware or rustle the plastic grocery bags stuffed beneath the sink. I note the brand of cereal and the kind of coffee he drinks. I hold a half-empty salt shaker to the light and see the tiny grains of rice mixed inside—my mother's trick to keep the salt from clumping. I read the ingredients on an unopened bottle of Blue Desert Barbeque sauce and drink from the plastic jug of Tropicana orange juice. I smell his dish towels to see if they smell like Tide (they don't) and sample a semi-stale chip from an opened bag of Doritos.

None of these things give me the answers I want, but then again, I'm not quite sure what I'm looking for anyway. After a while, I pad silently back to my Pottery Barn room and slip beneath the covers of the guilt quilt.

Staring at the dark ceiling, I promise myself that if things don't get better, I'll steal my father's credit card and book a flight back to New Jersey. I'll hitchhike to the airport if I have to.

It doesn't help to know that I can probably get myself to the airport and maybe even to New Jersey, but it doesn't mean I belong there, either.

FOUR

Paige

Emily Linton was not always my best friend. I was five years old when we met. My father was finishing up his PhD and working on a restoration project in New Mexico. Our parents introduced us, and even though Emily was nice to me, I knew she was just being polite. Mostly she was friends with the Navajo kids whose parents worked for my father. Emily had spent a year on the Navajo Nation and had even gone to a school there.

I was homeschooled by my mother, but it was my father's lessons that I craved. I was pretty proud of the fact that I could read petrogylphs and glue together the pieces of pottery that my father rejected. Before Emily, I was the child prodigy. I liked adults admiring my long, black hair, commenting on my pale blue eyes, and praising my archeological abilities.

I couldn't compete against Emily Linton. I couldn't speak *Diné Bizaad*. I wasn't as pretty or smart or popular. It sounds stupid now, but back then I feared my father wished that Emily was *his* daughter. I thought he loved me less because of her.

I gave myself up to daydreams and built elaborate fantasy worlds in which I was popular. I changed my name from Paige Patterson to Kylila Unitas and pretended it meant "girl with the yellow hair." It didn't matter that my hair was black—Emily's was blonde and that's what I wanted.

One morning I was excavating my favorite Barbie—Birthday Barbie, to be exact—from a shallow grave near the well where my father was studying an old burial ground. I was curious to see what Barbie would look like after being buried for a whole day—the longest I had ever let her spend in the ground. I wondered if she would turn leathery, like the remains my father found, and was happily in the process of digging her up when Emily Linton wandered up to me.

She peered over my shoulder. "What are you doing?"

I kept working and did not look up. When archeologists are about to uncover an important find, they do not let themselves get distracted. I kept slowly digging, ignoring her, like the way my father ignored me when he was working. My pulse jumped a little when I brushed the dirt off the face of my Barbie and her unblinking blue eyes stared back at me.

"Look," I said. "It's the bones of an ancient Anassie Indian. I've never seen a body so well-preserved. We'll need a tarp to cover the site."

I looked up, hoping she'd be impressed that I'd practically quoted my father about the tarp, but her arms were crossed and a smirk twisted her pink lips.

"It's not Anassie," she said. "It's Anasay-zi. And you've buried her all wrong. Her hair is braided when it should be loose on her shoulders. And she should be in a squatting position, not lying down. And she should be wrapped in a blanket, not wearing an evening dress."

My cheeks burned. I'd kept Birthday Barbie's hair braided so it wouldn't get ruined in the dirt. I wanted to argue that Emily was wrong about the hair and everything else, but I knew she wasn't.

Sitting back on my heels, I looked her in the eye. "Well," I said. "That would be true if this were an ordinary Anasay-zi, but this is an *Anassie* Indian princess, which is a tribe much older than the *Anasay-zi*. They buried her this way because she's not really dead. Her step-mother put a spell on her, and when the Indian prince kisses her, she'll wake up."

It was an obvious steal from Snow White and I was old enough to know that it'd be embarrassing if she called me on it. But Emily's eyes lit up like I'd said something really interesting and then she sat down next to me, so close our shoulders touched.

"I think the prince should have a prayer stick and a ceremony if he's going to bring her back from the spirit world." And then she very casually added, "I could make one if you want."

Part of me wanted to ask about the Navajo kids and why she didn't want to play with them. But a bigger part swelled with pride because she wanted to play with me—me, Paige Patterson, whose hair was black, not blonde, and who had strange, light blue eyes ringed with even weirder dark blue rims.

"Okay," I said and then honesty forced me to admit, "but we're going to need to make a prince, too."

She smiled. "No problem. We can make one out of grass."

"Okay," I said.

"There's a secret place I know," Emily said, "where the grass grows taller than anywhere else. Want to see it?"

I wasn't allowed to be out of sight of my parents, but when I looked over, they were with Emily's parents, examining a grave they'd found near the water. I knew they wouldn't notice if I was gone for a little while. Part of me was scared to break the rules, but another part of me knew that, no matter what the punishment was, it would be worth it.

"Come on," Emily urged, and together we ran into the field of tall grass that grew out from the edge of the water.

In the morning, Emily takes me on a room-by-room tour of the ruins. Although yesterday I acted like I couldn't care less when my father led me through the dark, soot-coated rooms, today with Emily as my guide, I can't help but be fascinated. Can't keep from staring at the charred remains of a fire pit and wondering about the family who lived here. Did they fight a lot or laugh? Did they fear the coming of night? Was there ever a girl like me standing in this same spot who wished she was anywhere else?

Emily walks up to me. "You look so serious. What were you thinking?"

Today she's straightened her hair, and it falls in a long, yellow ponytail with a razor-cut edge. She's wearing a lot of dark eyeliner and mascara. I almost smile thinking about how we used to barely comb our hair when we were kids. How we swapped clothing, even though hers was too big for me.

"I was thinking that it's weird how everyone who lived here just vanished. And no one knows why. It's sad."

Emily shakes her head. "I thought that at first, too—I kept wondering what happened to them. But then I started to see these ruins for what they are—a window into the past. Everything here tells a story. We're learning so much, Paige. We're going to find out what made them leave and where they went."

I think about my father—the clues he left behind—the few pens, pencils, and paperclips rattling around his desk and the nail holes where the pictures used to hang in his office. "Who cares what happened? They're gone."

"Who's gone?" a male voice says. We walk around the dividing wall and see one of my father's interns—the blond with the crew cut—squatting by the stone and plaster base. He has a net in one hand and a specimen jar in the other.

"Dale, you were eavesdropping," Emily says, smiling despite the note of accusation in her voice.

"If I were eavesdropping," he replies, returning the smile, "I wouldn't have asked a question."

"Yes, you would. Just so it wouldn't look like you were eavesdropping." Emily turns to me. "He's smart but warped." From the smile she gives me, however, warped doesn't seem like a bad thing.

"Not warped. Curious." His blue eyes turn to me. "Emily has been telling me all about you."

"Like what?"

"Stories about when you were kids."

I give Emily a sharp, sideways look. "What stories?"

Emily laughs. "Only the good stuff, Paige, like how good you were at excavation work. How you could look at a site and start making up all sorts of stories about the people who used to live there."

She holds my gaze a moment longer. Long enough for me to see that she hasn't forgotten the other stuff we did, the stuff we'd promised each other never to tell anyone else.

"Already flirting with her, Dale?" Another of my father's interns walks over to us. He's average height, with straight, dark hair and a lean, intellectual-looking face. "Don't believe a word he says—unless you give him a math problem." He extends a narrow, long-fingered hand to me. "Jeremy Brown," he says. As his grip lingers on mine, he adds, "We met yesterday."

I remember him. Dark, deep-set eyes, straight nose, and longish bangs that flop forward.

"Don't you have some wall you need to be studying?" Dale asks.

Jeremy's smile widens. "Better to study walls than bugs."

"It's their research projects," Emily says. "Dale is comparing the DNA he extracts from the beetles he finds in the ruins with the DNA of ancient beetles."

She starts to explain the focus of Dale's study, but behind her, in the distance, I see Jalen Yazzi coming into view. He's wearing another stretched-out, plaster-splattered T-shirt and a pair of loose basketball shorts. On his wide shoulders, he carries a barrel-shaped, red Igloo cooler, and between it and his height, he's almost too tall for the low ceiling. Yet he walks smoothly, gracefully maneuvering around the broken divider walls.

I try not to stare, but he's beautiful in a way that makes it nearly impossible not to. He gets within a few feet, and I feel my heart beat faster. I keep my gaze on him, but he walks right past.

I know he saw me, even if he didn't acknowledge me. Wiping the sweat from my brow, I wonder how obvious I was, if he guessed that I think he's hot, and I know that I was probably embarrassingly obvious. What was I thinking? I vow never to even look in his direction again. It must have been jet lag or I never would have acted like such an idiot.

Emily touches my arm and laughs. Fortunately she seems to have missed the whole thing. I quickly laugh too, but I have no idea why.

I try to put the whole thing behind me and focus on all the cool stuff in the ruins—the chamber where the skeleton of a child was buried in the wall and the petroglyphs carved in the stones.

I do a pretty good job of not thinking about Jalen until we break at noon. Emily and I retrieve our lunches from our backpacks. When I put my water bottle to my lips, it's full and the water is cold—way colder than it should be. I drink it in greedy gulps, and it slides down my throat in a long, cool stream.

I think of the Igloo cooler balanced on Jalen's shoulder. Did he refill my water bottle? If so, why?

FIVE

Paige

"Dale and Jeremy both like you," Emily states a few days later. "You should pick one and put them out of their misery."

Today she's taking me to see Tacoma Well, which—after the ruins in the cliffs—is the park's biggest tourist attraction, about a mile from the information center. The path, lined in small stones, is barely wide enough for us both and completely shadeless. Although it's barely nine o'clock in the morning, the sun is already blistering; it feels like heat is growing out of the ground like an invisible crop. I'm quickly coated in sweat and dust.

"I don't think they're exactly in misery," I tell her. "I just met them."

"I know," Emily replies, "but you should have some fun this summer. I want you to like it here. Dale is better-looking, but Jeremy has the brains."

I study the ground in front of us. As kids, we would never have stayed between the lines of a defined path. I almost want to kick some of the stones out of the way.

"Look, I'm not dating *either* of them. Besides, I'm already having fun." I say it in such a purposely morose tone that Emily laughs and pushes my shoulder.

"You'll like it here," Emily promises. "And you're right. You don't need either of those guys. It's going to be you and me—just like the old times."

I give her a quick, sideways glance. Is she going to talk about what happened? Do I even want her to?

"Look," she says, "we're here."

Tacoma Well is an enormous, round sinkhole filled by an underground spring with water the color of green JELL-O. The stones lining the well are rough, jagged, and porous-looking. It takes me a few minutes, but then I realize some of the black spots between the stones are not just gaps, but small caves.

"Hold on," I say as Emily starts to climb down past the rim. Pulling out my cell, I begin snapping pictures.

Emily strikes a pose, pretending to be falling over the edge. I snap the shot and then a couple more of her. We take some together, too—crazy ones that sometimes cut parts of our heads out of the photo because I hold out my arm and shoot without looking where I'm focusing.

Afterward, we climb down into the well. The pitch is steep, and the only sound is the shuffle of our hiking boots on the stone. It's so easy to feel time slipping away, that Emily and I are ten years old again and exploring, something that feels comfortably familiar and yet totally strange, as if I have dreamed the last seven years of my life.

We climb down several levels of semi-collapsed cliff dwellings. The blackened, caved-in openings seem more suited for giant bees than as the homes of prehistoric American Indians.

We're not the first people to hike down here. There's all sorts of graffiti cut into the rock, some even dating back to the 1800s. I bet it ticks my dad off to see it, and this makes me smile.

We spend the next couple of hours exploring some of the larger caves. Most of them are too collapsed to go into, but there's one large enough for us to crawl partially inside. Once we're sure there aren't any snakes or scorpions, we lie on our bellies in the shade and hang out, talking about everything and nothing.

When we were little, we used to do this a lot. I always thought that first impressions were the strongest—that the first breath of air, the first time you stepped inside an old pit house or a cliff dwelling, physically did something to you. The scent entered your body and brought the traces of whoever lived there to life. At least that's what I used to tell Emily and how every game began.

Of course, now I know that it was just my imagination, but back then it was so easy to believe it was something more. That Emily and I weren't playing house as much as we were reliving parts of the lives of the people who had lived there. In our fantasies, we were sister-maidens living out the mythology of the stories we heard our fathers tell us as we sat around the campfire every night.

Back then it felt so good to have a sister—even if it wasn't real. It doesn't justify the things we did, but maybe it explains what happens when the lines of what's real and what's fantasy get blurred.

On the way back from the well, I see Jalen emerging from a cluster of gnarled, small-leafed cottonwood trees growing out from around the banks of Otter Creek. He's with a thin, elderly man with a brown, wrinkled face the color of nutmeg and feathers braided into his graying black hair. Jalen carries a recyclable grocery bag in one hand, and a branch of cottonwood the width of my arm sticks out of the top.

"Hello," Emily says.

My gaze goes to the slight frown on Jalen's face and then returns to the fragile-looking man standing beside him.

"Who's that?" the man asks, looking straight at me.

Jalen's mouth tightens, and he steps closer to the older man. "That's Dr. Patterson's daughter. Come on, Uncle."

My cheeks burn. *Dr. Patterson's daughter.* He doesn't even remember my name. So much for hoping that he felt the same connection I did.

Jalen's uncle smiles at me. "She has pretty eyes," he says, smiling with almost childlike pleasure. "The blue corn maiden."

He's missing a tooth, and his hair is greasy. If I ran into him on the street, I'd think he was homeless, maybe mentally ill. But his eyes shine with intelligence, and despite his physical frailty, there's something solid and strong about him.

I can't help smiling back at him. "Thanks."

"Uncle," Jalen prompts. With one final glance, the older man allows Jalen to turn him in the direction of Otter Creek.

I stare at Jalen's back, feeling hurt and stupid for thinking maybe he was the one who'd filled my water bottle for me, that it was some kind of silent acknowledgment that he felt something for me. It's obvious now that my imagination is still capable of leading me into trouble.

"So that's why you don't want to go out with Dale or Jeremy," Emily teases as soon as they're out of earshot.

"Are you kidding me? He doesn't even know my name."

"He knows your name," Emily replies.

"Then why not say, 'This is Paige Patterson?'" I shake my head. "Not that it matters," I add the last part quickly and then firmly. "It's not like I care."

Emily laughs knowingly. "Yes, you do. You can't fight it, you know." She links her arm through mine. "Sometimes it just happens and there's nothing you can do about it except see where it leads."

"It's not going to lead anywhere. Seriously, Emily, you're making this all up. I don't like him."

But she isn't and we both know it. All these years have passed, and yet she still reads me so easily. I know suddenly that this is the test of a friendship. That time and distance don't matter. She's always been my best friend, and I should have fought harder to hold onto her. Instead, I listened when my mother said she was trouble.

Emily stops walking. "Ask him out," she urges. "You have to do it. You have to be the one to do it. You're the boss's daughter."

"Are you kidding? He doesn't like me, which is totally fine. I'm not interested in dating anyone."

"You say that," Emily says, "but even *you* don't believe it. Every relationship is a risk. Sometimes you just have to go for it."

I shake my head, but I think about Jalen, about how closely he walked beside his uncle as if he wanted to be able to catch him if he stumbled. What would it be like to have someone looking out for me? To care about me like that? I cross my arms and then release them angrily because I don't want there to be this deep ache inside me. And I especially don't want to rely on some guy to make it go away.

"No way I'm asking him out." I raise my brows. "I wouldn't go out with him if he begged me."

She rolls her eyes. "Paige," she says, teasing me in the way only a very old friend can get away with, "just who are you trying to fool? Stop dreaming and start living."

SIX

Paige

I don't ask Jalen out, but I fantasize about it. I imagine walking up to him, staring into those amazing dark eyes, and saying, *Hey, where's the nearest Starbucks?* And he smiles and says, *About a half-hour away. Why don't I take you?*

Of course the reality is that, if I asked him, he'd probably look tortured or give me directions without meeting my eyes. Emily wants me to go for it, but I have no intention of humiliating myself. Besides, what I told her is true. I'm really not looking for a relationship.

Still, as the days pass, my gaze keeps finding Jalen—on the other side of the ladders when I climb through the levels in the ruins, in a passageway, or walking by the river. We barely acknowledge each other, but his presence penetrates me anyway. Like heat or cold, he somehow gets inside me, but then we're past each other, he's gone, and all I feel is foolish.

On Saturday morning, the park stays closed as a *Diné* medicine man comes to perform a cleansing ceremony in the ruins. The purpose is to drive away any bad spirits before my father's restoration work. The ceremony is so private and so holy that, out of respect to the Navajos, nobody else is allowed near the cliffs.

I'm a little relieved because it means for the next several days there's very little chance I'll be running into Jalen. Instead, Emily and I stay in the information center and the blessed cool of the air-conditioning.

We spend most of Tuesday morning in the break room on our laptops. Emily blogs, and I spend way too much time composing a short email to my mom.

I'm sorry I haven't called. I always think about it at the wrong time.

(Lie. I've avoided calling her because I'm still mad at her). *I'm fine.* (Debatably a lie). *Guess what? Emily Linton is doing a summer internship here. Yesterday we hiked to Tacoma Well. More later, Paige*

I feel a little mean for mentioning Emily when I know it will upset her. But I'm justified. My mom sent me here. She has to deal with whatever happens.

Mid-morning, Emily and I buy some sodas and chips from the vending machines. And then, even though we're not supposed to eat in the museum section, we wander through the maze of exhibits.

We pass a wall of reddish-brown pottery—much of it broken—and turn a corner where some shelves house stone and animal-bone tools and weapons. Usually the exhibits are packed with tourists, so today, because of the medicine man, the park is empty and it feels like Emily and I have our own private gallery showing.

Pausing in front of a taxidermy display of desert animals, we stare at a doe who looks eternally frightened, and a tawny-colored coyote frozen in mid-trot. On the ground are smaller animals and reptiles. I squat to examine a coiled rattlesnake. Emily crouches next to me. Her breath is warm on my shoulder.

"Do you remember when we found that snake hole?"

Instantly I am nine years old and about to stick my hand into a round black opening in the earth. I remember how my heart pounded and my blood felt like hot acid in my veins. Emily sang and chanted as I knelt and then plunged my hand inside. The fear radiated in me, creating the power we believed was magical. That night, with the power still strong inside me, I dreamed of my grandfather, who had died when I was five. The last time I had seen him was in his bedroom in the nursing home, when my father took me to say goodbye. In my dream, his face floated above me, gaunt and colorless, watching me with a stern look. His lips did not move, but I heard his voice inside my head and he said the same thing he told me the last time I saw him. *The dark is coming.*

The way he'd said it sent chills down my spine, and I'd pinched myself hard enough to leave a bruise, hard enough to wake me if I were asleep. He was still there, floating like a horrible moon in the corner of the tent. The terror rose in me, and I'd cried out, loud enough to wake Emily, and she'd turned on the lantern.

Of course there was nothing to see, no ghostly head floating in the darkness, only Emily staring at me with wide eyes. When I told her what happened, however, she'd believed me. It seemed proof that fear could open doors to other worlds, that the greater the fear we produced in ourselves, the greater power it gave us to tap into those worlds. We did not recognize the essential truth about fear—that it exists for a reason. It warns you to turn back and stop whatever you're doing before it's too late.

"Girls," a woman's voice startles me so badly that my soda slops and I wipe my hand on my shorts.

Standing behind us is a tall, thin woman with very fair skin and reddish-blonde hair. She's wearing a pair of Bermuda shorts and a green silk blouse knotted at the waist. With her elfish features and long arms and legs, she looks a lot like Nicole Kidman, only older.

Emily jumps to her feet. "Mrs. Shum," she says, "we were just taking our snacks to the front of the building."

"Don't worry about it," she says. Her green eyes smile at me. "You're Paige, aren't you? Duke's daughter. Welcome. I'm Julia Shum, Dr. Shum's wife."

My father's boss's wife—instantly she's more interesting. Her nails are polished, her gold jewelry flawless, and her lipstick a shade of pink that my mother would say was too bright but then would secretly try to copy.

"Mrs. Shum is an artist," Emily explains. "You know that model in the front of the museum? Mrs. Shum made that."

I look at her with even more respect. "Seriously? It's amazing." It's a scaled-down version of the ruins, no longer crumbling and broken, but restored to what they would have looked like a thousand years ago, complete with tiny clay Native Americans climbing the ladders.

"Thank you." Mrs. Shum steeples her fingers and then places them over her lips as if she's hiding a secret. Her eyes sparkle. "I'm glad you liked it. Hopefully you'll like my newest exhibit. Would you like to see it?"

"Of course," Emily says, but when Mrs. Shum isn't looking, she rolls her eyes.

Mrs. Shum leads us through the pottery and weaponry exhibits and then stops in front of a pair of heavy, black curtains. "It doesn't look like much now, so you're going to have to use your imagination."

She pulls open the curtains, and we step inside an area partially framed with two-by-fours. The floor is cold, rough stone. Tools and bags of plaster lie scattered about.

"It's a backdrop," Mrs. Shum explains, "for the railings and plank ways that your father is extracting from the ruins. We're going to build an exhibit where people can actually see them—they'll be roped off, of course—but I'm going to recreate one of the passageways."

Vaguely, in the back of my mind, I remember my father saying something about some of the pieces going to research and others going to a museum, but I didn't realize it was this one.

"I'm going to texture the walls myself," Mrs. Shum adds, "and then paint the plaster black. I want people to have as close to the actual experience of being inside the ruins as possible. We'll use torches for lighting, that sort of thing."

"You should make it smell kind of smoky, too."

Mrs. Shum's eyes light up. "That's a great idea, Paige. I never thought of that."

"And the handprints. You should paint them into the walls, but make them almost invisible so you really have to look to see them."

Mrs. Shum's smile widens. I've impressed her. "Another good idea." She pauses. "Anything else?"

I look over at Emily, expecting her to say something, but she doesn't. It's odd because we've always played off each other's ideas, pushed each other.

Emily catches my eye and shrugs. "Well, Paige and I should probably let you get back to work." She doesn't wait for an answer. Turning, she fumbles with the curtains and then slips from the exhibit without saying goodbye.

I can barely keep up with her as she weaves her way through the rest of the museum to the exit door.

"Where are you going?"

Emily ignores me, pushes the glass door open, and steps outside. I follow her into the furnace-like heat and the sunlight that stabs like needles into my eyes. "What's the matter?"

She doesn't talk until we're halfway to the parking lot. "God. That woman. I just needed to get away for a minute." She takes a deep breath of air and then releases it slowly.

"What do you mean?"

Emily shakes her head. "She's just so phony. It makes me crazy."

"Why? She seems nice."

Emily gives me a scathing look. "That's what she wants you to think." She shakes her head, obviously getting more upset by the moment. "She was nice to me at first, too, and then when she found out how old I was, she tried to get me kicked out of the internship program. If it wasn't for your father, Paige, she would have."

I think Emily is just jealous because Mrs. Shum liked my ideas.

"My father, the hero." I say it automatically, sarcastically, because he's the clear villain in every story about him. I can't stand that Emily can't see that.

Emily's face tightens. "I know you're upset about the whole divorce thing, Paige, but so is your father. He feels terrible about what happened."

I glance sharply at her. A shot of bitterness stings me. "How do you know what he feels?"

"Because when he first came here, he came to our house. I saw him, Paige. He was lost. He wouldn't talk unless you asked him a question, and he wasn't eating either. One time he sat in the car for, like, fifteen minutes before he walked up to our house and rang our doorbell."

"Funny. He had no trouble getting in his car and driving out of our lives."

"You're wrong. Half the reason I got this job was that your father thought it would make you happy. Before you got here, he asked me a million questions about things you might like."

"And he sure listened because the refrigerator was stocked with hotdogs and frozen pizza. I *hate* hotdogs."

Her hands go to her hips. "Your room. You don't know how much he agonized over everything in it. He wanted it to be perfect for you."

For a moment, I just look at her. "What do you know about my room?"

"Everything. I helped him pick it out, and when the furniture came, we decided where everything should go."

Emily and my father decorated my room? Them together poring over my dresser? My vanity? I picture their heads together, studying the Pottery Barn catalog and talking about me. I hate that he's different with her—nicer, warmer—than he is with me. "Do you honestly think a Pottery Barn room makes up for what he did?"

The sun is full in her face, and Emily squints as she glares down at me. "Maybe he loved you enough to leave."

"Oh, come on," I give a false laugh. "Don't give me the 'it's for the best' crap. I've heard that before. You don't know what you're talking about."

"I know enough to know that it would have been worse for you if your father and mother had stayed married." She sweeps her yellow bangs behind her ear. "It would have sucked the life out of you—out of everyone."

I make an exasperated sound. Why does everyone always think they know what's best for me? "I'm not saying that they shouldn't have gotten a divorce. I'm saying that he didn't have to take this job. He could have stayed at Rutgers. He could have chosen *me*. Instead…this." I make a big gesture with my arms to include the whole park. Inside, anger boils. "He walked away from us. No matter how you look at it, that's what he did. He simply didn't care."

Emily's nostrils flare. "Just because he came here doesn't mean he doesn't care about you. You think I haven't seen what an unhappy marriage can do to people? It kills them. It's like taking a little sip of poison every day." Her cheeks turn red. "Grow up, Paige," she says and walks away.

SEVEN

Paige

For the next several days, I refuse to go with my father to his office and therefore manage to avoid Emily, who thinks she knows everything and really knows nothing.

She tries to call and text, but I ignore her. Every time I think about what she said—*grow up, Paige*—it makes me mad. She's the one who needs to grow up. Even worse is thinking about them hanging out together, picking out my furniture and decorating my room. I imagine them talking and laughing, Emily sharing her opinion and my dad peering into her face as if it were the most fascinating thing in the world. Why couldn't he ever look at *me* like that?

On the third morning of my isolation, after my father leaves for the park, I go for a run around the neighborhood. It's hot and I don't get very far. Afterward, I come home, take a long, cool shower, and then sit in front of the television wondering when Emily became more my dad's friend than mine.

Around four o'clock my father calls to tell me that he won't be home for dinner. He has a department meeting at the university—which he has forgotten about until now—and hopes to be home by nine. He says there's frozen pizza in the freezer or a box of macaroni and cheese in the pantry. Neither appeals to me. I end up eating a bowl of cereal in a house that is colder and more silent by the minute. Why did he even want me to come to Arizona when clearly he doesn't care I'm here?

I leave the bowl in the sink and then pad through the house to my father's room. His door is shut, but I feel no guilt whatsoever as I turn the knob and step inside. The room is neater than I would have expected. The bed is made with a striped tan comforter. On the dresser that used to be in our guest room in New Jersey, he's got a couple pictures of me, one of his parents, and one of himself and Dr. Linton standing on top of a shelf of rock with a breathtaking view of a desert valley behind them.

Starting in the bathroom, I systematically go through his things. I feel like an archeologist digging through the rubble of my father's life. I hold up a bottle of aspirin, a jar of Vicks VapoRub, rubbing alcohol, a small tube of Neosporin. The medicine chest says my father is relatively healthy—no prescriptions, nothing that really says anything about him.

I go through his closet, flip through the line of jeans on hangers, smell his shirts, and even check the pockets of the one sports jacket he owes. Nothing.

Inside the bedside drawer—he still has that stupid leather and lace comb holder I made him back in, what, first grade? My grandfather's Timex with the Velcro band is there, too, with the hands forever frozen at 3:12.

In the bureau, I plow through his sock and underwear drawer. In the second drawer, I flip through a stack of T-shirts—a lot of them from Rutgers—and then my fingers freeze as I touch something paper. An envelope.

It isn't sealed, but it's a little bulky and my father's writing sprawls across the top—*Chaco Canyon, New Mexico, 1989.*

Inside are three very old photographs—the thick, square ones that popped out of instant cameras. They're black-and-white, so at first it looks like two teenagers sitting together on top of a boulder, but then I realize they're pictures of my parents. They're both much skinnier, and my mother's hair is long, permed, a darker brown than she has it now. When I turn over the back of one of the photos I see my mother's writing.

D, love you with all my heart, A.

Another picture is of them kissing, on top of that same boulder, and then one of them laughing self-consciously as if they just realized they'd been caught.

I stare at the photos. My parents look so young—like my age—and in love. You would never guess they would end up hating each other so much that they would fight not just for the things they wanted, but for the things they didn't want the other person to have.

I put the envelope back in the drawer exactly as I found it and then open the next drawer. As my hands travel through yet another stack of shirts, I keep thinking about those photos. My father moved across the country to get away from my mother. So why does he have these in his T-shirt drawer? There are no displayed pictures of her. Why not just throw them away?

By the fourth day of staying home I have searched the entire house, watched hours of mind-numbing television, stalked my friends in New Jersey on Connections, and in a low moment, even called my ex-boyfriend, Aaron Dunning, hanging up before he answered.

For the second night in a row, my father works late. He says he has departmental business, but I think it's a form of what my mom calls "tough love." He wants me to get so lonely that I'll stop being mad and talk to him. Although I recognize this, I also realize that staying at the house alone all day is driving me crazy.

That's why, on the morning of the fifth day, I'm actually relieved when my father tells me the medicine man has finished the ceremony and asks if I'm interested in coming to the reopening of the park. I force myself to embody indifference. With a casual shrug, I say, "Whatever."

We stop for gas and pick up sandwiches that come out of a machine and probably have been there for ten years, but at least it's not cereal or frozen pizza, and if I get food poisoning maybe he'll send me back to New Jersey. Providing I survive. Providing I want to survive, that is.

We get to the park early, but John Yazzi and the rest of his crew are already waiting near the information center. My gaze goes immediately, uncontrollably, to Jalen, laughing at something one of the other men said. He doesn't make eye contact, but his smile fades as if he can sense me looking at him.

Emily sidles up to me. "I'm sorry," she whispers.

Although I've been waiting to hear this, something in me refuses to acknowledge or accept her apology. Instead, I straighten my spine and stare straight ahead at my father, who is going over the morning schedule.

Emily moves a little closer. Her shoulder is warm and soft against mine. "I'm sorry," she repeats. "I hate this—not speaking. Can we talk about what happened?"

I look at the white shirt on the back of the man in front of me. "What's there to say?"

"Lots. I was awful. I shouldn't have said those things."

"But you said them." And now she has to live with that.

"I wasn't thinking. Please, Paige. I can explain."

I let myself look at her for the first time. There're dark circles under her eyes and a tight set to her mouth. "You took his side. What's there to discuss?"

"I know it sounded like it, but I didn't mean to."

I'm not ready to forgive her, but I think of how alone and friendless I've felt. It's been like carrying a heavy weight, this anger. Not just at her, but at my dad, my mom, even my friends back in New Jersey who barely bother to send me any email. It's almost like dark emotions can put up a force field around you. No one can get through it to hurt you, but it gets awfully lonely.

"Please, Paige."

The rest of the summer stretches in front of me like the shimmering black strip on the highway to infinity. Besides, I've always forgiven Emily. And even though she hasn't said it, I owe her. I will always owe her, and we both know this. I grind the toe of my sneaker into the floor. "Not here. Not now."

She exhales in relief. "At lunch," she says. "I know a place."

Around noon, we climb down from the ruins and follow a narrow, twisting trail that brings us to the creek. A short distance later, Emily walks out onto a long gray rock that rises like the back of a whale above the slow-moving brown water.

She unpacks a container of blueberry yogurt and a bag of trail mix. I unwrap the ham-and-cheese time capsule.

"Listen," Emily begins, "about what I said. I'm really sorry." She stirs the yogurt. "I'm not excusing myself, but it's just that your dad has been really good to me."

"I'm happy for you." It's a lie, but I say it anyway and manage, just barely, to keep the sarcasm from my voice.

"I know you're really mad at him, but he's trying, Paige. He's trying to make things right."

I balance my bottle of Diet Dr. Pepper on the uneven rock. "Why are you taking his side? You're supposed to be *my* friend."

She fingers a silver chain around her neck. "I am your friend—that's why I want you to patch things up with your father. He loves you. I know you love him."

Shaking my head, I feel the anger burning inside me as hot as the full sun searing my shoulders. "Are you crazy? He walked out on my mom and me and I'm supposed be happy about that?"

"Maybe not happy," Emily concedes, "but you could try to see his side. Maybe if you understood why he left New Jersey, you wouldn't be so mad at him."

I break off part of my sandwich and then throw it into the water as a fresh wave of betrayal crashes over me. My parents gave me a generic "we've grown apart" reason. It kills me to think my dad talked to Emily, confided things he never told me—that he is a different person with her. I look at her and imagine them discussing me. Him saying how emotional I became—how I took my mother's side, refused his calls, deleted his emails. All true, but all justified.

I throw another piece of sandwich into the water. As much as I'm angry, I'm also consumed with a need to know what was said.

"What did he tell you? About the divorce?"

She finishes chewing and takes a long drink of Diet Coke. "He said that in New Jersey he was becoming a person he didn't like. That leaving the field and going into an academic career had been the wrong choice for him. He wanted to get back to where he started." Her green eyes are clear, marble-like, and I think she might be directly quoting him. "He thought he could be a better father here."

"How could he have thought that?" I snap. "All he cares about is work."

She shakes her head. "That isn't true. He was dying inside. He would have had nothing to give you."

"Is that what he said?"

She gives me a slightly sheepish smile. "No, but he didn't have to." She stays silent for a moment and then begins stirring her yogurt. "I have a friend at school, and her parents stay married but they don't love each other anymore. There're going to stay together until she graduates high school and then they're getting divorced. They think she doesn't know, but she does. She talks about it. How polite her parents are to each other, but they sleep in separate bedrooms. Her mom is so lonely, Paige, she cries at night." Emily shakes her head. "My friend wishes they would go ahead and get a divorce. Every day it's a little worse. Like taking a small sip of poison."

She's said this before, when she was talking about my father. I hate to think of him saying something like that to her, even though part of me knows it was true.

Emily fingers a turquoise bead on a long chain and then lets it fall back inside her tank top. "I read somewhere that infants need to be loved or they die. I think it's like that no matter how old you are. People either get love, or they start to die inside. It's how our brains are wired." She gathers up her unfinished lunch and climbs to her feet. "We'd better get going," she says, offering me her hand. "I've got to get my blog to your father by two." She pulls me to my feet and then looks into my eyes. "Friends?"

I think about what she said, about people needing love, about dying a little on the inside when they don't get it. I think maybe that's what's been happening to me, dying inside. At least that's what it feels like.

I nod slowly. "Friends."

EIGHT

Paige

Several days later, Emily takes me on a long hike that follows the creek south and winds us through a grove of wizened hickory trees frozen into painful, arthritic-looking shapes. The trees become sparser the further from the water we walk. After about ten more minutes, the tree line ends. Emily comes to a stop in front of a knee-high rock wall and wipes the sweat from her forehead. "We're here."

Looking over her shoulder, I see a small, cleared area enclosed by the rock wall. The ground is flat, the color of rust, and dotted by crumbling headstones. "A graveyard. You brought me to a graveyard."

"An ancient graveyard." Emily's eyes gleam. "Come on. It's way cool."

We step over the wall and move among the headstones. I feel like a giant in this city of graves. I pause by a marker so eroded the lines are no more than scratches. The name is too faded to read, but the date says 1590.

"A colony of Europeans tried twice to settle here," Emily explains, "but they all either died or disappeared. Just like the American Indians." Her voice lowers. "A lot of people claim the park is haunted. They've seen the spirits of people walking around the grounds or climbing up to the ruins just before dark."

We've told each other ghost stories far worse than this one. I frown. "Don't do this."

"Do what?" She walks over to one of the graves and lies down on top of it. "Take my picture," she says. "I'll post it on my blog."

She tries to hand me her cell, but I don't take it. "We're not little kids anymore," I snap. "Get up."

Emily pushes the camera toward me. "Come on. Just one."

I shake my head. "No."

Her brow furrows, and she squints up at me. "It's not like it's actually a grave anymore. There isn't anyone still buried here."

"I know, but I don't do that stuff anymore."

She looks at me for a long moment. "I'm not asking you to do anything but take my picture. Come on. I need it for the blog."

Annoyed, I take the phone from her hands. She lies back, folds her arms on her chest, and closes her eyes. "Ready."

I snap a shot, not caring how it turns out, and then hold out the phone. "Here."

She sits up, takes it, and then shades the screen with her hand to look at the photo. "Perfect." Pulling out her canteen, she takes a long, thirsty swallow. "Thanks."

"I can't believe my father is going to let you post that photo." Easier to imagine is my father's face turning red with anger that we were goofing around inside this cemetery. He was always like that, even when I was little. It had to do with respecting the past, honoring the dead. He once fired a man from his crew for making crude remarks about the skeletal remains of a 300-year-old woman they found near the Arizona/Utah border.

"Well, maybe not the photo," Emily concedes, "but as long as I keep the blog factually accurate, he's pretty chill." She pats the ground next to her. "Come and sit."

I plop down across from her, not on the grave but nearby. The earth is hot and crusty. As I stroke the blanket of dirt and loose pebbles, it feels like they are large crumbs of bread in a giant's fairy tale.

I realize that already I am imagining the start of the game I swore I would never play again, and I lift my hand from the ground. We were such idiots, but back then the games became so woven into our friendship I don't think either of us knew how to stop.

Emily tosses a pebble at me. I jump when it stings my chest. "Have you ever been in love?"

"What?"

"You looked so lost in thought I figured it had to be about a boy."

I blink at her, both relieved she hasn't brought up the game and trying to focus my mind on this new topic. "No."

"No, there's no boy at home, or no, you've never been in love?"
I think of Aaron Dunning and feel a stab of guilt. "No to both."
"No boyfriends?" Her voice is skeptical, the pupils of her eyes tiny
black dots in the sea of her green eyes.
My mind flashes again to Aaron Dunning, and another stab of guilt
pierces me. "Well, one."
"I knew it," she laughs. "You've been holding back on me. Tell me
about him."
I've never really talked to anyone about Aaron before, but part of me
always wondered why I didn't fall in love with him. I wanted to—I
seriously wanted to. But it never happened.
It takes a little more coaxing, but eventually I cave. I tell her how my
mother and Aaron's were friends. How we had pre-AP chemistry
together. One night he showed up at my front door and with flowers
and movie tickets. *You get them either way,* he said, *but I hope you'll want
to go with me.*
Every girl I knew wanted to be his girlfriend. It wasn't just that he
was tall, blond, and blue-eyed; he was nice. And he was smart—just a
little ahead of me in class rank, or at least where I used to be.
He did everything right, but after a couple of dates, I knew something was wrong. I didn't look forward to going out with him—instead
I felt tired just thinking about it.
Sometimes in the hallways, I'd see my friends walking with their
boyfriends. They'd have their arms linked, and their faces turned to
each other, like sunflowers to the sun. At first it made me jealous and
then just plain sad.
Everybody was shocked when I broke up with Aaron. My mom
tried to hide it, but I knew she thought I'd made a huge mistake. The
only mistake in my mind, though, was staying with him for so long.
Emily nods sympathetically when I try to explain how I kept telling
myself things would get better, that my feelings would change—that it
was somehow *my* fault.
"You did the right thing," she says. "You shouldn't be with someone
just to be with someone." She pushes back a sweat-soaked strand of hair
and looks at me very seriously. "Love should be something big. It should

be obsessive and a little dangerous. Something you can't control—it controls you. When you kiss, it should feel like a bolt of lightning slamming into your chest."

I laugh, but inside I'm jealous. It's never been like that for me. "When did you become such a romantic?"

"I'm not. But the thing is, the chemistry is either there or not, and you know it right away."

I think of the first time I kissed Aaron Dunning. He came to our house to watch *Australia*, which turned out to be the-movie-that-would-not-end. First, he'd put his arm around me, and then he'd stared sideways as me for so long it got uncomfortable. When I turned to comment on it, he'd leaned forward and put his lips on mine. I felt something in me pull back, although I didn't physically move an inch. It was like a very soft sea creature had attached itself to my lips and was moving slowly through the water, pulling me along with him.

Afterward, I'd smiled at him, but I had to fight the urge to dry my lips. I could tell Aaron was pleased, though. I told myself that this was the only thing that mattered. It took me a long time to realize that it wasn't enough.

A thought floats through my mind. What would it be like to kiss Jalen? I imagine the strength of his arms coming around me, his face lowering, his lips warm and firm. I think it would be good, but maybe it wouldn't. I decide it doesn't matter. I'm more likely to get hit by lightning than get kissed by a guy who won't even say my name.

I look at Emily. "How about you? You ever been in love?"

She drops her gaze, then pulls the silver chain out of her shirt and fingers the bead of turquoise. Her smile is sly. "I 'm focusing on my career now."

"I don't believe you. Tell me who he is."

She laughs, drops the bead back down her shirt. "Nobody," she insists, but her gaze slides away from mine. "I'm going to be an Ivy League girl and then graduate school. Your father promised to write me a good recommendation. And after I get my PhD, I'm going to travel. Meet people from all over the world and write a best-selling book." She gives me an appraising look. "You could come with me. We always were a great team."

It's my turn to laugh. "I could come with you as what? Your friend?"

She looks at me hard. "As an archeologist. That's what you always wanted. You saw things in a way I never could."

I shake my head. "The way I saw things almost got us killed, remember?" My hand flies to my mouth. Here I was hoping that Emily would never bring that summer up, and I'm the one who did it.

"That was an accident," Emily says firmly. "It shouldn't stop you. You love it, Paige, and you were good at it. Come on—we'll both get PhDs and really live our lives. Not just get some job that pays the bills."

The heat is so strong even my scalp is drenched in sweat, but it doesn't matter as much as what Emily is saying, offering. For a moment I'm interested, and then reality sets in. "I'm not getting into a good college. I totally tanked last semester, remember?"

Shaking her head, Emily flips her braid. "That was only one semester. You're smart, Paige. You're going to kill your SATs."

I almost laugh thinking about the PSAT I took last fall. I didn't read a single question, just bubbled answers in the pattern of a butterfly. Of course I'd scored in the lowest five percent. To be honest, I'd been hoping for a total fail.

"Even if I did, I don't think an Ivy League school is going to take me."

"You're the daughter of a man famous in his field. That counts for something."

"Like I would ever go to him for help."

Emily rolls her eyes. "You might not have to. Colleges look at more than your class rank. You have an interesting story—being home-schooled, traveling around the Southwest with your dad as a kid. Every college essay," Emily states with authority, "is basically about what diversity you bring to their school."

"Diversity?" I laugh. "I'm a white girl from New Jersey."

She shakes her head. "You weren't born in New Jersey and you didn't grow up there. Not many people have your background. And if you got involved with one of the research projects this summer, it'd give you material for a great essay."

"I'd have to go to my father and ask his permission. I'm not doing that."

"You don't have to," Emily's lips curve slyly. "All I have to do is whisper in a certain intern's ear that you're interested in assisting him on a project and he could go to your father and ask him for your help."

I actually find myself turning the idea over in my mind. The idea of research, of working in the ruins, has more appeal than I'm willing to admit to Emily.

"You could turn everything around," she presses.

"Who says I want to turn things around?"

She holds my gaze. "I think you do."

I shift. "Community college could be fun."

"And you could keep living at home. Is that what you want?" She pins me with a look that makes me wince.

I look away, seeing with painful clarity living at home and being my mom's best friend and companion. I love her, but it just suddenly feels scary, wrong, and yet somehow inevitable.

I know it's my fault. I've let myself drift and fail and use my parents' divorce as an excuse to stop trying. They may have turned our house into a war zone, but there was a part of me that was only too willing to let their problems consume my own.

"Just think about it," Emily says, "but whatever you decide, I support you." She pauses. "I'm your friend and it's your life."

She doesn't say the last part sarcastically. More like she isn't going to judge me or rub it in if she goes to Columbia or Princeton and I don't.

"It goes both ways," I tell her. "I support whatever you want to do."

She looks at me, eyes cat-like and curious. "You do?"

"Of course."

"What if it was something that you didn't like?" She's testing me, just like when we were little and she would ask me what scared me most.

"I told you, I'm not playing the game anymore." I climb to my feet.

"I wasn't talking about that," she snaps.

"Then what?"

She's silent for a long moment and then sighs. "Nothing." Rising, she brushes the dirt from her legs. "Just promise me, we'll always be friends."

"Of course." But the moment still feels unfinished. "You know you can tell me anything, right?"

Emily smiles and links her arm through mine. "I know that," she says. "Thanks."

NINE

Paige

As much as I try to deny it, the seed Emily planted in my mind takes root. Over the next few days, I find myself wondering if I could start over. What if I nailed my SATs? Wrote a great essay and got into a really good college? What if I stopped obsessing over my parents' divorce and started caring about my future?

Wandering the cool cliff chambers, I stop thinking of them as gloomy and haunted, but as a metaphor for the restoration of my own life, the seed of an essay. The Paige Patterson who came here can die, and a new Paige can be reborn. She can be whoever I choose her to be.

And so, even though it feels like I'm betraying my promise not to let my father think I find any part of being in Arizona interesting, I seek out Emily and tell her my decision. I find her in the locker room, changing from a pair of sweat-soaked Nike shorts and a tank top into a short denim skirt and a floaty, cream-colored top cinched at the waist with a belt. When she hears my news, she grabs both my arms and grins in excitement. "You're not going to regret this," she promises. "I'm so glad you're doing this."

"I'll give it a week," I tell her, trying to make it seem like it isn't a big deal even though inside I'm pretty excited. "And if it doesn't work out…" I shrug my shoulders.

"It'll work," Emily states. "Just wait and see."

Two days later, in the fourth-level chamber, the place I have come to call the airplane hangar, my father calls me over. My heart starts to beat a little faster because I'm pretty sure I know exactly what this is all about.

It's mid-morning and engineers have already removed about a fourth of the black railing. I walk past the tall, dark form of Jalen Yazzi, who, as usual, doesn't even glance in my direction. Although he doesn't know it, he has factored into my choice process as I have decided being attracted to Jalen falls into the category of self-destructive behavior. Something I will no longer allow myself to do.

"One of my interns just asked if you might be available for a few hours every day to help research," My father says.

I dig my sneaker into the yellowed stone floor and shrug. "Whatever." I hope he doesn't see the flush of blood that's rushed to my face. The interest that powers my heartbeat.

"It would be a great opportunity for you," he says. "Mostly it would involve taking samples and recording data. Some photography, as well. Are you interested?"

I count to five before answering. "I guess."

My father shifts. "You don't have to do this if you don't want to. In fact, if it doesn't interest you, I'd rather you not get involved. Indifference breeds mistakes. It isn't the attitude of someone I want working in the ruins."

It feels like he's slapped me in the face with the truth of our relationship—that these precious ruins mean more to him than I do. But I also recognize that letting myself get mad at him will only keep me trapped—that if I want to get out from under his control, if I want to move forward with my life, I have to swallow my anger.

I lift my gaze. "I'll do a good job."

He nods and then gestures to someone standing somewhere behind my left shoulder. "Jeremy, can you come over here for a moment?"

He says Jeremy's name so loudly that several heads turn around, including Jalen's. Jeremy detaches himself from the group and walks over to us. Although he's only a little taller than me, Jeremy's cute in a preppy, intellectual sort of way. His gaze lingers on me, and I feel increasingly confident about my decision as he comes closer.

After my father grants his approval, Jeremy turns to me. "We could get started right now." He pushes a long, dark bang behind his ear, only to have it fall forward again.

"Of course, of course," my father says, already looking past us at the iron railing that has begun to bow and yet still seems to desperately cling to its grip on the wall.

Jeremy smiles warmly. His teeth are small, but very white and even. I glance over at Jalen to see if he's noticed, but already his back is to me. "Just let me get my pack," Jeremy says. "I don't suppose you've ever had any experience with GIS systems?"

I shake my head, deciding now probably isn't a great time to tell him about my recent scholastic achievements, or rather, lack thereof.

"No matter," Jeremy says as I follow him to the side of the wall where he retrieves a battered canvas backpack from the ground and slips one of the straps haphazardly over his shoulder. His voice lowers a notch. "I'll teach you."

As we head down the ladder connecting us to the floor below, I glance back at Jalen one last time. For once I catch him watching me, and his scowl fills me with more satisfaction than it probably should. I give him a smug smile. He might not want to spend time with me. He might not like me. But I think Jeremy does.

For the next few days I spend a lot of time with Jeremy inventorying the walls. Basically, this means taking photos and then mapping the construction of the interior walls in the ruins. It's slow, tedious work, but I don't mind. It reminds me of when I used to watch my father all those summers in New Mexico. How slowly he would study a semi-collapsed pit house, remove the unsalvageable pieces, and then even more slowly put the rest of the structure back together.

I always liked that about archeology—that nothing happens in a hurry. You study things before you touch them. You look at something from every different angle before you decide what it is. You think about how the broken pieces fit and why someone might have built it to begin with. You have to daydream about it, let your mind play out different answers.

By Thursday, I begin to think that maybe that's how I saw Jeremy. When I met him, I made assumptions, but they weren't necessarily the right ones.

When he stands a little too close to me, I don't back away. When his hand accidentally brushes mine, I don't say anything.

We reveal ourselves to each other in pieces, discovering that both of us are only children, homeschooled, and raised by fathers who have unapologetically put their careers before their families (his is a neurosurgeon).

On Friday, we've just finished mapping an interior wall on the third level when Jeremy wipes the sweat off his forehead and closes his sketch pad. "We need a break. Want to go somewhere cooler for a little while?"

"Like the North Pole?"

He laughs. And this is something else I like about him. Even if I'm not that funny, he always acts like I am. "I've got somewhere closer in mind."

I get to my feet, stretching out my back, which feels tight and cramped after sitting on the ground for a couple of hours. Jeremy sips water from his canteen, watching, an amused smile on his lips. "Want some help?"

"With what?"

He laughs again. "Nothing."

We follow the passage past the dark mouths of chambers no bigger than closets where families once lived. Ahead of me, Jeremy moves through the gloom with the ease of someone who's done this hundreds of times before. I follow him through the third-floor passageway to the small ground-level chamber.

However, instead of leading us outside, he points to the ladder descending into the deepest chamber in the ruins.

"Have you ever been down there?" He shrugs his pack off his shoulders.

"Of course." Emily took me there when she gave me the grand tour. It's small and dark, almost well-like, and we didn't linger. I think it reminded us too much of things we would rather forget.

"Then you know how much cooler it is down there." He wipes the sweat off his thin face as if to emphasize how hot it is, but there's a different kind of energy coming off him than I've ever felt before. "I'll go first and turn on the light for you."

Turning around, he eases his body down the wooden ladder. The rungs creak as he disappears from sight. A moment later Jeremy's voice calls up, "You can come down now. Careful, though, it's steep."

A line of sweat forms on my upper lip. I hesitate, knowing he's right but not wanting to feel the claustrophobic press of the walls. But then I hear Emily's voice in my head, advising me to replace unhappy memories with good ones. I find the first rung of the ladder.

The tunnel between the levels is so narrow I can easily touch all sides. It almost feels like I'm climbing through a chimney—kind of like Santa Claus. The thought cheers me up and I make a note to joke about this to Jeremy, who appreciates my sense of humor. Not like Jalen, whose face would probably crack into a million pieces if he let himself smile.

I take another step and then another and another. The light gets stronger. I'm near the bottom when Jeremy reaches up to steady me. His hands span my ribcage, and he lifts me effortlessly, swinging me down the last few rungs and setting me gently on my feet. I'm aware how strong he is, how great it feels to be held, how his thinness is exciting. And most of all, the void of my own loneliness, screaming with the need to be touched.

In the beam from the flashlight, Jeremy's face is harsher, more angular, his eyes black and glossy. That shock of hair that won't be tamed has fallen forward, and he pushes it behind his ear. "Better?"

"Better."

The room is cooler, although a long way from feeling air-conditioned. The tribe's shaman lived here, and it is considered one of the most holy spots in the ruins. I know my father wouldn't like us being here. I feel a twinge of guilt and then tell myself we aren't harming or disturbing anything.

"Make a wish," Jeremy moving the beam of light across the ground until it comes to rest on a gaping black hole.

"You're joking, right?"

"I'm not saying we should throw a penny down there, but if you were going to wish for something, what would it be?"

"Three more wishes," I say and move closer to the opening of the *si'papu*.

In the velvet darkness, I can almost hear my father's voice telling me about how, a long time ago, the earth was lost in a great flood and then a new world came into being. Mankind didn't exist until a goddess named Spider Woman sang them into existence and led them through the four caverns of the underworld until they finally came to an opening—a *si'papu*—near the Colorado River.

There's more to the story, but what my mother and I loved most was the idea of God as a woman—a mother to mankind and also grandmother to the sun. My father, to his credit, had no problem accepting that women held the power. He and Dr. Linton spent hours discussing how Spider Woman "sang" people to life, and the idea of creation by thought. I didn't understand this completely, but I believed it because my father and Dr. Linton were the smartest people I knew.

I've seen dozens of *si'papus*, but none as deep as this one. I put my arm inside the hole and stir the black air with my hand. It feels lush—like liquid velvet. As my fingers continue to move through the darkness, I find myself reaching deeper and deeper into what feels like a bottomless pit.

"I know what I wish for," Jeremy says, kneeling beside me. He gently pulls my arm out of the *si'papu* and then laces our fingers together. I feel his thumb stroke the back of my hand back and forth, back and forth.

"World peace?" I say, but know that isn't what he's wishing for at all.

He laughs. "No."

My heart beats faster as a heavy silence falls between us.

"Can I kiss you?" he asks.

We both know the question is a formality. This has been building for days. Every casual touch, every lingering look has been adding up to this moment. I think, *Why not?*

Leaning forward, I brush back that shock of hair that won't stay out of his eyes. It's heavy, silken, jet-black against his skin. "Yes."

He clicks off the flashlight. The room implodes into pitch blackness. It's like one minute I have vision, the next I'm totally blind, like someone has cut out my eyes. "Where are you?" I punctuate the sentence with a nervous giggle.

"Right here."

I smell him—the faint odor of pine, like the woods at home. It doesn't matter, suddenly, if he's the right guy for me or even if I really like him. He's here. And then his lips—cold as river rock—land on mine.

The chill of his mouth is unexpected, and I pull back. "Jeremy…"

He swallows the word with a kiss, and although his lips are still cold, they're not as bad as before. I tell myself to give it a moment, to relax. He kisses me in a pulsing motion that's easy to follow. I close my eyes and lean into him, trying to get into the kiss.

He puts his arms around me and then pulls me forward, tipping me sideways onto the stone floor. His tongue traces the line of my lips, probing gently. I open my mouth just enough, and he slips inside me. He tastes of some unfamiliar, slightly pungent, dark spice.

We break free. He draws a quick breath, and then he's kissing me again. He touches my face gently, weaving his fingers as far as he can into my hair, loosening my ponytail. His hips begin to rock against mine.

I pretend it feels great, but inside I'm thinking it's Aaron Dunning all over again and a huge disappointment fills me. Is this how it's always going to be? It's not like in books, where the girl gets so turned on that she loses control of herself. It's not like getting hit by lightning. It's actually kind of gross.

When he comes up for air again, I put my hand on his thin, angular shoulder. "Jeremy…"

He strokes my face. "You're so beautiful. Do you know how beautiful you are?"

His voice soothes some part of me, reminds me why I came down here. He tells me I am desirable, that he has been hoping for a moment like this. I feel myself waver. "I don't know if I want to do this," I whisper.

"I'll stop anytime you want me to." He lowers his head, nibbling at my lip like a goldfish skimming bubbles off the surface of the water. His hand skims the hem of my shirt. "Stop?" he asks.

My mind whirls. He's older than Aaron, more knowledgeable, more experienced, more able to teach me how to do this better—how to enjoy it. And that's exactly what I want. I can't think of anything worse than to be like this, stuck at this stage, missing out on all the great stuff people are always talking about. I start to think about Jalen and then I shut that image down. I'm moving on.

"No," I whisper. "Don't stop."

I feel his smile before his lips begin the pulsing motion, pushing a little harder against mine this time. I don't protest when his hand slides under my tank top and spans the skin of my stomach. His fingers slide back and forth, a lazy, stroking motion that moves so infinitesimally higher that I might be imagining it. But then the top of his thumb brushes the band of my bra.

"Stop."

Immediately he withdraws his hand. Although it's dark, I can just make out the black sheen of his eyes as he pulls slightly back from me. "Stop?"

I almost say yes, but then I tell myself that I'm ready for this. Ready to grow up, ready to be a different, better version of myself. More than ready—I *need* to do this.

He kisses me, and I tell myself it's great. His hand starts the whole stomach-stroking move all over again. I concentrate on relaxing my abs and not slapping his fingers away. I tell myself that any moment it's all going to change and become magical. I just need to relax.

His hand glides upward, and this time his thumb slides under the wire band of my bra. My heart skips and for a moment I think this is what I've been waiting for, but then some instinct takes over and before I even know what I'm doing, I grab his hand away.

"Stop."

But Jeremy's mouth has mine pinned and only an unintelligible whine comes out.

Things accelerate. Before I know what's happening, his whole hand is under my bra and his hips are pushing against mine. I shove his shoulders enough to put him off–balance, and the moment my mouth is free I say very firmly, "Stop!"

He draws back, but his hand keeps moving over my breast. "Stop?" he coaxes.

"Stop."

He hesitates a long moment and then starts to kiss me again. A little more fiercely, as if he can *make* me feel. I try to push him away, and he resists. I start struggling for real then, twisting my head, breaking our kiss, slapping at his hands.

He pulls back. I can't see his face in the darkness, but I can hear him breathing, short and fast, and feel the quiver in his muscles, like electricity passing through him.

"You mean stop?" he whispers, and then squeezes my breast slightly harder. "Or do you mean *stop?*"

"I mean get off me!"

He doesn't say anything, but I can hear his breathing growing louder, a little angry-sounding. "Okay," he says quietly, but he doesn't stop. Instead he squeezes my breast so hard that I cry out, and then with his other hand he pops my shorts open.

Suddenly a voice calls from above. "Paige? Paige! Are you down there?"

It's Jalen. I've never been so relieved to hear anyone's voice in my life. Jeremy abruptly releases me. I push my tank top down and scramble through the darkness toward the sound of Jalen's voice.

My arms and legs shake so badly I'm afraid I'm going to fall backward, off the ladder and down into that pit. Jalen calls my name. I see his face almost lost in shadow, peering down. He stretches out his arm. When I get close enough, I grab onto it, and he pulls me up the last two rungs.

"Are you all right?" he demands and asks the question twice before I manage to nod. "What happened?"

His gaze moves over me, and even in the gloom of the chamber, it must be obvious to him—my swollen lips, my disheveled hair, and oh, God, my shorts undone. He reaches for me, but I rush past him holding my shorts closed. The light slants through the chamber's entrance. Misjudging the width, I scrape my shoulder on the masonry frame, but I hardly feel it. All I want to do is get as far from the ruins and what just happened as possible.

TEN

Paige

All night I lie in bed and think about Jeremy's hands on me. No amount of time in the shower can wash away the bruises that circle my left breast—reminders that when you play with fire, you get burned. At breakfast, I can barely choke down a cereal bar. For once I'm glad that my father is too preoccupied with his newspaper and coffee to notice that anything is wrong. We ride to the cliffs with the car stereo tuned to a news station. I look out the window, alternating between the dread of facing Jeremy again and the fantasy of telling my father what happened and him somehow making things right.

As we make the long climb up the series of ladders bolted to the cliff wall, I give myself a pep talk about not letting Jeremy see that he's hurt me, that he's changed me in any way. Maybe I gave him mixed signals, but that didn't give him the right to hurt me. And the more I think about it, the more I think he knew exactly what he was doing. It makes me mad, and I think about telling. But I'm not exactly thrilled about the idea of showing everyone my breast and then trying to explain what happened. I did flip-flop, after all.

All my worrying is for nothing, though, when we get to the top. Jeremy isn't in the ruins—probably hoping to avoid me as much as I want to avoid him—and I spend the morning staying closer to my father than I have the entire time I've been here. If he notices, he doesn't comment.

Jalen, however, keeps looking in my direction. He knows something's wrong, and I can see him trying to figure it out, making the connections between Jeremy's absence, the baggy T-shirt that replaces my usual tank top, and the way my eyes slide away from his.

Mid-morning, when we break, Jalen walks in my direction, but I see him coming and run. Everything is different now. I don't want Jalen to like me, not like I used to. I don't want him to see me at all.

At noon, I meet Emily at our usual spot on Whale Rock. We take out our lunches, but I can't bring myself to take a single bite. Instead I think about Jeremy, and in this fantasy, I'm pounding my fists into his thin, evil face, and blood pours from his long, elegant nose.

"What's with you today?" Emily complains, setting her water bottle on the rock. Today she's wearing a light-blue tank top with a deep plunge. I bite my lips, barely able to keep from snapping at her to cover up for God's sake—to stop dressing like a stripper. To stop dressing exactly as I did twenty-four hours ago.

I shake my head. "Nothing."

"You haven't heard a word I've said and you have these black craters under your eyes. Did you and your dad fight?"

"No."

I look down at my sandwich and feel sick. When I glance up again, Emily is chewing her sandwich and looking at me thoughtfully. "It's got to be your dad. What'd he do this time?"

"Nothing." I try to fake a smile. "I'm fine."

Her face twists as she studies me. I can tell by the expression in her eyes she doesn't believe me.

I lift my sandwich to my mouth and try to make myself eat.

"Then, what?" Emily pushes a bag of Doritos toward me. "Have one."

I push the bag away. "I told you. I don't feel well. It's too freaking hot to eat, anyway." I spit out the word "freaking."

Emily puts down the Doritos. "What's wrong?"

"Nothing. I'm just sick of one-hundred degrees. Why do we even sit in the sun?"

"What happened to your hands, Paige?" Before I can stop her, she takes my hand into hers. "And why are your hands and knees scraped up?"

"It's nothing." I pull my hand away. Truthfully, I don't even remember hurting them, although those scratches weren't there when I climbed down into that chamber with Jeremy.

I know he wouldn't have raped me. He wouldn't have dared—not with me being the daughter of his professor. But there was a moment I could feel him struggling for control of himself. Almost like a line he'd reached where, if he crossed it, there would be no turning back.

Standing, I leave my garbage on the rock and follow a stony footpath along the bank of the creek.

Emily scrambles after me. "Wait up. Where are you going?"

"Nowhere." I walk faster, head down, hugging myself like I'm cold even as the sun burns down on my neck. I hear Emily's feet on the gravel behind me, but I try to shut her out. If the trail were wider, I would run and run and run. And still not be able to get away from this thing inside me.

Emily's fingers curl around my arm, and she pulls me to a stop. "What's going on?" Her green eyes are wide and worried. Despite the sweat plastering her hair to her face, she still looks beautiful. "Why won't you talk to me?"

"There's nothing to talk about."

"Paige…"

"I just want to be alone." Actually it's the last thing I want, as I am the person I want most to avoid.

"Talk to me."

"I'm fine." My voice sounds like a girl with a thousand things wrong.

"Then what happened?"

"Nothing." But the word sticks like a fist in my throat. I clutch my hands and will myself to hold Emily's gaze.

"It's your dad, isn't it? What did he say this time? I screwed up last time, but this time I'll take your side no matter what it is. I promise."

I grab the hem of my boxy, ugly Rutgers T-shirt and twist it together. I only brought this shirt because I wanted my dad to see it and be reminded of the life he left behind. I never dreamed I'd be wearing it to hide in. "I really don't want to talk about it."

Emily touches my arm. "I'm good at keeping secrets."

I look up. Our gazes meet. In her eyes, I see the truth of her words— of the secrets that bind us together in a way that nothing else ever will.

"Come on. Let's go sit down." Emily leads me to a slab of red rock that forms a natural step rising from the creek. "Start at the beginning."

I'm reluctant. How do I start? What *is* the beginning?

"You can tell me," Emily coaxes. "Whatever it is, I'll help you—even if it's a smoke monster."

Just mentioning our childhood nemesis loosens my throat a little. I remember the night we tried to conjure up a man in a village who had died the day before. Only in my version—in this game—he wasn't just a spirit, but something far more powerful. A monster formed of smoke, coming at our call to snatch us back with him into the world of dead people. We sat terrified, watching the flames burn down and promising each other we wouldn't let go of the other no matter what crawled out of the smoke.

I wonder if I can trust her, and then realize I need to trust somebody.

"Yesterday, Jeremy asked if he could kiss me and I said yes." I hug my knees, trying to stay objective, to see it as a movie I saw rather than something that really happened. "It was okay at first, but then I asked him to stop."

Emily's brow furrows in concentration. "And did he?"

"Yes. But then I changed my mind and let him kiss me again."

She nods. "That happens sometimes. It's okay."

"But then I told him to stop again." I hesitate because the details now are getting a little fuzzy. I remember *how* I felt much more than *what* I said or how many times I said it. "But then he started to kiss me again and I could tell he was trying really hard to get me to change my mind. I didn't want to hurt his feelings, but I didn't want him to keep kissing me." I can feel myself getting furiously hot, as if the temperature inside my body is ten times stronger than the heat of the sun. "So I told him to stop."

Emily takes a deep breath and puts her arm around me. "And did he?"

My throat closes. It was my fault. I see that clearly now, and it takes me a moment to loosen my throat enough to speak. "Sort of. He said okay, but then he did this." I look around, confirm we are alone, and then lift up my T-shirt. Peeling back the edge of my bra, I let her see the red and purple bruises on the outside of my breast, the scratches lower on my stomach.

She leans closer. "God, Paige," she says, drawing back. Her eyes flash with anger. "No wonder you were so upset. What a jerk."

I wipe my nose with the hem of my shirt and try to force the question that haunts me out of my throat. "I know I gave him mixed signals." I pause and grip my hands together. "I want to know…and I want you to tell me the truth…was it my fault?"

"Of course not," Emily explodes. "How can you even think that?"

"Because even before we went down into that chamber, I was kind of flirting with him. And he asked me if he could kiss me."

Emily rubs the back of her neck and shakes her head. "You get to say no. You get to change your mind. There's no point where you can't tell a guy to stop. He hurt you, Paige. That's wrong."

I close my eyes, remembering the rage building inside him. How he punished me for being a tease.

I start to tear up, and Emily whispers that it's going to be okay, but I know that isn't true. I've messed up again. Not just with Jeremy, but with the idea of starting over, of making myself more competitive for college and destroying the pieces of myself that I didn't like. You can't change who you are, no matter how much you want to.

Emily and I sit like that for a long time, and when I finally sit up, she keeps a supportive hand on my leg. "We need to tell your father what happened."

I look up, wipe my eyes. Is she serious? "No way."

"You think he won't believe you?" Her face tightens with determination. "Paige, just show him your bruises."

"I'm not showing him anything." I put more space between us. "And he's the last person I want to know." I swipe my eyes, angry at how they keep filling up. "I just want to put this behind me."

Emily frowns. "He's your dad. He needs to know. If you won't tell him, I will."

I draw back, surprised. Didn't she just hear me? A rush of anger shoots through me. Why does she have to always take his side? "I thought you were good at keeping secrets."

Emily doesn't flinch. "This is different. The freak needs to pay for what he did. He deserves to be thrown out of the program. The next time I see him, that's exactly what I'll tell him."

"Don't say anything to him!"

"The hell I won't. I'll tell him to turn himself in to your father and apologize to you."

I give a bitter laugh. "He'll never do that. Besides, it's his word against mine."

"You have bruises."

"He'll say that we were fooling around and it got a little rough."

Her eyes narrow. "He hurt you," she says, "You told him to stop."

"He'll say that I said that before when I really meant the opposite."

"Anyone who sees those marks will believe you. Besides, you're underage."

She doesn't get it. She doesn't see that it isn't just exposing the physical marks, it's also the embarrassment of everyone knowing what I did, having to go to my father for help. "Like I want to flash my boob to the world." I glare at her because it's better to feel angry than helpless. "You want to be my friend? Stay out of this."

"Your dad will understand. He'll help you."

"My father and I are not exactly on close terms. He'll think it was my fault, anyway." I lace my voice with as much sarcasm as possible. "Kids should be allowed to divorce their parents if they want."

"Forget about the divorce. Tell him or I will."

"You can't do that. I don't *want* you to do that." A line of sweat rolls down my back. Another chases it. I find myself pointing my finger at her. "You tell anyone and we're finished."

She looks at me with fierce green eyes. Every inch of her tanned face is lined with determination. "You're my friend, Paige. My best friend. Maybe the only one I've ever had. I can't just do nothing."

ELEVEN

Paige

The rest of the day I worry that Emily is going to tell my father and this whole thing is going to blow up. I can't imagine anything worse than explaining what happened in that chamber. I think of how showing him the bruises would be as humiliating as getting them.

I text Emily a couple of times, begging her not to say anything, but she doesn't reply. I station myself at my father's side, hoping that if she tries to talk to him, I can intercept her. I wish I'd never told her.

I'm relieved when my father and I leave the park a little earlier than usual. He needs to make a stop at his office at the university and promises that we can pick up pizza for dinner. He doesn't seem to know anything is wrong. For once I'm grateful he's so clueless.

The drive to his office takes about thirty minutes. All of them he spends on his cell, talking at length about the restoration efforts. I watch the scenery flash and play games in my head. If my father hangs up before I count to ten, I'll tell him the truth. But it doesn't matter how many times I count in my head, he doesn't hang up. As we pull onto the campus, I feel the urge to talk to him fade.

I text Emily again: *Please*. She doesn't answer. I curse silently as we pull into a parking garage and I lose cell coverage.

The Melinda Carter Jones School of Archaeology is a square, four-story building marked by a bronze statue of what must be Melinda—a middle-aged woman wearing an old-fashioned skirt and blazer looking sternly into the horizon.

Just like his office at the park, my dad's office is a mess of papers, books, and miscellaneous things—like pieces of pottery in different sizes and shapes perched on top of the credenza. As he shuffles through some papers on his desk, I touch the spine of the textbook he wrote five years ago, the one that earned him tenure at Rutgers.

The sound of classical music from my father's cell interrupts the silence. "Hello," he says and then almost immediately his eyes go blank and his lips tighten. For a moment I think it's Emily, calling to tell him what happened, but then his lips thin and he says, "Did you want to talk to Paige, Heather?"

My stomach knots at my mother's name. I haven't considered it before, but if Emily tells, my mom is going to find out and she'll start threatening to send me to counseling, or worse, bring up Aaron Dunning—tell me all over again how perfect he is, how he would give me another chance if only I asked.

"Okay. I see." He pinches his nose wearily and looks down at the desk. "Why doesn't this surprise me?"

I glance away. What's left for them to argue about anymore? I wonder if it'll ever end, or if, for the rest of my life, I'll be the connection that allows them to keep hating each other.

Their conversation is short, mostly one-sided, and then my father hangs up. His eyes have a familiar hardness that I recognize from whenever he and mom fought.

"I have to step out," he says. Pulling a twenty-dollar bill from his wallet, he hands it to me. "There's a Domino's down the street. Why don't you pick us up a pizza and some soda and bring it back here?"

It isn't a question; it's an order. Before I can even ask where the Domino's is, he dials a number on his cell and storms out of the room. I weigh the value of sulking against going for the pizza, and in the end decide that hunger wins.

The security guard in the building points me in the right direction, and five minutes later I'm standing in line at Domino's. The few tables in front are filled with college kids, talking and laughing. Other kids are wedged into the corners, waiting for their orders.

I fiddle with my cell and try to ignore the table of guys at the table across from me. A week ago, I would have been flattered that they were checking me out, but after Jeremy, their gazes make me hunch my shoulders and pretend they're not there.

When my order finally arrives, I pay for it and then step out into the warm evening. It's dark, but not pitch, and the heat feels good after standing around in the air-conditioning. The street is quiet and empty, just a few cars, and I hurry down the block to the archeology building.

My father hasn't gotten back yet, but I'm too hungry to wait for him. I sink my teeth into the first steaming hot slice, and my eyes close in pleasure. The pizza is spicy and tastes exactly like the Domino's at home. For a moment, I'm back on the tomato-red microfiber couch, watching TV with my mom. I suddenly miss her so much more than I'm mad at her. I want to go home. I just don't belong here. When my father gets back, I'll demand that he book a flight for me.

Just as I am putting away my second slice and planning the details of my escape, he walks into the room. He's sweating, and the tight, unhappy look still hangs around the corners of his mouth. He uncaps a bottle of water and takes a long, thirsty drink before reaching for a slice.

"Sorry I had to step out—the reception is terrible in here."

His hat is gone, and his blond hair sticks out in all directions. There's a smear of dust on his cheek, and his eyes look funny, the pupils dilated. "You okay, Dad?"

It seems to take a long time for my question to reach his brain, or maybe just for him to form the answer. "Yes," he says, "everything's fine now." He doesn't quite meet my gaze, though, and mops his face with the crumpled blue bandana in his pocket.

He picks at the pizza, and several times I catch him staring at me. My skin prickles. Something is different. "You were gone a long time."

"I know. I'm sorry. I needed to sort through some things." He puts his half-eaten slice on his napkin. "Remember those Friday pizza and movie nights we used to have?" He pauses. "Do you and your mom still have them?"

The wistful note in his voice almost gets to me, but then I remind myself that he made a choice, that he walked out on us.

"No," I lie. He doesn't still have the right to know what my mom and I do on Friday or any other night.

"I wish I had been there for more of them," he says. "Especially last year."

I glance up in surprise. The words are the closest he's ever come to an apology. "Why weren't you?"

He shrugs and shakes his head as if the answer is as much a mystery to him as it is to me. "I thought it would only make things worse."

Strangely, I almost get that. Almost. I think about the last year. The cold war between my parents. The arguments that ended with my father getting into his car and driving away, presumably to his office. "How could that have been possible?"

He sets the slice of pizza down. I wait for him to answer, but he doesn't. It slowly occurs to me that it isn't that he's ignoring me, that maybe, for the first time, he's agreeing with me.

TWELVE

Emily

It makes me sad that I can't be with Paige tonight, but not for the reasons she thinks. The funny thing is that I almost let her know today at lunch what's happening with me, but then she told me about Jeremy. After that, I couldn't very well blurt out that I was in love, could I?

Neither of us meant for it to happen, but who could resist him? It started in the ruins. Whenever I was around him, I felt like a giant butterfly. My heart beat like wings, and my bones thinned until they felt as insubstantial as paper. He could crush me in his hands without even trying. At the same time, I wanted desperately to be held. It was agony to be around him and hide my feelings. My name on his lips— *Emily*—could burn my skin worse than the sun.

The first time our hands touched accidentally, I felt a rush so strong I thought I would pass out or cry out. But I held it together and then, as soon as I could, I ran to another part of the ruins. Standing at the window, I looked down at the ribbon of river far below me and ordered myself to breathe, to get it together. He was older, brilliant, on the fast track. What chance did I have?

However, he must have guessed how I felt. In the information center, a few days later, I was buying a Diet Coke out of the vending machine, and he just happened to be walking by. When the can landed in the bottom tray, we both bent down to get it. This time, when our hands touched, they stayed that way for a long time. I looked in his eyes, and my heart pounded so hard it had to be audible to him. A few days later, he asked me if I wanted to get coffee with him after work.

After that, we began stealing every moment we could. Sometimes it was just minutes; other times—the ones we lived for—were longer.

I know what I'm doing is wrong, but I can't help it. Being in love is an addictive drug. It rushes through your body and you'll do whatever it takes to get it. You'll lie to your parents, you'll lie to your friends, and you'll even lie to yourself. Because you have to have it.

I have a key to the park gate. The moonlight guides me to the cliffs. I walk quickly through air that wraps around me like Chinese silk. Just thinking of him—how he will undress me, how his breath will be warm and moist on my skin—makes me shiver.

I hear a rustling in the bushes—maybe a coyote hunting or a fat snake slithering deeper into the night. It's dangerous being here. I'm not stupid. I grew up understanding what nocturnal creatures live in the desert. It's not like I haven't considered what could happen. It's just that, when he tells me he can meet me, I can't resist. To deny him is to deny myself oxygen.

I reach the first ladder and lift my leg onto the bottom rung. I don't need the moonlight. I've done this many times. At night, heat radiates off the limestone like heat off a body. It seems to enfold me, to breathe with me as I climb higher and higher.

For a moment, Paige's face flashes through my mind. How I wish I could tell her everything. I can't, but I can make Jeremy Brown pay.

I reach the ruins. A soft yellow light flickers through the slit in the castle wall. The ache low in my stomach deepens, and my heart beats faster. This is our place—he's waiting. I can't see him, but I feel him.

I'm smiling as I step into the chamber. He's there and worth every risk I've taken, every lie I've told.

"Ya'at'eeh alah alah," I say, greeting him in the language we both love.

"Shi ayoo'nishi," he replies.

"Shi ayoo'nishi." I love you.

I slip into his arms and breathe him inside me, trying to pull the essence of him into my lungs. His strong hands tug the hem of my tank top. I shiver as he lifts the shirt over my head and tosses it to the ground. His smooth hands span my ribcage and then feel for the clasp of my bra. His touch is electric, moving higher, molding to me, burning me up from the inside, igniting the part of me that has no shame, no control, only this overwhelming need.

Closing my eyes, I press my hips against him. "Hurry," I whisper.

THIRTEEN

Paige

When I walk into the kitchen the next morning, my father is hunched over his coffee, scowling at the paper. I accidentally clang my spoon against my cereal bowl, and he about takes my head off.

The explanation is in the sink—a wine glass with a purple stain at the bottom. The empty bottle's in the trash. He's hung over. This is new. Does he know about me and Jeremy and it's driven him to drink? If so, why doesn't he say something?

His bad mood continues at the park. He lectures everyone on preserving the integrity of the ruins—basic archeology 101—and reminds us that being inside the ruins is a privilege, not a right.

"Glad you could join us, Mr. Brown," he says as Jeremy slips into the back of the room.

I look away but not before Jeremy flashes a smile at my father. "Sorry, Dr. Duke—car problems."

"I'll see you in my office immediately after this briefing." His tone promises that this is a conversation Jeremy won't want to hear.

A sick feeling fills me. I look around the room for Emily, but don't see her. I know she's here because I saw her Prius in the parking lot. It seems a pretty big coincidence that my father is angry, Jeremy is late, and Emily is conspicuously absent.

My father finishes the briefing, and the group breaks up. Jeremy leers at me as he passes. There's no hint of apology in his narrow face. It's more of a smirk, like we share a secret. I feel a rush of hatred for him.

"Paige," my father adds, "Stick around, please. I'll talk to you after I'm done with Jeremy."

I nod, but the tone of his voice tells me that, like Jeremy, I'm in trouble. As soon as his back is turned, I push past everyone else and head for the exit. I'm pretty sure Emily is avoiding me, but I know her. If she's hiding anywhere, it's in the ruins.

The sun has risen, but the temperature hasn't reached its full strength. I jog down the path, trying to get to the ruins before anyone else. I need to know what she told my father. My legs are strong from soccer, and it almost feels good to tear down the path, as if I can outrun the conversation my father and Jeremy are having.

I'm sure Jeremy is telling him how I led him on, how he thought it was a game we were playing. He'll make me look like a tease or, at best, a troublemaker. My father will probably believe him. See it as my way of acting out, of finding another way to hurt him.

So what? It shouldn't bother me. Let Jeremy say whatever he wants. It isn't like my dad has any power over me anymore. It isn't like I *care* what he thinks of me.

I climb the three ladders in record time. At the top, I'm breathing hard and soaked in sweat, but I'm still upset enough to keep going. The full sun hasn't hit the ruins, and the shadows in the windows are deep.

Inside, I scan the gloomy darkness for Emily. She isn't on the second level, so I crawl up through the tunnel between the floors. She isn't on the third level, either.

"Emily?" I say loudly, but there's no answer. As I listen in the silence, the hair on the back of my neck stands straight up. The walls seem to press a little more closely around me. "Emily?" I call, but softer.

Chamber by chamber, I search every inch of the ruins, every dark passageway. I use my cell, but it does little to illuminate the deeper rooms. I can feel a heaviness—a certain stillness in the air that doesn't seem right. I keep stopping, looking over my shoulder, and listening.

It's exactly like the hide-and-seek games that we used to play, especially the ones at night, when the moon was full. We would always hide where we knew it would scare the other the most to search. The fear, after all, was the purpose of the game.

"Emily! Where are you? I'm not kidding!" I yell as I climb into the fourth-floor chamber. It's huge, empty, half-dark, half-bathed in the morning light. The walls look torn, wounded by the railing half-pulled from the limestone walls.

I'm shaking with anger now—that she not only betrayed me, but now she's hiding, forcing me to wander through this graveyard in the cliffs looking for her. I turn slowly, studying the emptiness, my heart beating harder.

Maybe, I think, we're playing the game, only this time she's started it. And if so, then Emily has chosen the place I'll fear the most to look for her—the basement chamber.

It seems cruel to think she'd put me through that, knowing what she knows. But I can see her thinking that unless I face my fear of going down there, I'll never get past it. It's all bullshit, I think.

Anger strengthens my resolve. I'm not doing it. Not playing her game. If she's waiting for me down there, she's going to be waiting a long time.

Walking to the front, I stare out at the valley framed by the giant stone oval window. Far below, I see a group of people approaching the ladders. I know it's my father and the other interns. My face gets hotter, and my stomach knots with dread. There's still time to avoid my dad and Jeremy, but I'll have to hurry.

At lunch, I hike out to Whale Rock and spend a long, hot hour waiting for Emily. She doesn't show, and as the day stretches longer, it seems clear that Emily is avoiding me out of guilt. She must have told my father; she knows she betrayed me. She thinks I'm mad, which is correct. However, it doesn't mean I don't want to talk to her. She owes me that.

I forgive u. Just tell me what u told my dad.

I stare at my cell, willing it to light up with her response, but it doesn't. Like a fugitive, I stake out the information center, lurking among the racks of T-shirts and cheap souvenirs, skulking around the museum, waiting for Emily and ready to bolt if it's my dad or Jeremy.

By six o'clock, when my father comes down from the ruins, I've pretty much given up on her and resigned myself to face my father.

"Where have you been?" My dad steps into his office and sets his sweat-stained hat on top of a pile of books on his desk. "I texted you five times."

To my relief, his dusty, sunburned face looks more tired than angry.

"I know. I'm sorry. Have you seen Emily? I've been looking for her all day."

"No." He drags a metal chair from against the wall closer, and the sound makes me cringe, like he's scraping his fingernails across a chalkboard. "Paige, we have to talk." He sighs deeply. "Maybe you already know what this is about."

I focus on his hair. Sweaty now, a shade darker than blond. When he was younger, he was what was called a "towhead," which used to make me laugh and think of tow trucks.

"She told you."

He draws back a little, his brows furrowing in surprise. "Yes, but I didn't think you knew. She said she planned to talk to you about it tonight. I didn't want it to come as a complete surprise."

Why would Emily talk to me tonight? I look at him, puzzled. He's fingering an empty spot on the fourth finger of his left hand. When he had a ring there, he used to twist it around and around. "What are you talking about?"

He hesitates and then pushes hard at the skin on his jaw. "Your mother, Paige. She's getting remarried. To Stuart."

For a few seconds, my mind refuses to understand what he just said. I want us to be talking about Emily, but then it sinks in. Stuart—the short, balding guy with the overbite and weird laugh—is marrying my mom. "Her boss?"

It's a stupid question. Stuart Lowe is not only a partner at the law firm where my mother works, but also is the attorney who represented her in the divorce.

My father nods. "I know this comes as a shock, honey, but—" He runs his fingers though his hair. "—now that I've had more time to think about it, this could be a good thing for you." His expression softens. "So go easy on your mom, okay?"

I blink at him. Inside I'm shouting, *Are you crazy? Do you think you can drop this bomb on me like this and expect me to "go easy?"*

Standing up, I shove the chair behind me so hard it bangs into the computer table. Surprise flashes in my father's eyes.

"Go easy on Mom? What about me?" I don't wait for him to answer. "Why are you even bothering to tell me? It's obviously all decided."

"Calm down," he says, which only makes me madder.

I sweep the stack of his books and papers off his desk with my arm. As they crash and scatter, I run out of his office. It's after hours, so the lights are dim in the main room and the lady who sits behind the register is long gone. I tear past the exhibits and T-shirts, past Mrs. Shum's curtained-off exhibit.

My mother is getting remarried. She's calling me tonight. I'm supposed to be okay with this. I jerk open the glass exit door, and the heat engulfs me like I've stepped into an oven. Fine. It matches my mood—burning hot.

Stuart Lowe is going to be my step-dad. Stuart with that awful, nasal laugh and habit of winking after he says anything to me. Ugh. I want to die.

I'm halfway to the parking lot when I realize that my dad has the car keys, that we are in the middle of nowhere, and it's not like I can simply walk home.

So I stand by my father's Jeep for a humiliating ten minutes while the few people who are left get in their cars and leave.

How could my mom do this to me? She had "working" dinners with him, drinks sometimes, but I always thought it was work-related.

What am I going to say to her? *Congratulations, you've managed to completely ruin my life?* Or simply, *I hate you?*

I'm so caught up in my thoughts that at first I don't notice my father has come out to the parking lot or that he's peering into the window of one of the few cars still parked. My own thoughts are consuming me—choking me—so I don't connect anything until my father walks up to me.

"Were you saying something about not seeing Emily today?" He asks the question casually, but his eyes are a little too intense for him to pull it off.

Only then do I connect the Prius with Emily and the fact that I haven't seen her all day and I haven't found anyone else who has, either. Only then do I feel something hard and heavy hit me in my stomach.

Looking into my father's eyes, I understand that something potentially far worse than my mother's engagement is happening.

FOURTEEN

Jalen

My father steps out of Uncle Billy's room. I can tell by the way he closes the door gently, as if any sound might shatter it, that it's a bad night. He pauses in the hall, closes his eyes, and sighs.

From inside the bedroom, a drum beats slowly, and my uncle begins to sing. It is a song for the spirits of the dead to find their way to the next world. The keening, lonely, and admittedly slurred words fill the quiet of the house.

The music breaks my father's small trance. When he opens his eyes, I see in them what I already know.

My uncle is dead drunk.

Sometimes Uncle Billy can go for weeks at a time without drinking, and when he's like this, you see him for who he is—a brilliant man who knows the name of every plant, tree, and flower. How to cure an aching back with the gentian root and use skunk cabbage to treat asthma. He can sit and play chess—and beat me. He can pick up my AP pre-calculus book and solve any of the problems just by studying the examples. You start to forget that the other Uncle Billy exists, the wildly unpredictable man whose sickness—and make no mistake, this is a disease—takes over the house.

My mother comes up behind me. "I don't know how to help him."

She's still wearing her green scrubs from the hospital, where she works as a nurse's aide. I'm taller than her now, and it makes me see her differently, as if she's more fragile than the woman who stepped between me and a pit bull one Saturday morning.

"He'll be fine," my father says. "We just need to leave him be."

"Leave him be?" My mother's face creases with worry. "He's chanting a death song."

My father steps forward, past me, and slips his arm around my mother. His size all but eclipses her. "Give him an hour, and then I'll ask him to stop." He has to speak loudly, above the beat of the drum and my uncle's voice. "Come on, Lynn," my father urges, managing somehow to hide his exhaustion because he will not burden her with his own despair. "Let's just go sit down." He leads her to the family room, where my younger brother Harold sits on the couch watching television.

"He sounds like a howling coyote." Harold turns the volume up a little.

"Harold," my mother says sharply. "Don't say that."

"Why not? It's true. How are we ever going to sleep through that?" He keeps his gaze fixed on the television, watching the Red Sox take on the Yankees. He isn't a big baseball fan, but watching television helps him cope.

My mother, who has put up with my uncle's drinking for as long as I can remember, who has seen him dance naked in the moonlight, nearly set the house on fire when he tried to turn the bathroom into a smoke room, and endured more drunken tirades on the injustices endured by our people than I can count, sighs. "Because it's disrespectful."

We watch an inning, maybe two. Mostly I'm listening to Uncle Billy and feeling the tension in the house grow stronger with the drumbeat. We don't know what Uncle Billy is mourning—it could be a small earthquake in another country, or the death of a man he read about in the newspaper.

In any case, if you've ever lived with an alcoholic, you know that everything revolves around them. You love them, but you also fear them because when they're drinking, there are no filters—only intense, dark emotions. Hateful things come out of their mouths, words that shoot like bullets and hurt all the worse because you can't shield yourself from the truth in them.

Alcoholics are the storm *inside* your house. Until it blows over, the best you can do is to survive it. An unspoken, but understood, rule is that you don't bring anyone else into the storm. This means you don't return invitations, which means you stop getting them.

I try to go somewhere else in my mind—a field blanketed in orange and yellow poppies, the ivy-covered entrance gate to Harvard, sunrise at the top of Camelback Mountain. Tonight, however, my brain won't take me to the usual places. I see instead the slightly sunburned, blue-eyed face of Paige Patterson. I try changing the image, like surfing channels on the television, but it keeps coming back to her.

Paige's face is not a peaceful place, either. I keep picturing her scared eyes and chalk-white skin when she climbed out of the basement chamber. Afterward, that jerk Jeremy Brown tried to tell me that they were just playing, but I knew he was lying. He's a coward who'll wait for you to turn your back on him before he does something. I know guys like him at school. They're brave only when there's no chance of a fair fight.

I'm thinking about having a second little talk with Brown when my father's cell rings. We all sit up. My brother mutes the television, although most of the conversation takes place on the other end of the call. The crease that forms between my father's eyes sends me to the back door, where we keep our work boots in a basket. I'm just finishing lacing them up when my dad joins me, truck keys jingling in his hand, and tells me there's a problem at the park.

FIFTEEN

Paige

By nine o'clock, we know several things—Emily has not been seen since yesterday afternoon, she didn't come home last night, and her parents believed she was with me.

Standing next to Emily's Prius, my father and I wait in the heat and fading light for the Lintons. Our silence is broken by the occasional ring of my father's cell as the park rangers check in every fifteen minutes or so with the discouraging news that there's no sign of her.

I tell myself that Emily will show up any minute, smiling, her eyes alive with an adventure she can't wait to tell me. Or she's hiding somewhere, waiting for me to come and find her in one of those terrible games of hide-and-seek we used to play.

Finally, a police car pulls slowly up to us—no lights flashing, no sirens. Two officers, a man and a woman, step out of the squad car. They are from the sheriff's office and introduce themselves as Detectives Zulie Rodriquez and her partner Manuel Torres. The policewoman is short and wide. The male officer is her exact opposite—tall, thin, and balding.

"Sarah," my father says as Emily's mother gets out of the squad car's back seat. He hugs her, and she sags against him. It's been years since I've seen Mrs. Linton, but even so, she's aged so much I barely recognize her. Her short hair is more white than blonde and sticks out in all directions as if Emily's disappearance has hit her like a windstorm.

"Any news?" Dr. Linton asks, hurrying around the car to place his hand on his wife's shoulder. He's gotten fatter, and his short brown hair is sprinkled with white.

"None. I'm sorry." My dad steps back as Mrs. Linton emerges red-eyed and weary-looking from his arms. His voice softens. "We'll find her."

"Ma'am," Detective Rodriquez says, snapping on a pair of latex gloves and then pulling a flashlight out of a holster on one side of her expansive belly. "Is this your daughter's car?"

"Yes," Mrs. Linton says and claps her hand over her mouth.

The detective shines her light into the dark interior and strains to see, as if Emily might be crouching in the back seat. My father and I did the same. All we saw was a half-opened package of Skittles in the passenger seat and a crumpled bag from Jack in the Box. The other detective pauses at the left rear tire and then squats down. "Was the tire flat this morning?"

My father and I look at each other. I can't remember.

My father shakes his head. "I don't know. I didn't notice it until this evening."

"I don't see a puncture," he says.

"You think someone let the air out?" Rodriquez asks.

"It's possible," he says, climbing to his feet. He dusts his pants and turns to the Lintons. "Do you have a key?"

Mrs. Linton hands her a spare hanging from the chain on a feathered dreamcatcher. My stomach does a slow lurch as I realize they're going to open the trunk, and I'm afraid suddenly of what they'll find inside.

The hatch opens with a popping sound. Inside, a dark-colored blanket covers something large and lumpy. My father steps in front of me. "No, Paige," he orders, "Get back."

I twist around him in time to see Detective Torres poke the blanket with his flashlight. He pulls it free, and Mrs. Linton cries out. It sounds like distress, but it has to be relief because Emily isn't lying dead in the trunk. Instead, I recognize her tan Urban Outfitters backpack and her black nylon gym bag.

Detective Rodriquez unzips Emily's gym bag. She holds up a pair of Nike shorts as the policeman shines his flashlight on them. Next, they pull out a pink, ribbed tank top. I'm embarrassed for Emily when they fish out her lace push-up bra.

"No panties," Torres comments with absolutely no expression in his voice. He bends over, peering once more inside the gym bag, and then straightens.

"Maybe she didn't bring a change." Rodriquez glances at her partner. I can tell they're wondering what this says about Emily, if they think maybe she's the kind of girl who leaves her underwear at home.

"It's in the shorts," I blurt because somebody has to defend Emily, and the Lintons seem incapable of doing anything but standing there looking like shadows of themselves. Both officers look at me as if I'm talking another language. "The underwear is built into the Nike shorts."

Rodriquez's face opens as she gets it. She nods and then turns to Mrs. Linton. "When was the last time you saw Emily wearing these clothes?"

Mrs. Linton blinks rapidly, and then she frowns. "Maybe yesterday morning? I'm not sure. It was early." Her eyes glisten with tears that shine in the dim glow of the overhead parking lights. "I don't remember. She's always wearing Nike shorts."

I look at the clothes lying in the gym bag and picture Emily standing with the sun blazing down on us on the banks of Otter Creek. "She was wearing those yesterday morning. After lunch she changed into denim cut-offs and a white sleeveless shirt."

It was cute, and I remember being a little jealous because it showed off her tan and her breasts. I wished I were her—that I had someone to interview, a park blog to write, a great body, and a great future waiting for me at Columbia. Instead, I had a father who barely spoke to me, a mother who didn't care enough about me to fight for me, and bruises from someone I'd hoped would be my boyfriend.

"When did you last see her?"

"I left the park around six," my father replies, although the question is directed at me. "I think she was still here."

The female detective's sharp black eyes focus on my father. "You are?"

"Dr. Patterson. Duke. I'm with the university." He pushes the skin on his face wearily. "I should have waited." His shoulders sag, and he looks over at Emily's parents. "I'm sorry, Tom, Sarah. I never thought…"

Mrs. Linton begins to cry, and Dr. Linton pulls her against him. "Shh," he says, "We'll find her. It's going to be fine."

"You don't *know* that," Mrs. Linton pushes him away harshly. "It doesn't *feel* like everything is going to be fine. Someone obviously disabled her car and took her. That doesn't sound like everything is okay to me."

The detectives exchange long looks, and then the policewoman glances up at the parking lot lights shining high above us. "We're going to need the tapes from the security cameras."

My father shakes his head. "You'll have to talk to Tom Blackstone. He's in charge of park security. He's searching the grounds for Emily just in case she wandered off…" His words trail off, but not the thoughts. Emily could be lost, and there are all sorts of poisonous creatures in Arizona.

"Who else was at the park when you left last night?"

My father's brow wrinkles. "I don't know. I didn't see anyone in the information center, but there could have been some maintenance people on the grounds." He adjusts his hat on his sweat-plastered hair. "With a park as big as this one, it's virtually impossible to be sure everybody is out." He starts to say something and then hesitates. "Surely you don't think somebody who works here had anything to do with this?"

"We're just trying to get as much information as possible," Detective Torres says. "You locked the entrance gate when you left, right, Mr. Patterson? So if Miss Linton did try to go back into the park to get help, someone would have had to let her inside."

My father nods, not bothering to tell the officer it's *Dr.* Patterson, not *Mr.* Patterson. "I suppose. But I don't think…"

Detective Rodriquez cuts him off. "It's unclear whether she disappeared from inside or outside the park, so we're going to be part of this investigation. I'll need a list of people who work at the park. Also include any volunteers, contractors, or anyone who had access. If there's a log book of visitors, I want that, too." She turns to her partner. "The girl's been gone twenty-four hours. Call in the alert and get a team out here to search the car." She looks at my father. "I want to talk to Blackstone. Now. And I want the tapes from the security cameras. I'm also going to need a recent, good head shot of Miss Linton. The sooner, the better. If you have any on your phone, that would be a good start."

I have pictures of Emily on my cell. "I've got some." I scroll past the pictures we took at Tacoma Well—it already feels like years since we took them—and find the shot I'm looking for. Emily is sitting on Whale Rock, squinting into the strong sun. Her French braid pulls the hair off her face and shows her features. She's tanned and smiling confidently, like she has everything in the world going right for her.

The detective glances at the shot and then skims through the other pictures on my cell. When she looks up, her black eyes fix on me with an interest that wasn't there before. "You and Miss Linton were good friends, Miss…?"

"Patterson," my father replies before I can. "Paige is my daughter."

"While we're waiting for Mr. Blackstone," Detective Rodriquez says casually, "I'd like to speak with Miss Patterson."

A wave of heat crashes over me, and the night feels airless. With the police staring at me and the Lintons looking so broken, it all starts to hit home. Emily has vanished. She could even be dead. Rangers are combing the park for her, and now detectives from the county sheriff's office want to question me. A voice inside me that I've been struggling not to listen to is getting louder. It's saying that maybe Emily's disappearance is my fault.

"Of course," my father says. "Anything we can do to help."

"I'd like to see her alone," Detective Rodriquez says.

There's a moment of silence, and then my father says, "Paige is a minor. I'd like to be present."

"That is your prerogative," Rodriquez agrees, but her eyes narrow and she tilts her round face to meet my father's gaze. "Sometimes kids speak more freely when their parents aren't around."

"I understand. I'd still like to be present." His lips have a tight, thin set that means his mind is made up.

"Oh, for God's sake, Duke," Mrs. Linton explodes, "just let the police talk to her. She might know something that could help us find Emily."

"I'm not saying she can't talk to the police," my father replies. "But Paige is a child."

The words jolt something awake in me. He thinks I'm a child? What a joke. And suddenly he has my best interests at heart? "Dad," I snap. "I'm seventeen. I want to help."

"It's not negotiable," he says flatly.

My hands clench. Of course it isn't. Nothing in my life is negotiable. He always has to control me. Why?

"Just calm down," Detective Rodriquez says, gesturing as if we are cars going too fast. She gives me a sympathetic smile and then turns to my dad. "Dr. Patterson, you're welcome to join us. Is there somewhere more comfortable we can talk?"

"My office," he says, not looking at the Lintons, who stare at him as if they no longer recognize him.

SIXTEEN

Paige

My father's desk chair creaks under the detective's weight as she wedges her body between the arm rests. She scoots it forward, and the chair squeals as if in pain. Patting her round face dry with the sleeve of her shirt, she sighs. "Thank God for air-conditioning."

The room is a mess, with stacks of books and papers littering the floor. It feels like days, not hours, ago that I swept them off my father's desk. I can't even begin to let myself think about my mother and Stuart.

A radio crackles. Rodriquez presses a button and speaks into her shoulder. "Good," she says a couple of times, and then her brow wrinkles as a voice on the other end squawks out something unintelligible. "Make sure you get the names of all the searchers and run background checks on all of them. Anyone leaves without showing you an ID, I'll have your ass." When she finishes, she pushes back in the chair. "So," she says, looking at me, "You're what? Sixteen? I have a son—thirteen going on twenty-one." She chuckles, but when neither Dad or I comment, she keeps going. "He's always texting. I started him out on five hundred texts a month and then had to upgrade to an unlimited plan. The penalties were killing me."

After a long, silent moment, my dad says, "I'm glad you worked it out."

"What kind of plan are you on? I'm always looking for a better deal."

My father hesitates. "We have a family plan."

"A family plan," Detective Rodriquez repeats. "That would be how many phones?"

"Three. Paige, my ex-wife, and myself."

The policewoman nods. "An ex-wife."

"She lives in New Jersey," my father says.

Detective Rodriquez appears to mull this over and then dismiss it. "So you have unlimited texting?"

"Yes."

What about Emily? Why isn't the detective interested in her? I clench my fists to keep from screaming.

"Internet? My son wants that."

"Of course," my father says. He gives me a half-smile.

"Unlimited data?"

I try not to squirm. Aren't the first forty-eight hours supposed to be the most important? Or is that just for television and movies? My father starts drumming his fingers along the edge of the desk as the detective rambles on about the merits of various cell phone plans.

"Mr. Patterson," the detective says, leaning forward, "would you mind telling me how you got those scratches on your hand?"

My father's drumming stops abruptly. For the first time, I notice the three claw marks standing out in vivid red against his freckled skin. My stomach clenches.

"A cat," my father says, pulling his hand out of sight. "It was sitting on top of the Jeep this morning. It scratched me when I tried to shoo it away."

The detective nods sympathetically, but her black eyes fix unblinking on my dad's face. "Neighbors' cats can be a nuisance, can't they?"

My father swallows, and his Adam's apple bobbles. A hint of sweat shines on his face. "I don't think it was a neighbor's—it was probably feral. I didn't see a tag."

The detective steeples her fingers and holds her gaze steady on his. "So there's no way of verifying your story," she states, pleasantly, almost sympathetically. "Would you mind telling me when the last time you saw Miss Linton was?"

My father shakes his head. "Look, I had nothing to do with Emily's disappearance."

"Then you won't mind answering my question, Mr. Patterson. This is just standard procedure."

My father shakes his head. "I don't know," he says. "I suppose I saw her at yesterday morning's briefing…" He thinks hard. "Things got busy…"

They're doing it again—wasting time—and I can't take it any longer. "You need to talk to Jeremy Brown," I blurt out, and both of them look at me.

I feel my cheeks get hot as the name hangs in the air, like a bad smell waiting for me to claim it. My heart thumps in the quiet room. I realize I'm twisting my hands in my lap and force myself to stop.

"Who's Jeremy Brown?" Rodriquez asks.

"Jeremy?" my father repeats, disbelief all over his face. "Why would you say that?"

"Just who is Jeremy Brown?" Detective Rodriquez's voice carries a note of authority that makes it clear her questions overrule my father's.

"One of my PhD students." My father stares at me. "Why would you think that, Paige?"

I'm sweating now, despite the air-conditioning. Just thinking about him brings everything back—the darkly pungent taste of him, the suffocating intensity of his kiss, the strength of his hands. "Because he's a jerk."

"Talk to us, Paige. Tell us why he's a jerk." Detective Rodriquez leans slightly forward, her plump lips forming an encouraging smile.

I almost laugh, although it isn't funny. She's treating me like a child, or as if I'm injured, in shock, and she has to be careful or I'll completely shatter. It's Emily, though, who's missing. Emily who needs me to tell them what happened.

The minute hand on the wall clock clicks loudly. It's ten-thirty. As the seconds tick by, I think of Jeremy Brown touching me as I lay there waiting for something magical to happen, and then the anger that flowed into those hands when I asked him to stop. I imagine Emily provoking him, Jeremy losing it and shoving her hard enough to make her stumble, hit her head…

It's difficult to talk about, but I make myself start at the point where I went down into the basement chamber. I admit that I gave Jeremy mixed signals, but that, when I asked him to stop, I was very clear about it.

Next to me, my father shakes his head as if he can't believe what he's hearing. I can't bring myself to look into his face, but I hear the changes in his breathing—the sharp intake and the longer, sad-sounding exhales. When I get to the part where Jeremy got angry, my father stops breathing all together. I glimpse his white knuckles clenched on the armrest of his chair.

When I finish, there's silence. I look down at my hands, twisted in my lap, different somehow, as if they belong to someone else. I jump as my father tentatively touches my arm. He says my name like a question, but I don't have an answer.

"So this boy..." Detective Rodriquez says very slowly, "Did he rape you?"

My father flinches at the word.

I shake my head, trying not to imagine what my father is thinking. "No. Jalen came, and Jeremy stopped."

I imagine Jalen's dark face peering down into the tunnel—his eyes flickering with what looked like rage and concern, the strength of his hand pulling me up the last rungs.

"Who's Jalen?"

"God, Paige," my father says gently. "Why didn't you tell me?"

"Mr. Patterson. Please. Who is Jalen?"

"John Yazzi's son. He works in maintenance," my father replies impatiently. He turns to me. Beneath his brows, his eyes are intensely blue and the black pupils barely larger than dots. "Are you okay?"

I twist my hands together again, wishing he'd just be mad. I don't want him suddenly pretending that being my father means something. Like he really cares what happens to me. We both know that's a lie. I shrug with an indifference I don't feel and force my face as blank as I can make it. I ignore the part of me that wants to curl up in his arms and let him handle everything.

"You could have told me. I would have listened."

I look away from him. And then what? Kicked Jeremy out of his precious program? I don't think so.

"Paige," Detective Rodriquez prompts, "what happened after Brown let you go? Why do you think he did something to Emily?"

"After, I...I wanted to forget what happened, but the next day Emily guessed. She was angry. She wanted to confront Jeremy." I take a breath to steady myself because I have to stay calm. They have to believe me. "And tell him to resign from the program or she'd go to my father. We fought about it. She wouldn't listen…" I squeeze my eyes shut picturing her hard, set face. "You can't ever make her listen when she doesn't want to."

"When did this conversation happen?" Detective Rodriquez asks.

"Yesterday afternoon. Around one o'clock."

"The day after the alleged assault?"

My father sits up straighter. "If my daughter says there was an assault, there was an assault."

"I need evidence." Her eyes narrow as she looks at me. "Physical evidence. Bruising…torn clothing…witnesses."

"There are bruises." I think of the red and purple marks circling my left breast like a ring of fire. The scratches just below the line of my shorts.

"Can I see them?"

I look sideways at my father, silently begging him to turn away but he doesn't. I lift the hem of my shirt, show her the scratches on my stomach. I don't show her the bruises on my breast. Hopefully the marks are enough to make her understand that Jeremy is dangerous and she needs to send the police to his house.

Frowning, Detective Rodriquez narrows her gaze at me. "Shit," she says. Then she sits back in her chair and folds her hands together, obviously thinking, deciding if she's going to believe me or not. Finally her gaze lifts to my father's. "I want you to take Paige to the emergency room right now and have her examined by a doctor. Any bruising should be documented. And I'm going to need a statement."

"I don't want to go to the hospital! I don't want anyone taking pictures of me! You need to go to Jeremy's house!" My voice gets louder, but I can't seem to help it. "You need to go there *now*."

My father puts his hand on my arm, and I jump at the touch. His face is ashen; his lips are tight, shrunken-looking. It makes him look a hundred years old. "Paige," he says wearily, "we need to do exactly what she says."

Someone knocks on the door. "Just a moment," Detective Rodriquez calls. "It's very important that you do this, Paige. I know it's hard, but I wouldn't ask you to if it wasn't absolutely essential. It needs to go on record."

"But Emily…" I begin and then stop. All of this needs to be documented *because* of Emily. Because the policewoman believes me, believes in the possibility that Emily is missing because of Jeremy.

This isn't a story I made up in my mind, something to scare myself so I would feel fear, like Emily and I did all those years ago. Detective Rodriquez is building a case against Jeremy Brown because she believes he might have done something even worse to Emily than he did to me.

I taste something thin, bitter at the back of my throat, and my stomach clenches. Standing, I look around desperately as everything gets worse—the vile taste rising in my throat, the rolling of my stomach. I barely make it to the wastebasket before I throw up.

SEVENTEEN

Paige

In my bed, I lie with the covers pulled high looking up at the ceiling. Although I've been trying for hours, I can't sleep. The room feels cold, much colder than usual—as if the thermostat is set around fifty degrees. I flip over. It's just after two o'clock in the morning. I'm so tired my hands tingle, but I can't sleep, not when Emily's missing. I wonder if the police have Jeremy in custody. If they've found Emily. Another chill goes through me, and I tuck the quilt more tightly around my shoulders.

I'm thinking of getting up and putting on a pair of sweats when my door creaks and Emily walks into the room.

In the moonlight, her hair looks disheveled. Half her face is in shadow, but as she nears, I see it's not the lack of light, but dust coating her left cheekbone.

"Oh my God! Emily!" I sit up straight. "You're okay!"

"Paige!" She hurries to the edge of my bed. Her long pale hair falls forward as she leans over me. "I've been trying to get in touch with you."

"Where were you?" I study every inch of her. She's very pale, and there are small chunks of something plaster-like dangling in the strands of her hair.

"I got lost," she states, a little sadly. "I've been walking for a while." She looks down at her feet. "I lost my sneakers. Isn't that funny, Paige? They disappeared when I was sleeping. I just woke up, and they were gone. Have you seen them?"

The question is odd, but I'm so happy to see her I don't care. "No."

Her shoulders sag. "Oh."

"They're not important," I assure her. "What matters is that you're back and you're okay. What happened to you?"

Her face wrinkles. "I don't know." Her eyes move to the top left corner of their sockets, as if she's thinking really hard. After a moment, she shakes her head. "I can't remember."

"Were you in a car accident?"

"I don't think so." She feels the back of her head with her hands and then grimaces. "God, my head hurts."

Throwing my covers off, I swing my legs over the side of the bed. Emily stands very still as I throw my arms around her. "Stop trying to remember. It doesn't matter what happened. I'm just so happy to see you."

She smells strongly of roses, as if she has doused herself in perfume. It's so unlike her that it takes my mind a second to register that her body is stone-cold in my arms and her skin feels hard and smooth as polished marble.

Stunned, I pull back far enough to look into her face. Only instead of Emily, she morphs into my mother, who leans over me, the strap of her silk nightgown slipping from her pale shoulder, her eyes black and angry.

"You didn't see him, Paige," she says. "You were dreaming."

My alarm goes off, and I jolt upright. Heart pounding, I fumble for the off button and switch on the lamp. The room is empty, and it's 2:13 in the morning. I pick up the clock to reset the alarm and discover it's already set for six—my usual time. So why did it go off? The dream was about Emily. So why then did my mother say, you didn't see *him*?

What was a dream—and what wasn't?

Emily's face is on the television when I walk into the kitchen. My father and I sit at the butcher-block table and stare at the small flat-screen television on the counter. It's the photo I gave the police, the one I took at Whale Rock. Emily's pale hair looks more silver than blonde against the back drop of the blue sky, and she wears a wide, confident smile.

In a flat, detached voice, the reporter summarizes her disappearance, the Amber Alert, the search underway at the park. Viewers are given a number to call if they have information, and then it's over. The next story starts and it's like Emily never was.

I glance at my father, stroking his unshaven face, the circles under his eyes dark as bruises. He catches me looking at him, gets up, and dumps his uneaten cereal in the sink.

"We need to talk," he says, rinsing the bowl.

I eat a bite of Honey Nut Cheerios. They're mushy and flavorless, and they stick in my throat like dread. Maybe he knows something more than the report on the television. "Did they arrest Jeremy?"

He shakes his head and pours himself a cup of coffee. "No. Look—I didn't want to talk about it last night, but why didn't you tell me what happened with you and Jeremy?" He leans back against the sink. "Did you think I wouldn't believe you?"

Even soggy Cheerios float. I push them down with my spoon and they pop right back up like things you don't want to think about.

"Paige," he tries again. "I'm on your side."

Maybe that was true a long time ago, but I'm not the same little girl who idealized him. And he's not the father who read me petroglyphs or fixed my Barbies, knowing I would only pull them apart again, excavate them, and then pretend I was an archeologist, just like him, and try to piece them together.

"Damn it, Paige. Why won't you talk to me? I'm your father."

I drown more Cheerios. The answer is so clear it doesn't need to be spoken. Being my father doesn't mean he has the right to know what I'm thinking or that he can make me explain myself to him.

"Paige," he prompts.

I look up. "Why did you walk out on me and Mom?"

My father doesn't answer. The goose bumps rise on my arms. Why is it so cold in here? It reminds me of the cold in my room, of my nightmare of Emily walking in, her long hair tangled and matted and her face half-coated in fine, white dust.

"I didn't walk out on *you*," my father says. "Your mother and I divorced."

"I know, but why?"

He shakes his head. "We've talked about this. People grow apart. It wasn't right for a long time. You know that, Paige." He rubs the empty place on his fourth finger. I wonder if he even knows what he's doing.

"You flushed it down the toilet," I say, and he looks up, startled. "Your wedding band. Don't you remember?"

The color rises in my father's face, and his hands drop. "Yes," he says evenly. "I remember. I shouldn't have done that, but it's in the past." His mouth tightens. "I know you're still angry at me for what happened, and I don't blame you. I've never been good about telling you that I love you, but I do."

I drop my spoon with a *clang* onto the table. "Were you having an affair, Dad? Is that why you left Mom and me?"

My dad's head jerks back as if I've hit him. "What?"

"Were you having an affair with a student at Rutgers?" I make myself look him in the eye, but inside I'm a mess, just one step away from losing it. Maybe this is why I can finally ask that question.

He takes a deep breath and releases it slowly. "Why would you even think that?"

He hasn't denied it, and a sick feeling spreads in me. "I heard you and Mom arguing in your bedroom. She said something about all those little girls hanging out in your office, that she knew about them and she wasn't stupid."

My father considers my words for a long time and then he pinches the bridge of his nose. "I never had an inappropriate relationship with any of my students."

Part of me wants to believe him, but another part of me feels like he isn't telling the full truth. I clench my fists. Arguing with my father is pointless. It's like he wears a verbal shield and you can hit and hit and hit him but never touch him. Have I not witnessed this a hundred times?

"Paige," my dad says. "I love you."

I stand so I look down at him. "You don't love me. You don't love *anyone*. All you love is being *Dr.* Duke Patterson—digging up dead things and then spending all your time looking at them, thinking about them. It's all you care about!"

"That's not true," he says.

"Isn't it? Other fathers actually like to hang out with their kids. They go to their games. They cook pancakes in the morning and grill dinners. I think you would like me more if I were dead, a skeleton you could examine."

"I'm sorry I'm not who you wanted me to be," he says, and even then his voice isn't angry, just kind of sad and resigned, as if what I've said is true. "Someday, maybe, you'll figure out that being like everyone else is overrated. Just because I don't barbeque doesn't mean I don't love you."

"Just forget it, *Dr. Patterson*. I really don't care anymore." He flinches at the coldness in my voice. I feel mean and bad about myself, but don't let it stop me from walking out of the room.

Access to the park is restricted, but the ranger recognizes my father and unlocks the gate. The grounds look empty, but then we see a skinny German shepherd sniffing the ground just past the cactus gardens. The handler jogs to keep up with the dog, who runs in increasingly wide loops. I could have told them Emily's scent would be strongest by the saguaro where we argued about my father and lead to the banks of Otter Creek where we sat eating lunch.

Inside the information center, the largest conference room is crowded with police, park officials, and rangers. Jalen and his father are there, too, studying a map with Tom Blackstone.

Jalen leans on the table, bracing himself on his arms, the muscles so clearly defined I could trace each one with my finger. His black T-shirt fits the width of his shoulders, then hangs loosely over his hips. He feels my gaze and looks up. I look away quickly, disgusted with myself for the feelings I shouldn't have, especially now.

At the long conference table, Detective Rodriquez sits at the head, an exhausted-looking Mrs. Linton on her right. Dr. Shum, also seated at the table, acknowledges my father with a weary nod. Beside him, Mrs. Shum lays her hand on top of her husband's.

"Any word?" my dad asks.

"No." Dr. Shum's eyes have deep purple circles beneath them, and the collar of his green park shirt stands up on one side as if he put it on without looking in the mirror. "The Equine Search and Rescue is on its way, and the search parties will go out as soon as the dogs finish."

"Dr. Patterson," Detective Rodriquez says with exaggerated emphasis on the word *doctor*. "I was wondering if I could have a word with you privately." She lifts her heavy body up from the chair and walks toward my father.

"Of course," he says. The two of them disappear out the door.

The minute he's gone, I'm surrounded by the Lintons. Mrs. Linton links her arm through mine and leans into me, uncomfortably close. "Paige," she says, "I know this is hard for you, but if you have information, you need to tell us."

She smells a little. Not terrible, but sour enough that I don't want to be near her. Her eyes are terrible—bloodshot and watery. I try not to breathe too deeply, and then I try not to breathe at all. "I told the police everything."

"I know. But there's more, isn't there?"

I shift. "What do you mean?"

"You asked her to talk to him. You even offered to cover for her—that's why she lied to us. Told us she was spending the night with you. She never would have, otherwise. I can forgive you that, but we need to know where she was going to meet him."

My gaze falls to the gray linoleum floor. It looks dirty and soiled, a pattern so trampled it'll never be clean. I know I should leave, but my legs feel bolted to the floor. "No, it wasn't like that. I never asked her to talk to him." My throat closes, and I can't squeeze out that I didn't want Emily to get involved.

"The police are questioning Jeremy Brown right now. I know you know more than you're telling."

I shake my head.

She closes her eyes as if she's trying to keep control of herself, but when she opens them, her pupils are as sharp as pencil points. "You were always leading her into trouble. Even as a little girl. I tried to talk to her about you, but she wouldn't listen." Her lips quiver, and she doesn't speak for several seconds. "How could you let her face him when you knew he was a monster?"

My heart pounds, and my legs start to shake. It feels like she's growing taller, stronger, while I'm shrinking, dying inside. I try to look away, but the room is a dizzying kaleidoscope of faces.

"Why couldn't you just leave her alone?"

Dr. Linton pulls ineffectively at his wife's arm. "Sarah," he says quietly. "Don't."

"It's her fault," Mrs. Linton insists. She leans closer, and her voice drops to a sour whisper. "It should have been *you*. Whatever happened to her should have happened to you. It's *all* your fault."

The venom in her voice is like poison in my bloodstream. Heart pounding, I turn, knocking into someone and spilling their coffee and pushing past, out of the room. Running down the hallway, Mrs. Linton's voice repeats clearly in my head. *Your fault. Your fault. Your fault.*

I run through the maze of exhibits. Where can I go where I won't see Mrs. Linton's accusing eyes? Where do you go when the person you most want to avoid is yourself?

I race past the taxidermy display, the wall of bronze tools, the shelves of pottery, and the curtained-off area, and then I'm in the gift shop.

I veer away from the floor-to-ceiling windows that face the cliffs and then push my way past the racks of T-shirts, the postcard stand, and the shelves of stuffed animals to a corner where an ancient-looking soda machine stands along the wall. I lean forward against it, breathing hard, absorbing the heat coming off its surface.

A voice makes me jump. "So what kind do you want?"

I turn slowly. Jalen is standing behind me, still as a shadow. His eyes are black, serious.

When I don't answer, he takes a dollar bill out of a worn brown wallet and peers past me at the selections, although he probably already knows most have been empty since the day I arrived.

"Water, water…or water?"

"Nothing. I'm fine." I shift an inch backward and feel the heat of the machine at my back.

He leans around me and feeds the limp dollar into the slot. A bottle bounces to the bottom with a *thump*.

His hand looks huge as he twists off the cap. As he gives it to me, our fingers touch. The contact startles me. A spark. I almost laugh, not because it's funny, but because it's either laugh or cry. His hand moves away abruptly, leaving me with the cold weight of the plastic bottle.

I take a small swallow of the icy water and mumble "thanks." I hope he'll go away.

I lift my chin. "You didn't have to come after me. You don't have to try and make me feel better."

"I know," he says.

But he doesn't *know*, or he wouldn't keep standing there as the seconds tick by. I want to ask why he came after me, why he never says my name, and why he's still standing there. And yet I say nothing at all.

Yet there's something comforting about his presence, as if he's a wall between me and the rest of the world. But as much as I'd like to hide behind him, I can't let myself do that.

"I'm fine."

"I know."

I lift my gaze from the slimy blue label around the water bottle. "You can go."

"I know." The hint of a smile softens the straight line of his lips.

"So why don't you?" I would cringe at the coldness in my voice if I didn't need it so badly to hide how scared I am. How guilty I feel.

He shrugs. "Because you're so pleasant to be around?"

His face is so serious I have to study him hard to see if he's joking or not, and even then I'm not completely sure.

"I'm not going to fall apart."

He nods as if this is a given but then doesn't budge an inch. "Good. You want to sit down?"

"Are you babysitting me?"

He smiles. "A little. There's a bench just outside the door in the cactus garden. It's quiet there."

"You're trying to keep me away from the Lintons."

His smile fades. "They've been up all night. Their daughter is missing. You can't take anything she says seriously."

But I can. And I do. Because she's right. It should be me who's missing. Me who should fight her own fights.

It isn't until we step outside of the information center and into the heat of the morning that I realize how cold I am. How welcome the sun rays feel, soaking into my skin as if they're going all the way to the bone. We take a seat on some wooden benches that face the cliffs. The police dogs are gone, and the landscape stretches out as far as I can see, empty of people, empty of any birds or animals. I don't know if I'm more terrified that they'll find her body, or that they'll find nothing at all.

Next to me, Jalen is quiet. His eyes are watchful, fixed on something in the distance. If as much as a rabbit moved, I think he'd see it. I have the feeling he can sit this way for hours, not speaking but soaking up thoughts. I take a sip of water and hear myself ask. "What do you think happened to her?"

"I don't know."

I start peeling the label off the bottle and ask the question that haunts me. "Do you think she's alive?"

He takes a long time to answer the question. "I hope so."

"I hope so," I mimic in frustration. "You must have heard something. Last night, or earlier before I got here. What did the police say?"

His lips tighten. "The dogs keep following a scent into the park, but there's still a possibility that she was abducted from the parking lot."

I compare this to my own theory, and it comes up short. "Mrs. Linton said the police were questioning Jeremy Brown. Do you know anything about that?"

He shakes his head. "No. But Detective Rodriquez questioned me about him. What happened on Tuesday afternoon between you and him."

I hold his gaze. "What did you tell them?"

"That I heard noises coming from Chamber One and when I called out if everyone was okay, you came up the ladder looking upset."

He had pulled me up the last few rungs. I still remember the power of his grip, the strength of his hand lifting me. For the first time, however, I realize that the story didn't end with me running out of the ruins. "Did you see Jeremy?"

"Yes."

"What did he say?"

He shrugs. "Nothing."

"I don't believe you."

"He was in a hurry. He asked which way you'd gone."

"Did he seem...mad?"

"No. When I asked him what was going on, he told me to stay out of it."

"And then what happened?"

He turns to meet my gaze and blinks a couple of times. "I told him you climbed up into the third level."

He lied for me. He saw me run through the doorway out into the open. Although nothing in his face moves, something in his stillness gives him away. He's holding back. "That's it?"

My suspicions are confirmed when Jalen does another series of slow blinks. "Well, he was kind of in a hurry to get to the ladder and he accidentally tripped over my feet. I helped him up and told him that he should be more careful, that accidents like that could happen pretty easily around here."

I don't know what to say. I'm not even sure how I feel about him defending me. Part of me feels glad, and yet I also realize that, once again, I've let someone else stand up for me. It's like I'm five again and Emily is explaining the rules of fear—*it either helps you grow or makes you less of yourself.* Maybe there's more truth in that than either of us thought.

Before I can either say thank you or tell him that I can look after myself, the door to the information center opens. John Yazzi sticks his head out of the opening.

"Jalen," he snaps, "we need you inside."

EIGHTEEN

Paige

For the next several days the park stays closed to the general public as the search for Emily Linton intensifies. The days are cloudless, searing hot, over a hundred degrees, but it doesn't stop volunteers from showing up before dawn and staying until the rangers make them leave.

Equine rescue teams arrive from Scottsdale and Houston. The riders divide the park into grids and search in pairs. Although they cover more ground, at the end of the day the riders return, like me, sunburned and exhausted.

I spend an afternoon watching a team of divers search Tacoma Well. When they break the surface, the black hoods of their wetsuits remind me of the heads of turtles I used to feed in the pond near my house in New Jersey.

The dogs find a faint trail that leads from the parking lot to the base of the cliffs. The dogs, of course, can't climb the ladders to follow the scent, and for a while there's talk of men carrying them up into the ruins, but that doesn't happen. Instead, Dr. Shum and my father lead teams of officers up the cliffs. They spend several days prowling around the honeycomb of rooms, jagged stone corridors, and hollowed-out crevices in the walls.

Rumors fly. Emily has run away and is sunning herself on the sandy beaches of Southern California. Emily was the victim of a serial killer who preys on girls at national parks. Emily's disappearance is part of a publicity stunt to bring more tourism to the park. Emily met the same fate as the hundreds of Native Americans who vanished from the cliffs more than six hundred years ago.

One night, as my father and I eat our respective microwave dinners in front of the television, the news flashes the same photo of Emily and the reporter repeats the story of her disappearance and the discouraging news that there are no developments.

After the story ends, my father turns off the television. "Listen, honey, I know Emily's disappearance is disturbing, but there's something else we need to talk about. Ray came by my office today." He pauses. His blue eyes are intent behind the black frames of his glasses. My stomach tightens. "The police have cleared Jeremy."

A bite of Stouffers's lasagna lodges itself in my throat. "What?"

"He has an alibi. He was home all night with his mother."

"That's impossible. He's lying."

"He was home with his parents. The story checks out."

"He could have slipped out, met Emily at the park."

His eyes look skeptical behind his glasses. "The odds of that are small." He pauses, pushes the skin on his face as if he dreads delivering the next bit of news. "Ray and I talked about you and Jeremy." He pauses, giving me a long, dreadful moment to imagine them discussing the details, maybe even passing back and forth the pictures the police took at the hospital. "We're going to temporarily suspend Jeremy from the university. Dr. Shum is going to talk to him and the other interns before he makes a final decision."

"Great. Maybe he can make copies of my photos from the hospital and pass them around." Or they could post them, I think bitterly, next to the flyers of Emily.

"He promises to be discreet, but this is a serious charge against Jeremy. The university has a very strict sexual harassment policy."

"I don't want to press charges. I just think that he isn't who he seems. He comes across as nice, but he has a temper, Dad. Don't you think it's more than a coincidence that Emily disappears the day after I told her what happened to me?"

My father cleans his glasses with the hem of his shirt and then replaces them. "I don't know what to think," he admits. "It's still possible she'll turn up."

"And it's also possible that Jeremy's mother lied to protect him. Wouldn't you lie to protect me?"

He shakes his head. "I hope I would never be in a position to have to answer that."

It isn't the answer I want, and I shift impatiently on the couch. "Come on, Dad. He's lying. I want to talk to him."

"No," my father say in a tone of voice that says the conversation is finished.

"I'll know if he's lying." I know the taste, touch, and scent of him. I know both more and less than I want.

"No, Paige. This is for the police. Stay out of this."

"Are you kidding me? Emily is missing and you don't want to get involved?"

"Of course I want to help. Look, Emily's disappearance—it's terrible…" He mutes the television and shifts on the couch to face me. "It's beyond terrible, actually. But you're my priority. He hurt you. You need to stay away from him."

"But he might know something."

"Paige. This whole…incident between the two of you is serious. The Browns have spoken with Dr. Shum. They're hiring a lawyer. They say…the statements you're making about their son are false and inflammatory. Until everything is resolved, any communication has to go through the university."

"What if there's still a chance Emily's alive and he knows where she is?"

"He doesn't know, Paige. If he did, the police would have found out."

"The police don't know him. I do."

My father shakes his head. "When I pictured you coming here, I thought it might be like when you were little. You loved going on-site with me. I thought it…" His voice trails off, and for a moment I think he's going to say that he hoped it would bring us together. His eyes fix on me, unblinking. "Maybe it would be best if you went back to New Jersey."

"You're kidding me."

"I want to do what's right for you."

My fingers trace a small dark stain on the sofa where I spilled grape juice when I was little. I was terrified my father would be mad, but all he said was that I'd given the couch a history, a story, a memory. He said it was a good thing, but Mom always turned the cushions over when we had company.

"I don't want to leave—not until I know what happened to Emily."

His gaze softens. "We might never know. Sometimes bad things just happen."

"I thought you cared about her."

"I do care about her. I'm just saying that sometimes things happen and you wonder if you could have changed them if you'd done something differently." His brow furrows, and his face forms that faraway look he gets when he slips into professor mode. "You can second-guess the choices you make, but you can't change anything. The truth is that sometimes it is our fault and sometimes it isn't. Ultimately, either way, you have to let go and move on."

What is he talking about? What choices have either of us made when it came to Emily?

"Are you serious?" I'm supposed to accept that Emily is missing? That there's nothing I can do about it? I'm on my feet before he's finished. "You can't give up on her, Dad. You just can't say, 'Okay, it's been a week. Time to move on.'"

"Look, I'm still going to do everything I can to find her." He takes a breath and releases it slowly. "I'm just trying to make sure you're prepared if this doesn't turn out the way we hope. I know we've hurt you in the past. I don't want to do that again."

The last sentence stops me from heading to my room. It's the first time he's ever admitted that the divorce happened to me, too. I've been waiting for him to say this for so long now, and yet suddenly I'm afraid. I make myself hold his gaze. "Why did you divorce Mom? She wanted to try to work things out. She told me."

He takes off his glasses again. His blue eyes look larger, somehow younger. "Is that what she told you?"

"Yes. She said she wanted you to go to counseling with her. She said you wouldn't."

He replaces his glasses. "That's true. What you need to know, honey, is that what happened between me and your mom had nothing to do with you."

"How can it have nothing to do with me when it happened to me, too?" That was something I was supposed to think, not say. He isn't allowed into my head, into my thoughts. He isn't allowed to see he can make me cry or laugh or feel anything at all.

The couch cushions shift under his weight, and then he sits beside me. "I know," he says. "I know it happened to you, too." His arms go around me, but I make myself go away so that he can't reach inside me. I stay absolutely still, and after a moment his arms fall away.

"I love you," he says, searching my eyes. "I don't say that enough. I'm sorry. I'm sorry about the divorce. It was never about leaving you. I just couldn't stay there anymore."

"Why?"

A wry, ironic-looking smile lifts the corners of his mouth but doesn't touch his eyes. "I thought that I could give you more if I started liking myself again."

"You give me more by moving two thousand miles away?"

"Back in New Jersey…it was all academic. It was never going to be right for me." He shakes his head. "It was never about leaving you, Paige."

Of course it was about leaving me. He chose. It wasn't like I had the same ability. No one asked me where I wanted to live or took my feelings into consideration. Yet when I look into his eyes, I could swear he's telling the truth. He's happier here. He belongs here. I don't want to admit it, but it's the truth. And maybe he does love me—not a lot, but enough to do what he thinks is best for me. But then I remember that night I heard them arguing. The word *affair* rising just above the crack of a slamming door. Maybe Mom thought he was having an affair, but he wasn't. He might be this really famous archeologist, but sometimes he's a total geek. I almost cave in, let myself reach for him, but then my mind wanders back where I don't want it to go—to the night Emily disappeared. My father sent me to get the pizza, but where did he go? What if the real reason my father wants to send me back to New Jersey isn't because he loves me and wants to protect me, but because he's somehow involved?

NINETEEN

Paige

When we get to the information center the next morning, I tell my father I have cramps and won't be joining one of the search parties. I hang out in the ladies' room until I hear the building go silent, and then I slip out the back exit.

Hurrying through the parking lot, I pass an assortment of cars and trucks. Two equine trailers fill the air with the sweet aroma of hay and the darker, pungent odor of manure.

It's about six miles to Jeremy's house and should take less than two hours to get there, if the directions on Google maps are correct. More than enough time for what I need to do.

I glance over my shoulder as I start down the long driveway leading to Highway 59. No one sees me, and I pick up the pace a bit, a little scared and also a little excited. It's still early, and when I reach the highway, the road is clear for miles, flat and sunbaked. Along the shoulder, cactus plants with leaves as big as hands grow in clusters.

Emily and I used to challenge each other to jump over them. And more than once we scraped ourselves bloody. A couple of cars rocket past in a gust of hot air. According to my phone, I've gone about half a mile when the rumble of an engine pulls up behind me. I motion for it to pass, but the pickup keeps pace behind me.

Someone's following. Too easily, I imagine Emily walking the highway at night and the lights of this same pickup pinning her in their glare. A faceless man offering her a ride. Could this be an awful coincidence to have the same thing happen to me? I hunch my shoulders as the truck pulls alongside me.

"I thought it was you," Jalen says. "What are you doing?"

I release a breath I hadn't realized I was holding. "Shit, Jalen. You scared the crap out of me."

"Where are you going?"

I shrug. "Nowhere."

He accelerates past me and then jerks the truck to a stop on the shoulder of the road. When he steps out of the pickup, my heart sinks. It would be so much better for both of us if he just stayed out of this.

When I get close enough to move around him, he blocks me. I glare up at him. "What are you doing?"

"Trying to talk to you."

I try to cut around him, but he blocks me a second time. "Just get out of the way."

"Not until you tell me where you're going."

"Why do you even care?" I study the smooth planes of his face. There's no trace of anger in his eyes or the set of his jaw, which in a way makes it harder to be mad at him for stopping me.

"One girl's missing. No need for there to be two."

I lift my chin. "I can take of myself."

He just looks at me. I don't know how I know he's thinking of me, clinging to his hand and fighting panic as he lifted me out of the basement chamber, but I know he is. It doesn't help that he's right. I'm still scared of Jeremy.

I shift my weight. "Shouldn't you be at work?"

"Shouldn't you be at the park?"

A car rockets past us. Jalen steps toward me as if he would protect me from it. It tells me even more than words that he isn't going to leave me alone. "Look, I need to do something... It's better if you don't know what it is."

He shakes his head. "Why doesn't that surprise me?"

"So you should just go. Pretend you never saw me. You're good at that."

I didn't mean to say the last part—and especially not to say it so bitterly, as if I care if he sees me or not. Jalen's head jerks as if I've slapped him, but then he turns around and walks back to the truck without saying a word. I'm a little surprised he's given in so easily, but mostly I'm relieved.

The engine rumbles. I wait for the pickup to pass, but it doesn't. At first I think he's just watching, but then when I look over my shoulder, I see the truck trailing behind like a dog that won't go away.

After a quarter-mile or so, I realize he isn't going to give up. It's humiliating. It's like he feels obligated to look after me, and I keep making things worse by saying things and doing things that make us both uncomfortable.

I stop walking, and when the truck rolls up alongside, I lean against the passenger-side door. "I'm going to Jeremy Brown's house. If you're going to follow me the whole way, I'd appreciate it if you didn't let him see you."

"Why are you going there?"

"Because I think he did something to her." I clench my fists, but can't keep the frustration out of my voice. I mean, how obvious can it get?

"And you think you'll find her locked in his basement?"

His sarcasm makes me even madder. "Better the basement than the freezer."

It's a terrible thing to say, and part of me can't believe it came out of my mouth. Emily's alive. She has to be. And Jeremy *knows* what happened.

"You think he's just going to let you wander around his house looking for her?"

"No, but I'll figure something out."

He's silent a long time. "Does anyone even know where you're going?"

I don't answer. The heat of the truck pours off, making me even hotter. "Yes. My father."

His lips tighten at my obvious lie. "You think this kid had something to do with Emily's disappearance, and yet you're going to his house, alone, without telling anyone?"

"I have to! Nobody will listen to me!"

I walk away from the truck, trying not to let myself doubt what I'm doing, not to see that Jalen's words had any truth in them at all.

A moment later, Jalen's truck pulls alongside me again.

"What?" I shout.

"If you're going to search the house," he says, "you're going to need someone to distract Brown long enough for you to do it. Get in the truck."

I stare at him in disbelief. "What?"

"I can probably get you five minutes, but not longer. The guy's a jerk, and any longer than that I'll end up punching him."

I hesitate, but looking at Jalen's face, I know there's really no choice. The passenger-side door opens with a groan, I get in, and minutes later we're driving to Jeremy's house. The shocks in the truck are gone and every bump jolts me hard. Cranking the windows is slow and hard. There isn't even air-conditioning, so we ride with the wind streaming in our faces, too loud to speak. But not too loud to swap gazes, for each of us to wonder what in the world we're doing.

When Jalen exits the freeway, however, it's less noisy, the silence more pronounced. I try to turn on the radio, but when it doesn't work, Jalen shoots me a quick, sideways smirk as if he expects me to complain. I look at my cell.

"Take the next left," is all I say.

What I don't tell him is that the truck smells like summer and feels unstoppable, as if we're driving a tank to Jeremy's house. The air blowing on my face reminds me of riding through the desert in the old Jeep with my parents all those summers ago. They would sit in the front, and Emily and I would bounce around in the back, laughing and clutching each other as my father drove through the bumpy, unpaved desert.

The memory fades and my stomach clenches, however, as we turn into the Mesa Verde development. All the houses here are brand-new, most of them sprawling concrete-and-glass buildings. Some are under construction, consisting of no more than frames of what look kind of like giant Popsicle sticks.

Deeper into the development, I look at a bed of concrete on a newly poured foundation and think it looks like a perfect place to hide a body.

Jalen pulls to the side of the road in front of a large, sand-colored, concrete one-story with an interesting grid on the front, like a gate molded onto the exterior. There are no neighbors on either side, only taped-off lots with scrubby trees and underbrush. Behind Jeremy's house, the humped shapes of mountains loom.

My mouth goes dry and my heart hammers as we step up to the mahogany front door with its black, medieval-looking hinges and criss-crossing bars. I'm shaking inside as I press the doorbell.

As if someone has been watching us through the window, the door swings open immediately, and suddenly Jeremy Brown is standing in front of us. The sight of his thin, evil face fills me with so much hatred that I can't speak.

"Hello, Paige." He smiles warmly. "Nice to see you."

I swallow. "Hello, Jeremy."

"Well," he says, "to what do I owe the honor of your visit?"

"I need to talk to you about Emily Linton."

He shakes his head. "I've been told not to talk to you without a lawyer present."

From inside, I hear a woman's voice asking who's at the door. Jeremy turns his head. "Friends from the park, Mom."

"Well, invite them in," she says.

He pulls the door wider, and suddenly I'm glad Jalen is with me. We step onto a white marble floor with dark-colored veins running through it. A few pieces of Native American artwork hang on the white walls, and we pass a three-foot bronze statue of a running horse tucked into a niche in the wall.

Jeremy's mother—a thin, dark-haired woman with large hazel eyes and small, airy bones—greets us. When she hears my name, her expression freezes and her lips thin.

"What are you doing here?" she says, and her voice is cold as ice.

"Relax, Mom," Jeremy says, "I've got this."

"You've got this?" Her voice rises. "What you've got is a suspension from the university."

"What I've got," Jeremy says calmly, "is a chance to work things out with Paige. Now go to your bedroom and give us some time alone. If I need you, I'll let you know."

"I don't trust her," Mrs. Brown says and gives me another hateful look. "I think you should leave."

"Mom," Jeremy says, "you want this to go away, don't you?" He doesn't wait for an answer. "You have to trust me. Now leave us alone."

With a final glare at me, she disappears down a hallway off the kitchen. Her high heels clack crisply, echoing her disapproval. After she goes, Jeremy offers us iced tea, but we decline. He pours himself a tall glass and then leads us to a glossy black leather sofa in the family room.

"I'm really glad you're here," Jeremy says, sipping his tea and settling himself more comfortably into a matching leather chair angled toward us. "I was going to call you, but then this whole thing with Emily happened." He leans forward, features creasing. "I'm really sorry, Paige. I know you two were close."

I look around the room—a painting of a desert sunset centered on the massive mahogany mantelpiece, shelves of painted pottery; a set of bleached antlers supporting the glass-topped coffee table in front of us. My gaze drifts to the floor-to-ceiling windows. Across what looks like several lots, a bulldozer is clawing at the land.

"When was the last time you saw Emily?" Jalen asks.

Jeremy sets the glass down on the end table. "The day she disappeared."

The day I told Emily about him attacking me. And the day she lied to her parents about spending the night with me. "What time?"

Jeremy shakes his head. The expression in his eyes is earnest, like someone trying really hard to give the right answer. "I don't know. Sometime in the afternoon. I was in Chamber Seven, doing some measurements." His gaze returns to mine, ignoring Jalen. "She was very upset. You'd just told her what happened between us, and she had it in her head that I should withdraw from the program."

"You're admitting that?" The surprise in my voice is clear even to me.

He nods. A lock of his long, dark bangs falls forward, and he pushes it behind his ear. "Why wouldn't I?"

"She would have gotten you thrown out of the program."

He shakes his head. "I'm sorry for what happened in that chamber, Paige, but it was a miscommunication, nothing more. I have nothing to hide."

Speechless, my mouth gapes open, and it takes a few seconds to get anything out at all. "Are you crazy? You attacked me." Next to me, Jalen tenses.

When Jeremy speaks, his voice is very patient, as if I'm a young child and he's explaining something complicated. "Paige, you knew why I brought you to that chamber." His eyes hold mine. "You wanted me. You said you did."

"I told you to stop." I make myself hold his gaze, but inside I'm shaking. I said those words, thought I meant them. Remembering what he did, however, is humiliating. I wipe my sweaty palms on my shorts and hope my face isn't as red as it feels. I can't even imagine what Jalen must be thinking.

"Not to piss off your new boyfriend—" he pauses to shoot Jalen what seems like an apologetic half-smile "—but you kissed me back. You gave me mixed signals. Look, I'm sorry about what happened, but there was fault both ways. You need to ask your father to lift the suspension."

I search his eyes. They're wide open, innocent, truthful. In his light blue polo and neatly pressed tan shorts, he looks clean-cut and all American. There's no trace of the violence or ugliness inside him. I feel myself waver.

"I already told my father the truth."

"All of it?" His eyes get a little more intense.

I clench my fists. "Yes. And I think it's pretty convenient, too, that your mother is your alibi. What TV show did you say you were watching?"

"Why would I admit talking to Emily if I had something to hide? I had nothing to do with her disappearance. Nothing."

"But you know something," Jalen says. It isn't a question as much as it is a statement. "I've seen you. You like to stay late at the ruins. You like to watch people, don't you? What did you see the night Emily disappeared?"

Jeremy shakes his head, completely covering one eye with his hair until he pushes it back impatiently. "Nothing. I was home, remember?" He folds his hands together, and a sly look comes into his eyes. "But it doesn't mean I wasn't at the park late on other nights." He looks directly at me. "The two of you were even more alike than I thought."

"What did you see?" The bones in the back of Jalen's hands stand out as he grips his legs.

Jeremy ignores him and keeps looking at me. "I'll tell you," he says, "because I want you to stop going around saying that I had something to do with Emily's disappearance. Paige, I'm asking—no, begging—you. Tell your father the whole truth about us."

Just what is the truth? That I was sad and lonely and starving for someone to touch me, to hold me, to want me. Jeremy was there. Did I lead him on? Did I deserve what I got? It's suddenly hard to say. I realize I'm twisting my hands and stop. "I already told him everything."

"Not everything," Jeremy says gently. "Or I wouldn't be suspended."

Our gazes lock. Mine drops first.

"I know you'll do the right thing," Jeremy says. "So I'll do the right thing, too." He pauses and then releases his breath slowly. "About a month ago, I stayed late at the park to update the database in Dr. Shum's office. As I was leaving, I ran into Emily on the path between the information center and the cliffs. She said she'd been in the ruins, getting background for a blog, but there was something about her... She blew me off pretty fast when I tried to ask her what she was writing about, and her hair was loose, messy...like she'd been making out." His eyes gleam as if he's remembering us making out. "It wasn't the first time I saw her late at the park, either."

"You told the police all this?" Jalen asks.

"Of course. I liked Emily. I hope the police find her." He pushes back that lock of thick, brown hair that almost-but-not-quite fits behind his ear. "If you ask me, they not only need to be looking for her, but also the person she was meeting after hours at the park."

TWENTY

Jalen

The first thing I do after I drop my boots by the back door is to head for the kitchen. I'm hot, hungry, and angry. The air-conditioning isn't working in the truck again, and I skipped lunch. Normally, none of these things would bother me, but today everything and everyone gets on my nerves. Especially Paige Patterson, who is determined to get into trouble and has somehow become my responsibility.

In the kitchen, my mother pushes around ground lamb in a skillet on the cooktop. It smells delicious. Reaching around her, I grab a sample off the top and pop it into my mouth. She hits me lightly, but the smile in her eyes forgives me. "Any news of the missing girl?"

"No." I think of Jeremy and grind my molars into the now-tasteless lamb.

"God," she sighs. "I was hoping today..." Her words trail off, and she gives a small shake of her head. "Go wash up. Dinner in fifteen."

I head through the living room where Harold sits in front of the widescreen television, playing a video game. He doesn't look up as I turn down the corridor to my room.

The back of my shirt still clings to my skin from the hot ride home in the truck, as does the dust from the park, but instead of heading to the shower, I walk up the three steps that lead to Uncle Billy's room.

Pausing outside the door, I listen. All day, the need to talk to him has played in the back of my mind like a song stuck in my head. The fear of what he might say wars with the need to ask him. I know he won't soften his words; if there's blame, he will lay it without hesitation on my shoulders. I already carry the burden of things he's said.

And yet, here I am, hesitating at the doorway. I'd head for my room if it wasn't for Paige. Am I wrong to help her? At this point, how can I not?

Leaning forward, I strain to hear inside the room. Is he drunk? Sober? Can I really trust what he says in either case? I hold my breath, frozen in doubt.

And then, as if he sees me clearly through the wood, my uncle calls, "Come in, Jalen."

The handle sticks, and the wood bows a little as I put my shoulder into it. It pops open, and the heat of the room wafts across my face, at least five degrees hotter than anywhere else in the house, which I guess makes sense. The room used to be an attic before he moved in with us. Fifteen years later, it still looks like an attic with its low ceiling, sloping walls, clutter of unpacked boxes, and mismatched furniture.

The room smells stale, airless, slightly sour. Uncle Billy has forbidden my mother from cleaning. It's probably been years since the rug has seen a vacuum, never mind dusting. Yet this is the place that pulls me like none other in the house. Here is the past—hidden sometimes in boxes, but visible in the artwork on the walls, the shelf of *kachina* dolls, a feathered headdress that was my grandfather's, a sheepskin rug worn bare in the center. Here there is no fusion of cultures, no walking a line between two worlds. Everything here is Diné. To Uncle Billy, I am completely Diné, and this is where I belong. The fact that my mother is white is insignificant.

To be defined, to be able to point to a heritage and say "this is who I am; on this side of the line I stand" is not a bad thing.

My uncle looks up from his desk. His eyes are deeply hooded, and the lines carved into his cheeks make him look years older than my father, although he is younger by three years.

"How is the hunt for the girl going?"

To get to him, I have to twist around the boxes and stacks piled on the floor. "The same," I tell him. "They haven't found anything."

My uncle nods. I strain to read the level of alcohol in his eyes. They look a little red, moderately shiny. A mug sits near his elbow. I'm sure it holds whiskey.

"What are you making?" I ask. It isn't the question that's bugged me all day—the same one that's burning me up inside and has been since Emily disappeared.

He looks down at the block of wood in his hands and then holds it up for me to see. "A *kachina* doll," he says, although this already is clear to me.

Over the years, he has made quite a few of these. For a long time, my father used to try to convince him to sell them at the park, like the other people who spread blankets and sell their jewelry on the grass near the entrance.

"The tourists will pay good money for them," my dad said. "Your craftsmanship is exceptional."

"They would not be used correctly," Uncle Billy said scornfully. "They are not idols or household decorations."

"You're not selling our people out," my father argued. "You'd be making a living."

"Food can be found," Uncle Billy told him. "But who we are needs to stay with us, to be honored by us. What would we be teaching our children?"

"That our people cannot isolate themselves from the rest of the world. Our cultures have always traded. This is just another form of it."

My uncle looked him in the eye. "Trading?" he scoffed. "They steal our children and you call this *trading*?"

Looking at the nearly two-foot-long block of cottonwood root in my uncle's bony hands, I realize it has been a long time since he has carved anything at all. "What kind of doll are you making?"

His face softens. "The yellow corn maiden."

Why the corn maiden? When he puts the doll down and lifts the mug to his lips, I want to knock it out of his hands. He hasn't told me what I've come to ask him, what I'm still afraid to ask.

"Uncle," I say as he takes a long, slow sip and then half-closes his eyes as if he savors every inch of the liquid's passage through his body. "The girl who disappeared. The one you played the drums for. Was she the one you told me about?"

He opens his eyes and looks at me. The puzzlement in his face makes him look almost childlike. "What?"

"The night the girl at the park disappeared. You sang the death chant."

His brow wrinkles, and he cocks his head as if the memory is a sound that might be heard if he listens hard enough. Finally he sighs. "She came to me. She was lost. I wanted to help her find her way." He gestures to the doll. "I need yellow yarn for the hair, and more paint. Will you take me to Walmart?"

I lean closer, see the spiderweb of gray claiming what was once hair as black as mine. "Is she the one you warned me about?"

He shakes his head. "What are you talking about?"

"The girl in your dream, uncle."

"I told you. She was lost. I was trying to help her find her way."

"And was she the same one you dreamed about before?"

His brow furrows. "I dreamed about her before?"

He doesn't remember. All the anger that was slow-burning in the back of my mind leaps to the front, and I want to shake him until he tells me what I need to know. "Think, Uncle Billy. Is the girl who's lost the same one you warned me about, or are there two girls?"

He shakes his head slowly and then picks up a piece of black sandstone and rubs it gently over the wood. "I'm sorry, Jalen," he says. "I don't know what you're talking about."

I stare at him. How could he forget the night he came into my room, stood beside my bed, and screeched like an eagle to wake me?

"You've got to remember, Uncle. You had a dream and you came into my room dressed as the Eagle *kachina* and told me about it."

Uncle Billy looks at me blankly. I can tell he doesn't have a clue what I'm asking. Too late, I remember something else about alcoholics. When they've been drinking, when their blood alcohol rises to a level you can measure in their eyes, they will forget things. You can tell them what they said or did, and they will deny it and believe with every fiber in their being that you are making it up.

They will not remember that they were drunk or that they woke you at two in the morning dressed in Eagle's feathers. They will not remember that they told you that you would be responsible for someone else's death.

TWENTY-ONE

Paige

All night I think about Jeremy Brown's words—that Emily was secretly meeting someone else in the park after hours. My mind probes this problem like a loose tooth. It hurts to go there, but I can't seem to help it.

Could Emily have been meeting my father?

Of course not. That would imply an inappropriate relationship, and my mind refuses to accept that. There has to be an explanation for Emily's disappearance that doesn't involve him. At least that's what I tell myself. Any one of the other interns, including Jeremy, could have been meeting her.

While my dad holds the morning briefing, I head for the ladies' room. Although the police have already searched Emily's locker and probably taken anything that might give a clue, I want to see for myself. I know her a lot better than they do.

Her lock dangles from the front of the locker, like an ugly charm on a necklace. The combination is part my birthday, part hers, and it opens on the first try. As I feared, it's mostly empty—just her canteen and a Vera Bradley bag holding deodorant, sunscreen, a spray bottle of Victoria's Secret body scent, and an assortment of makeup.

The air in the locker smells sour, and I spray the body scent. The odor of vanilla and lavender hangs in the air like a ghost. *If you were seeing someone, why didn't you tell me?* I picture her lips curving into a slow smile. *Well, Paige, I couldn't very well blurt out that I was dating your father, could I? You were mad enough at him as it was.*

I slam the locker door shut, but the conversation, like the body scent, lingers.

Remember those nights he worked late at the park? Emily's voice asks. *You don't think he was working, do you? It was right there in front of you, Paige. Only you kept closing your eyes. The way you did in New Jersey. The truth was right there in front of you. The way we looked at each other…the photo of us on my Connections page…the way I always defended him…*

Walking out of the room, I cover my ears with my hands. *Shut up,* I tell the Emily voice. *I won't listen to you. You're not even Emily—you're me making up a story, letting my imagination get out of control.*

Why do you think he wanted to send you back to New Jersey? the Emily voice persists. *You and I were always good at keeping secrets. Well, it turns out your father was, too.*

I walk faster down the empty hallway. *Shut up! Shut up! Shut up!*

I'm passing Dr. Shum's office when his deep voice booms, "Paige! Could you come here please?"

Shit. My stomach clenches. Part of me wants to keep on walking, but I know he's seen me. A fresh wave of heat sends small beads of sweat sliding down my back. *Not now*, I think, struggling not to let anything show on my face.

"Paige," another voice says, and my heart drops like a stone.

I step inside. My father is seated across the desk from Dr. Shum. For a moment our eyes meet, and then my dad shakes his head as if to warn me not to say anything.

"Have a seat," Dr. Shum waves me toward an empty chair. Although he smiles, he doesn't quite meet my eye. He takes his time shuffling and reshuffling the papers on his desk. "How are you doing this morning, Paige?"

How does he think I'm doing? I perch on the edge of a straight-backed chair with a long tear in the fabric seat. "Fine." I swallow. "You?"

"Pretty good. Thanks." His smile fades, and his brown eyes turn serious. "Paige, we need to talk." He scratches the side of his nose and then runs his hand through his thinning blond hair in a distracted way. "It's about Jeremy Brown."

I close my eyes briefly. "What about him?"

"I need to decide if he's going to return to the program or not."

Beside me, my dad pinches the bridge of his nose as if he already knows whatever Dr. Shum says is going to be painful to hear.

"There are some discrepancies I'm hoping you can help clear up." He leans forward, fingers laced and eyes hard. "He says that you came to his house yesterday. Is that true?"

I freeze. How much trouble am I in? I look at my father, but his gaze stays fixed on Dr. Shum. "Yes."

"Weren't you afraid of seeing him again?" Dr. Shum's head cocks to one side, and his brows push together sympathetically.

"Not really."

Now those thick blond brows lift. "That surprises me. Considering that he allegedly attacked you."

"Allegedly?" My voice rises. "You think I lied about that?"

Dr. Shum picks up a piece of paper from the top of a pile. "In your statement to the police, you say that he sexually assaulted you. But according to Jeremy, you were the one who initiated the physical contact." His brown eyes seem sad as he stares at me. "Now, who's right? Whose word do we take? Can you see, Paige, why we have a problem?"

My stomach drops and inside I'm shaking, but I make myself hold his gaze. "I asked him to stop. The guy's a creep."

Dr. Shum sighs and sits back in his chair. Pressing his palms together, he seems to be thinking hard. "The problem," he says, "is that, according to him, you said no several times, but you meant yes." He holds his hand up to stop me from speaking. "If you were so afraid, why did you go to his house?"

I glance at my father for help, but he seems to want to hear the answer as much as Dr. Shum. "Because I think he has something to do with Emily's disappearance."

Dr. Shum steeples his long fingers and sighs. "He never left his house that night. The police have cleared him. But back to the situation at hand—as far as what happened between you and Jeremy, I'm afraid it's always going to be a he-said, she-said thing."

Finally my father comes to life. "Ray, you can't ignore the bruises he put on her. I don't want him in the program."

"I know you're upset," Dr. Shum says, "but I've talked to the boy, and he's genuinely sorry. I see no reason for further disciplinary action. He's reinstated into the program effective immediately." His brown eyes hold my father's gaze. "In light of the circumstances, however, I'll be supervising him. That's my decision."

My father's already sunburned skin gets even redder. "Paige, go outside. I'll talk to you later."

I can't get out of the office fast enough. I tear down the hallway and into the maze of museum exhibits. I race past the cases of bronze tools and then accelerate past the taxidermy display. I'm almost through when Mrs. Shum steps out from behind the curtained-off exhibit and we nearly collide.

"Goodness, Paige, you're in a hurry." She smiles, but the expression fades as she searches my face. "You're upset. What's wrong?"

For the first time I see she's not alone. The tall, balding detective—I can't remember his name—is with her. "I'm fine."

Mrs. Shum smiles. A pair of oversized, wiry gold earrings swings from her earlobes. "I was just showing Detective Torres the new exhibit. He's fascinated with the ruins and wants another look up there. Is your father still talking to my husband?"

"Yes." Any minute he's going to come out of the office, and my thoughts are so jumbled, I don't know what—or who—to believe. Before Mrs. Shum can press me further, I run out the door.

My feet pound the bed of gravel lining the path in the cactus garden, and then carry me down the concrete path snaking around the sand-colored walls of the cliffs. The ruins sit in their niche, their broken walls smoothed by the distance, and black, empty windows gaze back at me as if they've seen every bad thing in the world.

I keep moving, even though my father is going to kill me for not waiting for him. I run until my lungs burn and my legs turn to rubber. And then I push myself farther. But what am I running from? Jeremy? My father? Myself?

The sweat streams over my body when finally I stumble to a stop. Breathing hard, I look around. I'm past Tacoma Well, basically in the middle of nowhere. Around me the barren landscape seems huge and as foreign as the surface of the moon. The posed cacti, scrubby hunched-over trees, and stubble of browned-out grass look like the sole survivors in a war the sun has long since won.

I wipe my hot, sweat-slick face and take a deep breath of burning air. I should go back; I'm going to have to eventually. But I press forward, daring whatever happened to Emily to happen to me. Stupidly, I want to prove to myself that my father wasn't involved. Even if it means I get killed, it's worth it. The thought is irrational, but nothing, I'm discovering, is really very simple. You can love someone and hate them at the same time. You can think you know someone and then suddenly they seem like a total stranger. You can look in the mirror and not see the truth about yourself.

I randomly follow the trail of trampled grass along an irrigation ditch. What really happened to Emily? What is it that I'm not seeing?

Close, close, a voice inside me whispers. I keep going, not understanding how far I intend to go. The heat increases. The sweat pours off me, reminding me how stupid I've been to run into the desert without water. I should turn around, but I don't. I don't know why.

I walk until I come to a corn field. The plants aren't quite as tall as me, but they're lush, packed together tightly, and utterly motionless. My mind flashes back to another time, another field. I hear Emily's childhood voice in my head. *There's this special place I know…*

All at once goose bumps break out on my arms, and the back of my neck prickles. I stare at the field, picturing Emily, not as a teenager, but as a ten-year-old in a frayed pair of denim shorts and an oversized pink T-shirt knotted at her waist. She smiles, the gap between her front teeth giving her a slightly mischievous, slightly sinister look. She beckons me forward.

Somewhere deep inside the corn field, a cricket begins to buzz. The single rattle quickly swells into a loud and insistent chorus as if thousands of crickets are buzzing. It's almost like the insects are calling me, daring me to walk into the tangle of corn leaves.

"There's a secret place I know," Emily said, "where the grass grows taller than anywhere else. Want to see it?"

It wasn't grass, though, where she brought me. It was a corn field with tightly packed plants and stalks as thick as my legs.

"Come on," Emily pulled me by the hand.

"Emily, I…"

"It'll be *fun,*" she said.

And it *was* fun, at first. The corn smelled warm and sweet. We walked deeper into the field until all we could see were the stalks. Emily giggled and then raced ahead, zigzagging through the plants.

It was hard to keep up. Leaves slapped my face, and a couple of times I almost tripped on the tangles of old, broken stalks. Suddenly Emily turned, and I couldn't see her at all.

I stopped. Panting, I looked around. "Emily?" It was very quiet. I called a little louder. "Emily?"

Spinning slowly, I looked for her. A jungle of giant plants surrounded me, blocking my view with their long, green leaves. Had Emily fallen? Was she hurt? My father's stories spun in my head—snakes and scorpions and iguanas big enough to carry off a child.

Something behind me brushed my arm. I whirled, but it was only a leaf. As soon as I pushed it away, another touched me, this time on the back of my neck.

"Emily!" I shouted.

The plants swayed, reaching for me. I tried to shrink, but they surrounded me. They seemed suddenly alive, capable of movement, of lashing their leathery leaves around me like ropes.

I sank to the ground, sobbing. And then suddenly Emily burst from between plants, laughing.

"Got you!" she sang out. "Now I'll find you!"

I looked up. "You scared me!"

She studied my face and then wrinkled her nose. "Why are you crying?"

"I'm not."

"It was just a game."

I stood up. She was taller, but I was really angry. "I don't want to play with you anymore."

"I'm really sorry," she said. "We'll make the corn prince now."

"I want to go back."

"Okay," she said, "but please don't be mad at me. My dad says if you don't face the things that scare you, you'll never grow up. You'll be a little girl forever."

"We need to go. The corn's alive," I told Emily. "It moves when you're not looking. It wants to catch you and turn you into a scarecrow."

Emily's eyes got bigger with excitement. "We'll fight it together. We'll steal the leaf from the tallest plant and destroy it." She reached for my hand. "I won't let the corn hurt you. I promise you that. We're best friends now."

I turn away from the field and its memories. And then I see him, standing less than a dozen yards from me. He's so still he seems to blend into the scenery. His presence is dreamlike, as if he would vanish if I blinked. Only moments ago, I dared the universe to have whatever happened to Emily happen to me, and now here he is.

I square my shoulders and ignore the way my heart suddenly slams in my chest.

"Jalen," I snap because I don't want him to see that he's scared me. "What are you doing here?"

TWENTY-TWO

Paige

Sweat rims the neck and under the arms of Jalen's black T-shirt. He walks toward me slowly, and despite my mood and my doubts, I cannot take my eyes off him. He moves like a lion, all muscle and bone and grace. But the question remains—why is he here?

"Jacob saw you run from the information center. I came after you. What's wrong?"

"You were following me the whole way? Why didn't you let me know you were there?"

He closes the distance between us, and suddenly I'm standing in the shade of his body and have to tilt my head to see his face. If he wants to kill me, there's no way I can match him physically. And yet even as I'm thinking this, I'm not scared.

He simply shrugs as if there is no need to explain.

I fold my arms. "It's creepy," I tell him. "I turn around and you're there. That time in Chamber One with Jeremy…you just showed up. When I was going to Jeremy's house, you just happened to be there with the truck. Why is it that every time I'm upset, you know to be there?"

"Just lucky," he says, stone-faced.

His joking voice is the same as his serious voice, but I get it. I shake my head. "Seriously, Jalen, how do you always *know*?"

His eyes meet mine, and I see, even if he won't say it, even if he doesn't want it to be true, there's something between us.

"Here." He lifts the strap of his canteen over his head and hands the battered metal container to me. "Drink."

"Thanks." I take the canteen from his hands and drink so greedily that I choke a little and small drops trickle down my chin.

I push the canteen back at him, and when he takes it, our fingers touch. It's just a brush, but just like before, it's electric, magnetic. But I have to pretend that I don't feel anything because I know that's what Jalen wants. I just don't know why.

He screws the cap on with more force than necessary. I feel his sudden tension, even if I don't understand it.

He pulls the canteen and strap over his head, and they nestle against his side, drawing a perfect line of where I would like to be. It makes me angry that I can't control thoughts like these, that when I look at him, I start thinking about how I want him to touch me, kiss me, *want me*. He makes it easy to forget that Emily is missing and that finding her is all that's important.

I dig the toe of my hiking boot into the hard, pebble-crusted earth and try to crush the thoughts I don't want to have. "Dr. Shum is reinstating Jeremy Brown."

He doesn't speak, but his frown deepens.

"Effective immediately," I continue. "Dr. Shum is satisfied with the police report. Jeremy's not a suspect, and there's enough ambiguity with what happened with me to reinstate him into the research program."

I hold Jalen's gaze even as the heat of memories burns my face. I don't want to think about Jeremy's thin fingers clawing at me, and even worse is the thought of Jalen picturing me like that, too.

"That's a mistake. He's an asshole."

"Totally."

"He's not coming near you," Jalen states.

I shrug, although inside I'm thrilled at the totally serious tone of his voice. He wants to protect me. He cares. "Maybe this is a good thing. Maybe I can make him slip up."

"I don't want you around him."

"I don't want to be around him, either, but I really don't have a choice. How else will I find out anything?"

Jalen's mouth tightens. "What if I told you I think you're going in the wrong direction?"

"What do you mean?"

He shifts, as if to ease the pressure of the words he doesn't want to say. "Jeremy told us he saw Emily at the park after hours. That she might have been meeting someone."

"He also said Emily was a slut. He's a liar." I have to force myself not to get angry all over again.

"He's a liar," Jalen agrees, "but even liars know the best stories mix truth with fiction. What if he actually saw her? What if she *was* secretly meeting someone?"

"That's crazy. I'd know." But my thoughts immediately jump to my father and the possibility that he and Emily were having an affair. Oh God, does Jalen think this, too?

Where, I wonder, does the line between loyalty to my family and loyalty to Emily lie? And on what side do I want to stand?

Behind me, the crickets begin a loud, shrieking chorus that rattles through the heat like demented laughter. I want to cover my ears from their terrible noise, my terrible thoughts.

"Maybe you know more than you think."

It's the worst thing he could say to me other than come right out and accuse my father. "If she were seeing someone, she would have told me." I say it a little defiantly. "We should go."

He doesn't argue, only follows me as we pick our way through a line of dirt that only barely resembles a path. Over us, the sun beats down so hot on my head it feels like my hair will burst into flames.

We follow the irrigation ditches leading from the well. Although these have been searched, I can't help looking into the murky water and picturing Emily's long blonde hair tangled in the reeds growing out of the banks.

I think about all those summers when Emily and I were kids. We were close in a way that I've never been with any of my other friends. Or probably ever will be again. I can't stop trying to find out what happened to her, even if it means that I might not like the answers.

I sigh. As much as I want to dismiss Jalen's observations, I can't. "So you think Jeremy was telling the truth about seeing her after hours at the park?"

"Yes."

"But she didn't tell me anything."

Jalen lets a moment of silence pass. "Maybe she couldn't. Maybe she promised someone she wouldn't."

We pass a towering saguaro, and I try to see a face in its prickly green barrel, a game Emily and I used to play. We never did, but it was good because, if we saw a face, it meant a person would die. "Then how are we going to find out who it was?"

Jalen stops walking and looks into my eyes. Suddenly he seems very old. "You knew her," he says, "who she was and who she liked. To find her, we need to start thinking like her."

"Until this summer, we hadn't spoken in years."

"It doesn't matter," he insists. "People don't change. What was she like growing up?"

Bold. Adventurous. Beautiful. I shake my head. The adjectives don't do her justice. "It was a long time ago. I don't know where to begin."

"I think you know exactly where to start."

We pass another cactus, but I'm too afraid to look for a face. I'm afraid I'll see Emily's. I take a deep breath, and then without looking at him, I start at the beginning.

TWENTY-THREE

Paige

"We played games." As we walk, my hiking boots make soft crunching noises as if the ground has been starched. "They were all about fear—feeling it and then using it to give us magical powers." I pause, hoping he won't laugh. He doesn't. "At first it was just running across a corn field by ourselves, but then it escalated. Before long, we were sneaking out at night, holding secret ceremonies, trying to talk to the dead."

Jalen doesn't talk or try to interrupt me as I try to summarize the next several summers—the risks we took, how our secret adventures bonded us so closely that neither of us could have other friends, nor did we want to. We shared everything about ourselves—our deepest, most private thoughts—and these became elements that I wove into our games. I feared snakes, so of course we sought them out, even touched them. Emily feared being alone, and so I would lead her blindfolded into the desert at night, leaving her in the scariest places I could find, to find her way back to camp.

There were fantasy creatures in our games. Coyumans—dangerous beasts who were half-coyote and half-human, but could be kept away if you could imitate their howl perfectly. And spirits—smoky dark creatures who moved through the night like shadows and possessed your body if they touched you.

The greater the fear, the greater the power it gave us. We believed fear let us tap into the power of the universe—even into the multiple worlds my father described in the myths he told us. We both claimed, one night, after inching along a crumbling canyon wall a hundred feet off the ground and no wider than our feet, to have seen the faces of old people watching us from the craggy face of the rocks.

By the time we were ten, we were very, very good at playing the game. It was our secret, and if we came home with bruises or cuts, our clothes torn, we were always able to explain it. It went on for years, I tell Jalen, until that final summer.

We found the cave by accident, one morning when we were exploring the rock formations rising in Macizo Canyon in New Mexico. It was well-hidden, the opening so disguised it looked like a shadow between two rocks. I stuck my face into the darkness. I couldn't see much, but I knew it was a perfect place to play our game.

Emily grinned. "The best-told stories are the stories told just before dark."

I hesitated. The last time I had played the game, I'd almost fallen off a very tall rock. For a long time now, I had wished we could stop playing these games. I actually thought what our fathers were doing was a lot more interesting, but I'd always done what Emily wanted me to do. The bottom line—I didn't want to lose her friendship.

I promised myself this would be the last time. "Okay, but I'll have to get inside before I'll know the story."

To prove I wasn't afraid, although I was, I went first. What little light there was vanished almost immediately, but I moved slowly, waving my arms around like a blind person, making noise, and taking tiny baby steps. The air grew cooler, smelled musty.

"We're in a *si'papu*," I said, pausing as Emily shuffled up behind me. "And we're going backward in time, to the world that existed before ours."

Emily's hand dropped on my bare shoulder, connecting us, but startling the hell out of me. "Shit," I said, and she giggled. The noise echoed in a terrible way.

With Emily's hand on my shoulder, I led us deeper into the cave. It was very dark, but we were used to it. The deeper we went, the more the walls became increasingly narrow. Each bend became harder to squeeze through.

The sounds became magnified, or maybe we were just breathing harder and harder. My heart thumped loud and fast, and my sides scraped against the rock that was pressing now on me from both sides even though I was mainly turned sideways. I told Emily that the cave had a heart and lungs, and if we listened closely enough we could hear them. I stopped. We listened.

"Oh, shit," Emily whispered. "I hear it. I'm totally freaking out."

"Let's go back." I thought about lying, saying that the cave ended. It was too tight for her to pass me. She'd never know. But I didn't. Instead, I led us deeper, embellishing the story, releasing my fear in the story I told as we inched our way through the darkness.

The bat came out of nowhere. I didn't even hear it until it was flapping by my head. I ducked to the side, and then it happened. One minute there were walls and floor, and the next they were gone. I had long enough to realize I was in serious trouble, and then the ground flew up at me. I heard something crack, and then Emily's weight smashed into me.

My leg exploded into a thousand knife-points of pain. It blazed up my body, took my breath, and lit my brain on fire. I had to clamp my teeth together to keep from screaming.

"Emily... Emily..." I croaked out. "Are you okay?"

"I think so," she said. In the darkness, it seemed like her voice was everywhere—around me, on me, even inside me. She shifted off me. "Are you okay?"

The pain was terrible. I couldn't keep myself from making a horrible groaning noise. "I...I think my leg is broken. And I'm bleeding."

Emily sucked in her breath. "Oh, shit," she said, and for once there was no excitement in her voice, only fear.

"How did you get out?" Jalen asks.

We've stopped walking. His irises are as dark as that cave was, but the darkness isn't absolute. There's a light in them, a way out of this story and all its terrible memories, and I hold onto this. "After a while, Emily climbed out of the hole we'd fallen into and went for help."

Jalen's lips tighten. "After a while?"

I cross my arms. "She didn't want to leave me. I was cold, and she lay next to me, trying to warm me up. I finally managed to talk her into leaving."

There isn't much more to the story, but every time I try to summarize something, Jalen stops me, asks for clarification. He wants details, to know how I felt. I find myself admitting to him things I've never told anyone else. How scared I was, how angry that I had not listened to myself and stayed out of the cave. How part of me had wondered if Emily would ever come back or if she'd just leave me there as the ultimate end to our games.

But she came back. And they Life Flighted me to Phoenix. My heart stopped three times on the way. I'd lost so much blood. They immediately operated after we landed—the first of three surgeries on my leg... and the end of my friendship with Emily. She came to see me in the hospital, and I pretended that everything was okay. But it wasn't. I blamed her. Her parents blamed me. A couple of months later, my father took the job at Rutgers, and we moved. I got busy, and it was easier not to be best friends anymore.

"Your leg...it's okay?"

We both glance down at my calf, at the scars marbling the length of it. He touches it tentatively, and I feel a rush of warmth shoot through me. "Yes."

He takes his hand away, but keeps staring at my leg. "I'm glad."

"I never told anyone about the game Emily and I played. We promised each other it would be our secret."

He falls silent but I know that he will never tell anyone else. Even if he were tortured. There is something strong and infinitely patient about him. "Is there any chance she was playing the game again?"

I look up. "No. Of course not."

"You're sure?"

"Yes. I made up the stories. Always. I think that's what she always liked about me. I dreamed them up, but I never would have acted them out without her."

"What if someone else—say, a man—played your part?"

"Impossible." But is it? What if she was playing the game at night, here in the park, and something bad happened? She got hurt or...

killed. The person she was playing the game with might not have come forward because he was afraid he'd get blamed. My stomach turns at the thought of her lying broken, like I was, in some lost, dark tunnel.

"From what you've said, Emily liked taking risks and was an adrenaline junkie. But if she were doing that, why couldn't the search dogs track her?"

Part of me still can't accept that Emily was playing the game without me, but Jalen has a good point. "I don't know. The dogs kept bringing the police to the base of the cliffs."

Jalen's brow furrows. "The police have searched there. I've searched here. There's no trace."

Yet something about the ruins feels right. The small, dark chambers, and the twisting passages and niches would be perfect for playing hide-and-seek, especially at night. I close my eyes, thinking hard, trying to imagine what could have happened and knowing I have no idea. Jalen's right. Every inch of the ruins has been searched multiple times. I have to accept that she isn't here. But then my eyes snap open.

"The police looked everywhere in the ruins, but what about the cliffs above them?"

"The ladders end at the shelf of the ruins."

"But what's above the ruins?"

"Just limestone."

"Isn't there a small gap between the roof of the ruins and the rise of the cliffs?"

"There is," Jalen concedes.

"Is there a way of getting up on top of the ruins?"

Jalen hesitates. "Just some old stone steps, but they're in bad shape. Nobody uses them anymore."

"I want to see them."

"They aren't safe."

"It doesn't matter." I climb to my feet. "Don't you see? A place like that is exactly where she'd go."

"They're not safe," Jalen repeats.

I feel the rush—half-fear, half-excitement. Just like when Emily and I played the danger game. I had forgotten that electric tingle that shoots through me now, unleashing something in me I didn't know still existed. "Show me or I'll look for it myself."

TWENTY-FOUR

Paige

We argue all the way back to the cliffs, through the ruins and to the corner of the parapet wall where the ruins intersect the cliffs. Ironically, I realize it's probably the longest conversation we've exchanged since I arrived.

Searching the planes of sand-colored limestone, I don't see the stone staircase at first, but then I notice an irregularity in the wall, a series of creases in the stone that must be what Jalen calls steps. My heart sinks. We're going to need ropes if we want to climb them.

"Now you've seen them," Jalen says. "Let's go."

The bossy note in his voice makes my head come up. I study the steps, following the chipped risers until they end at the slab of rock over us. "I think we can do it."

Jalen puts his hands on his hips. "Look at the drop if you slip."

The ground dips a dizzying hundred feet straight below us, making the concrete path look like a squiggle in the dirt. "I've climbed worse."

And then, before I let myself think too much about it, I step onto the parapet wall and slide my leg over the edge. Before I can reach the first step, Jalen clamps his arms around my waist and lifts me into the air. Settling me on my feet, he looks at me. "No." His eyes blaze.

I hit his arms until he release me. "Don't tell me what to do."

He lets go, but doesn't back away, making it clear that he has a good six inches and a lot more muscle than I do. "You're not going up there."

Our eyes lock. "You can't stop me."

He doesn't blink. "I just did."

And he'll do it again if I try to climb. I fold my arms. "I'll just wait then. Until you're not here."

"I'll tell your father."

"What—we're five? I didn't think you were a tattletale."

"I didn't think you were an idiot."

We glare at each other. Jalen folds his arms, mirroring me and physically blocking me from the edge of the cliffs. A dribble of sweat rolls down my face, and I push it impatiently away. All we're doing is wasting time, going around and around in circles

I release my breath in exasperation. "Just walk away, then. If you won't help me, at least get out of my way."

Jalen's nostrils flare. "I want to help you," he says, "but this is just crazy. I've been up there. There's nothing but a rock ledge."

"Fine." I start to step onto the parapet, but his fingers on my arm stop me. I turn slowly. "You know I'm going up there. There's no way you can stop me."

The muscles around his eyes tighten. He's mad. Good.

"If we do this," he says, "and I mean *if*, I go first. You watch where I put my hands and feet and then you copy me exactly, and if I get out there and say it isn't safe, then you have to accept that."

I nod, impatient even as I'm suddenly worried for him.

He mutters something under his breath—probably cursing me out—and then steps up onto the parapet wall. Sliding his long leg onto the side of the cliff, he feels for the first step. He tests it and then in one smooth move puts his weight onto it. He's on the wall now, and my heart pretty much stops, seeing him pressed against an almost-vertical rock. He moves his left leg next, finds the foothold, and pushes himself upward, grabbing a rock above him.

He climbs slowly, but with a grace and strength that makes it look easy. Within minutes, he's at the top and looking down at me from the jut of the ledge. "Did you see where I put my hands and feet?"

"Yes."

"Okay then," he says.

It's my turn. My hands tingle and my heart starts to race.

I wipe my sweaty palms on the pockets of my shorts and close my eyes, visualizing myself scaling the wall of the cliffs. The fear of falling is there, but I push it to a corner of my mind. I wasn't lying before. Emily and I have climbed worse.

I feel for the first foothold and then step off the wall onto the side of the cliff. For a few seconds I don't move, just let myself absorb the feeling of great height, the crust on the rock, the slickness of the sweat running down my legs. I press my face against the limestone, breathing in the sun-bleached smell of the rocks. And then I feel for the next step.

My fingers clamp like steel onto it. The sky feels like an invisible hand on my back, inviting me to turn around and look. *Or better yet*, it taunts, *lean back into my palm. I'll hold you.* Panting, I pause, and then without thinking about it, I look down.

My stomach drops. It's crazy. I'm standing on a stone step that, at best, is maybe three inches wide, and the ground is a million miles below me. I freeze, splayed against the wall.

"Move your right leg up about two feet," Jalen says. "There's a step a little to your left."

My muscles shake, but somehow I find the willpower to move my leg onto the jut of rock. My hands are really wet with sweat now, and I wipe my fingers before reaching for my next hold. Just that simple motion, the swing of my arm, makes me realize how precarious my balance is. How one false step could make me fall.

"Now take your left hand and reach up. It's about two feet right above you."

"You're bossy," I snap.

He keeps coaching me and I keep telling him that I don't need his help, but then suddenly his hand locks onto my arm just behind my wrist. He's lying on his belly, leaning as far as he can over the edge. His dark face frowns in concentration as he drags us both backward.

The relief to be alive—to have climbed up here safely—is so intense that I want to laugh. But then I look at Jalen's face, just inches from my own, so serious, and the feeling dies. Sweat beads on his forehead like diamonds, and his brows are thick and shiny black. Our eyes meet and everything stops.

His fingers stay wrapped around my arms, holding me, connecting us. Every second is somehow better, but also harder because the longing inside me only gets worse.

The moment stretches out, just like before in the chamber, when I thought he might kiss me. I sense him wanting me, yet struggling with himself. Before I chicken out, I shift closer, touch his face, trace the sharpness of his cheekbone with my thumb, and then slide my hand over his silky hair, pulled back in a tight ponytail. He closes his eyes, but cannot stop the small groan that escapes his lips.

Following an instinct I didn't even know I had, I close my eyes and kiss him.

It is the bolt of electricity that Emily said it was, and it's also something stronger, something that isn't gone in a flash. I move my lips against his, savoring the warmth and shape of them.

His arms go around me, lifting me onto his chest, and then he kisses me urgently, completely, as if everything he's kept bottled up inside himself has finally overflowed. He tastes like me, only better, stronger, and the smell of his sweat is exciting, deep and rich like the earth.

And then suddenly he pulls back. "I can't do this." He shakes his head, and the muscles in his arms ripple, as if in protest. But against what? Me? Himself? "I just can't do this. I'm sorry."

At first I can hardly focus on what he's saying—my whole body feels strange, shocked, shaky.

"I'm sorry," he repeats. His black eyes are intense, his facial muscles so tight his cheekbones stand out, almost skeletal. Obviously kissing me didn't have the same reaction for him as it did me.

"It's okay," I tell him, although it isn't. My body still feels different where he's touched it, and his taste is still in my mouth. Pride makes me turn away.

"I'm sorry," Jalen repeats for the third humiliating time.

"Don't worry about it." I try for a smile and end up with something that feels like a grimace. "I'm not going to run to my father and say you attacked me." It's supposed to be a joke, but he doesn't laugh.

"It's not that I don't like you," he says. "It's just better if we don't... I mean, we should stay friends."

Friends? How could he say that after the way he kissed me? I wave my hand as if his words mean nothing. As if they don't hurt when every humiliating one stings. "Don't worry about it."

Rising to my feet, I glance around at the wall of limestone on one side of us and the open sky on the other. For a moment I picture myself throwing myself off the edge. I wouldn't do it, but it's the only action big enough to describe the despair and humiliation I feel.

"I shouldn't have let that happen."

I cringe because that kiss was the best of my life and he regrets it. "Seriously, Jalen. It's no big deal."

I turn my back to him, in case the truth—that I will never think of him as just a friend—is visible on my face. Bending forward against the pitch, I follow the stone ledge higher, tracking the cracks and trying to move past what just happened, but I can't. It makes no sense. He kissed me back, and I definitely didn't imagine that.

On my left, the great wall of limestone stretches skyward and on my left is a sheer drop. Jalen was right—the views here are stunning, but this shelf is exposed and narrow. What was I expecting, anyway? A hidden cave? Emily's body?

I don't even want to think about climbing back down. Staying as close to the cliff wall as possible, I study the cracks and pores. Mostly though, I am thinking about Jalen, sulking, somewhere behind me, after the disappointing experience of kissing me. I put my palms on the warm limestone and close my eyes.

How do you turn it off—the feelings you have for someone who doesn't feel the same way?

The irony of the situation isn't lost on me, and for the first time I have a clue how Aaron Dunning must have felt. It's even more depressing because I realize that being attracted to someone isn't something you can force. It's either there or it isn't. I could be with Aaron for a hundred years, and he could never make me feel the way I do when Jalen kisses me.

But obviously he doesn't feel the same.

It takes a lot of concentration not to look at Jalen. Only once do I slip and see him staring out over the valley with his face tight and fierce, like he's been slapped hard but doesn't want to admit it hurts.

I've walked the length of the wall twice before I see it—the tiniest speck of pink almost lost in the shadow of one of the deeper cracks in the limestone. I step back for a better angle, but then lose sight of it completely.

Walking back to the wall, I reach up as high as I can, but can't quite reach the slip of pink in the small, black gap. Coming to stand next to me, Jalen silently studies the hole above us and then reaches his fingers inside. His mouth tightens, and even before he pulls his hand out, I know he's found something.

My heart beats harder, and a wave of heat passes through me. In Jalen's hand is a woman's white Nike sneaker with pink geometric lines across the side and heel. It's Emily's sneaker, of course. Who else's could it be?

Jalen looks at me. For once I can see the surprise and horror in his eyes. And then his dark brows push together in puzzlement as he reaches his fingers into the sneaker and pulls out a handful of dried corn kernels. Spilling them softly back into the shoe, he looks at me.

"What the hell..." he says.

TWENTY-FIVE

Paige

Jalen goes for help. He's faster than me and so he goes alone. After he's safely down the side of the cliff, I return to the spot where we found Emily's sneaker. Sinking to the ground, I pull my knees to my chest. *Have you seen my sneakers?* Emily asked as she leaned over my bed with her long, dusty hair falling forward. *I was sleeping and when I woke up they were gone.*

Well, here they are, I think a little hysterically. *But where are you, Emily?*

Close, close, the cliffs seem to whisper. I hug my knees tighter and order myself not to freak out. But the nightmare replays itself in my mind. It feels like I'm being watched. If I could only turn my head quickly enough, I would see Emily in the shadows of the cliffs.

Come on, Paige, I tell myself. You're not five years old anymore. Corn plants can't plot murder, and these cliffs cannot whisper.

But I'm afraid to look around. Emily's Nike sits silently next to me like a gift I don't want. The white laces are neatly knotted, and the multicolored kernels lie scattered inside. I want to pick them up and drop them one by one back into the sneaker for the dreams that aren't going to come true for her.

She isn't going to Columbia to get a degree in linguistics. She isn't going to write a book or fall in love. She'll never get married or have kids or travel the world. She'll never go skinny dipping, and she'll never kiss a boy like I just kissed Jalen.

Jalen. My fingers trace my lips where he kissed me. I close my eyes, trying to relive every exact detail. I felt his heart pound. And yet he pushed me away. Why?

I open my eyes and they go automatically to the Nike. My eyes close. Oh, God. Emily.

Time passes slowly, I don't know how long before I hear my father's voice call from below, "Paige, are you okay? I'm coming up now."

"Dad!" Rising, my legs shake, as I follow the slanting ledge to where the cliffs and ruins meet. I'm just in time to see my father's hands, his forearms, and then his head appear as he pulls himself over the edge of the rock shelf.

"Paige," he says, dripping with sweat. I hear the relief in his voice, and then he's hugging me hard. My nose smashes against the buttons of his polo shirt and his hat flips backward. He holds me for a long moment and then pulls back, the cowboy hat perched at an awkward angle. "When Jalen told me you were up here…" He shakes his head, presses his lips together as if his thought is too terrible to speak.

"Dad—we found her sneaker."

"Duke," Dr. Shum's voice calls up, "I thought you were going to throw down the rope and make it easier for us."

My father throws down a safety harness and rope. He wraps it around himself and then stands well back from the edge. A moment later, Dr. Shum appears. His green park polo is sweat-ringed and dusty. Although dark glasses hide his eyes, his smile seems warm.

"Glad to see you in one piece, Paige." He mops his brow with a bandana he sticks back in his pocket.

Jalen climbs up next and swings easily over the lip. He's taller than either my father or Dr. Shum, but more muscular. His eyes seek me and then scan me as if he's making sure I'm okay. I look away. I don't want his comfort, not if all he wants to do is be friends.

My father uncoils a rope from his shoulder and, with Jalen's help, lowers it over the ledge. A few moments later, they pull Detective Torres over the lip. Sweating heavily, the detective eases himself out of the rope swing. After a long uneasy glance at the slant of the ridge and then at the unprotected drop, he sighs. "They don't pay me enough." Turning to me, he says, "Show me where you found the sneaker."

It doesn't take long to lead the group to the highest point on the rock shelf. The detective removes his sunglasses and begins snapping pictures of the lone sneaker on the ground, the cliffs, and the nook where I first glimpsed the flash of pink.

After the detective has shot at least a dozen pictures, he puts down the camera and takes out a pair of latex gloves. He's too short to reach the opening in the cliffs, but accepts Jalen's offer to boost him up.

He peers so long into the hole that my already-dry throat seems to swell shut and my stomach clenches tight as a fist. And then he slowly extracts the other shoe, puts it in a plastic evidence bag, and then hands it to my father. He reaches back into the hole and pulls out a folded square of paper. It looks like part of a page ripped from a paperback novel.

Nothing in his face changes. After a long moment, he looks up and begins to read: "Why why you're asking here's why her hair. I mean *her hair!* I mean like I saw it in the sun it's pale silky gold like corn tassels and in the sun sparks might catch. And her eyes that smiled at me sort of nervous and hopeful like she could not know (but who could know?) what is Jude's wish. For I am Jude the Obscure, I am the Master of Eyes. I am not to be judged by crude eyes like yours, assholes."

There's a long moment of silence. The officer's gaze moves over each of us. "Anyone recognize the passage?"

No one answers.

"Can I see it?" Jalen asks.

The detective holds the ripped page out to him, letting Jalen take a closer look without touching it. Jalen frowns and studies the words. "No idea."

"How about you, *professor?*"

"No," both Dr. Shum and my father reply at the same time. They exchange glances and then turn back to the police officer.

"Someone climbs up here, fills a sneaker with dried corn kernels, rips out a page from a book about a girl with blonde hair, and you have no idea what it means?" The detective's voice sounds casual, but his gaze fixes intently on my father's face.

My father shifts his weight. A fresh line of sweat trickles down the side of his face. He shakes his head slowly. "You asked about the excerpt you just read. I have no idea where it comes from."

"But the shoes and the corn," the officer presses. "They mean something to you?"

My father pulls his hat lower on his head. "Maybe," he admits.

The detective waits, rereading the words on that torn page, but when it's clear that's all my father is planning to say, he looks up. "You have a theory? Tell us, Dr. Patterson."

Something about the way he asks the question makes me nervous. My father wipes his face with a dirty-looking bandana. He hesitates, and then says, "I think the sneakers and the corn are symbolic. A lot of ancient tribal burial ceremonies involved placing moccasins and food along with the body of the loved one. The moccasins symbolized a swift journey to the next world, and the food was to provide nourishment along the way."

"So, theoretically, Miss Linton is dead and her body is buried somewhere near here?" Detective Torres's voice is friendly, as if he and my father are having an intellectual conversation, not discussing murder. Emily's murder.

Why doesn't Detective Torres ask Dr. Shum these questions?

"I have no idea what happened to Emily Linton," my father says. "I'm just telling you what I think these items mean."

"I have a theory as well, *Dr. Patterson.*" The detective smiles, revealing a row of even, white teeth. "I think someone was obsessed with Emily Linton. Maybe he lured her or maybe she met him willingly, but something happened. Maybe she slipped climbing up here—an accident—or she changed her mind about sex and things got rough. So this man, who never meant to hurt her, finds himself with a dead girl. A dead *underage* girl. He knows it looks bad, so he hides the body. He knows this park so well that he knows exactly where to put it so no one will ever find her. But this man—he's not a monster—he feels bad about what happened. He can't sleep, can't get her out of his mind. His guilt is eating him alive, and so he holds his own little funeral—complete with a Native American twist—for her up here. Is that what happened, *Dr. Patterson?*"

My father's mouth opens, but no sound comes out. "My God," he sputters. "You think I…" His voice strengthens, becomes indignant. "I had nothing to do with Emily's disappearance."

"Accidents happen. Why did Stuart Lowe take out a restraining order on you, Dr. Patterson?"

Stuart Lowe—my mother's boss and new fiancé—filed a restraining order against my father?

Surprise flashes in my father's eyes. He opens his mouth, but nothing comes out. "That was a misunderstanding," he says at last. "We had words. There was custody involved. The man's a lawyer. He knows how to work the system." He doesn't look at me.

I feel myself start to freak out. What does he mean, there was custody involved?

"You had more than words," the detective prompts. "You threatened the man's life. Why? Do you have a temper, Dr. Patterson?"

My father's expression hardens. "No," he says coldly.

"I think you do. We've got a missing girl, and her supervisor has a history of violence. I'm giving you a chance to explain your side of the story."

My father squares his shoulders. "What happened in New Jersey has nothing to do with whatever happened to Emily."

What happened in New Jersey? I study his face. How much more don't I know about him? In a small, distant part of my brain, I realize that Jalen has moved next to me, stationed himself beside me.

"Duke," Dr. Shum cautions, "don't say anything else without a lawyer present."

My father shakes his head. Beneath the tan, his face looks strained, incredulous. "I've done nothing wrong." His voice rises. "I have *nothing* to hide."

The detective shrugs. "We're going to find out where this passage comes from, and eventually, we're going to find Emily Linton. So maybe it's a good idea, *Dr.* Patterson, if you have that lawyer ready."

TWENTY-SIX

Paige

While the police search the ledge, I escape to Whale Rock to be alone. Dangling my legs into the murky waters of Otter Creek, my mind spins. Emily dead? My father her killer? I try to picture him tying bows on her Nikes, scattering corn kernels inside, and then placing them with the page of a book—like a eulogy—into the crevice, but I can't.

But then, I guess, what daughter thinks her father is capable of murder?

I kick my legs and watch the diamond beads scatter on the surface. It's hot on the rock and I can feel the skin on my shoulders burning, but I don't care. My mind wanders back to Jalen—why did he kiss me in the first place?

"Paige," my father's voice says.

I turn around, disappointed that it's not Jalen who has come to tell me that he's changed his mind, that what he feels for me is more than friendship.

My father squats down on the rock next to me. "You okay? I've been texting you." Behind his dark glasses, his eyes are impossible to read. "It's time to go."

"Okay." But I don't get up, and after a moment he sinks onto the rock beside me. I stare straight ahead, into the creek. It looks still and serene, but I know you can't see the current or the water snakes beneath the surface.

"Do you remember the time you gave your Barbie a water burial?" He doesn't wait for me to reply. "It rained and the current got her. You didn't cry. You tested the flow of the stream with different-sized sticks and saw where they got tangled. It took you three days, but you found your Barbie."

I remember that, but I'm surprised that he does and that he would bring it up now. When I glance at him, I see he's taken off his sunglasses. His blue eyes, for once, are soft.

"You're strong, Paige. You're going to get through this." His gaze stays steady on my face. "I've hired a lawyer. Her name is Bonita Begay. If something happens, if the police arrest me, I want you to call her. And then call your mother. I've arranged for you to stay with the Shums until she can get here."

He hasn't said he's innocent. I ball my hands together so tightly my fingernails bite into my skin. "Why did Stuart Lowe take out a restraining order against you?"

He goes very still, as if the question holds him at gunpoint. A line of sweat rolls down the side of his face, but he makes no move to wipe it away. And then his shoulders seem to sag a little. "Because I threatened him."

"Why?"

"Because I was angry. I made a mistake."

"What happened? How am I supposed to believe you didn't have anything to do with Emily's disappearance if you won't talk to me?"

He opens his mouth as if he's going to speak and then shuts it again. Finally, he says. "You have to trust me, Paige. What happened in New Jersey has nothing to do with whatever happened to Emily."

He wants me to let it go, but I can't. "You told the police it was about custody. Were you and Stuart fighting over who got me?" Is it wrong to hope they were? That my father wanted me—wanted me so badly he lost his temper?

He gives me a small half-smile. "No, honey. You had nothing to do with it."

I look away. It's never about me and never will be. When am I going to figure that out and stop hoping for more? And still, something tenacious and unrelenting won't let me drop it. "If it wasn't me, wasn't about the custody, why did you tell that to the police?"

"It became a custody issue, but it didn't start out as one. Let's drop this, okay? We really need to get going. The lawyer's office closes at five."

He starts to rise, but I stay exactly where I am. "Stop treating me like I'm a little kid. Why won't you tell me the truth?"

"Because you're my child. I love you."

"That isn't love." I feel the frustration and fury shoot through my veins like acid, eating me up inside. Pulling my knees to my chest, I lower my head. He'd rather be arrested than tell me about Stuart Lowe. What could possibly be so bad?

He taps my leg. "Let's get going. I'll even spring for takeout pizza tonight."

"Did you threaten him verbally or physically?"

"It doesn't matter."

"It matters to me."

He sighs. "Physically, but I didn't mean it. I just got carried away."

What could possibly make him so mad? If it wasn't me and it wasn't custody, then what? The only person left is my mother. My mother?

I look up. He's turned so that he's facing the water and seems so lost in his thoughts he might as well be alone.

"Why did you keep those photos of you and Mom? I found them in your drawer."

He stiffens. "You were in my room?"

"You hate her, and yet you kept those photos. Why?"

"You shouldn't have been going through my things."

"You physically threatened Stuart Lowe, who just happens to be engaged to Mom. It was about her, wasn't it?" And then suddenly another piece falls into place—the dream about my mother. *You were dreaming, Paige. You didn't see him.* What if it hadn't been a dream but a memory?

"Don't, Paige," my father says, but it's too late.

I remember the night my parents were arguing and how the word *affair* came out, sharply, like a curse. But it wasn't the college girls hanging out in my father's office. He hadn't been the one having an affair. The truth explodes inside me, shattering me in a thousand new ways and leaving me feeling incredibly stupid for not seeing it.

"Mom was having an affair with Stuart Lowe. You found out and threatened him. That's the affair I heard you and Mom arguing about that night."

His face is somehow terrible in its stillness.

"Mom was having an affair." Repeating it a second time doesn't make it any less awful.

"There are things you don't understand."

"I think I understand this pretty well." My voice rises. "How could you not tell me? Why did you let me believe you were to blame?"

He looks at me a long time. I see the weariness in his eyes. "The marriage failed. Leave it at that."

"Mom cheated. How long?"

"It doesn't matter." He holds up his hand. "Before you start blaming your mother, being angry at her, I want you to know that I don't blame her for what she did. Well...maybe a little." He smiles wryly. "But the truth is that I closed my eyes when I knew she wasn't happy. I took jobs that kept me away from home for weeks, months sometimes. People get lonely. I haven't always understood that very well." He looks at me sadly. "But I do now."

When was the last time my father and I talked like this? Have we ever? It hurts to look at him, to see the pain in his eyes. And I remember Emily telling me what a broken, lonely man he was when he arrived in Arizona. I never saw that person until now.

"You should have talked to me. You should have said something. You barely even said goodbye. Dad, you acted like you didn't even care that you were leaving."

"I'm sorry. I just didn't know what to say to you." He shakes his head. "I'm so sorry."

He'd had plenty to say to my mother. I think of their arguments in the weeks leading up to the divorce. He closed me out. Why was it so hard to talk to me? And then I know the answer—because I wouldn't have listened. I was too angry. Every time he came near me, I'd wanted to hurt him as much as I could. I took Mom's side without ever giving him a chance to tell his.

I see the deep lines on his face and the sadness in his eyes. When he puts his arm around me, I lean into the warmth of his body. He was protecting my mother by not admitting that it was her affair that caused the divorce, and he was trying to protect me, too. He knew me well enough to understand that, if I'd discovered what she did, it would make me hate her, as I hated him, and he didn't want that to happen.

I still have so many questions, but right now, letting him hold me, knowing what he did was done out of love, is enough.

TWENTY-SEVEN

Paige

At the park the next morning, my father shields me from the reporters clustered around the entrance gate. A flashbulb goes off, and voices shout on top of each other: *Dr. Patterson! What evidence was found in the ruins? Dr. Patterson! Why are police calling you a person of interest?*

One reporter wiggles her way along the fence line and catches us as my father unlocks the gate.

"Dr. Patterson, I need to talk with you." She has bright red lipstick, dark hair cut short and straight, and a scary sharpness to her gaze. When my father shakes his head, she thrusts a card into his hand. "I have photos of you with Emily Linton at Pottery Barn. Why were you with her? Don't you want to tell your side of the story?"

My father pockets the card. "No comment," he says and shuts the gate behind us. Closing his fingers around my upper arm, he pulls me away from the crowd that continues to shout at us.

"Why didn't you tell her what really happened?"

My father's steps don't slow. "You can't trust the press. They're looking for a good story, not the truth."

Jalen, John Yazzi, and the rest of the maintenance crew are waiting outside the information center for their morning assignment. Jalen's gaze meets mine briefly. His eyes ask if I'm okay. They are the eyes of someone who cares about me, but only as a friend. I give him a fake smile that hopefully falls into the friend category. A spot between my shoulders tingles as I turn away. I'm pretty sure his gaze follows me into the information center.

The lights are on in the building, but no one is in the gift shop or the museum. I head for my father's office and shut the door. His ancient chair creaks as I collapse into it and then scoot it closer to the desk.

If it wasn't my father, then who left those sneakers in the cliffs, and where did that page in the book come from? I try to remember the exact words. It was some funny wording about her hair. Something like, *Why why you're asking? Her hair?* And then there was something about it being yellow and the sunlight.

Spinning the chair around, I turn on the power on a PC that wheezes and groans and slowly grinds itself to life. I go to Bing and type in, "Why Why her hair." I get about a zillion hits ranging from "why does my dog have gray hair" to "why does Melissa dye her hair with Kool-Aid."

I try a different search. "Hair like sunshine." Again, the results are meaningless. I don't give up, though. The page was important to whoever left it in the cliffs. The detective said the person was obsessed, and so I search, "obsession + blonde hair + book." I get some interesting titles on Amazon, but after an hour, I sit back in frustration. Nothing is working.

I decide to turn to social media and post the excerpt on my Connections page. I ask my friends if they can identify the book the passage came from, and if they can't, to post it on their pages. I'm pretty sure someone will recognize it.

Almost immediately my friends start replying. Unfortunately, most are more curious than helpful. I keep my answers vague because of the investigation, and am in the middle of talking to my friend Missy from the soccer team when someone knocks.

"Come in," I call out. Instinctively, I shut down the website.

Mrs. Shum stands in the doorway, her strawberry-blonde hair tied back with a colorful scarf. She's wearing tight capri jeans and a paint-stained, long-sleeved shirt. More than ever, her elfish features remind me of Nicole Kidman.

"Hello, honey. Hope I didn't disturb you."

"No. I was just surfing."

She reaches the desk and perches on the corner. "I've been thinking about you. How hard it had to be for you to find those sneakers."

I look up into her green eyes. "It was. But I'm okay." When she doesn't say anything, I add, "Thanks."

She nods, her gaze never leaving my face. "I'm finished early, and with everything that's happened, I was wondering if you'd like to have lunch with me. After, I'll take you to my studio."

She's nice, but the thought of spending time with her isn't very appealing. I remember now that Emily didn't like her. "Thanks, Mrs. Shum, but I'd better hang out here. My father..."

"...thought it was a great idea." She leans forward, and I smell the faint odor of paint and turpentine. "Honey, you're skin and bones. Let me feed you, show you around, and then bring you home." Her smile widens. "It might be good. More of those reporters are around, trolling for stories. Honestly, they're like sharks."

Even so, I don't feel like hanging out with Mrs. Shum or anyone, but then I see Jalen, hovering in the doorway, probably waiting for Mrs. Shum to leave so we can talk, so he can ask how I'm doing, be my friend. It makes me tired, thinking about the energy it'll take to act like our kiss never happened. I've been avoiding him, but it's been exhausting.

I turn back to Mrs. Shum. "Actually, that sounds like a great idea."

Mrs. Shum smiles brightly. "Excellent," she says.

Jalen watches us pass. I sense his disapproval, which makes me happy. On the way to Mrs. Shum's car, she dismisses a couple of reporters hovering at the gate with an impressively scathing look. I resolve to practice this expression later in the mirror.

"So tell me about the sneakers," she says, pulling an oversized pair of dark glasses out of her purse. "How did you find them?"

I don't want to talk about it, but it seems rude to ignore her question. "I just looked up and they were there."

"In a crevice in a rock," Mrs. Shum finishes. "But how did you *know* to search the crevice?"

"I didn't."

We walk through the shimmering hot parking lot to her black Expedition. She unlocks it with a chirp from the key fob and opens the door for me. "What do you think those sneakers mean?"

I don't reply and take my time with the seatbelt while she walks around to the other side of the car. Why is she asking me all these questions? I thought the point was to get away from here for a while.

Mrs. Shum gets in the car. When she looks at my face, her expression softens. "I'm sorry. I don't want to make it harder for you. I just know how much Emily meant to you, how hard this is. Sometimes, it's better to talk. I want to help. So does Dr. Shum. We're on your father's side."

I feel myself relax a little. "I think the sneakers mean that whatever happened to Emily happened in the park."

Mrs. Shum turns on the air-conditioning. As it blasts out hot air, we sit in silence, and then she says, "I agree. We get so many transients coming through the park. It's impossible to make it completely safe."

Although I want to believe it was a total stranger, there's a ritual aspect to the corn and writing that I can't ignore. "You think a transient would put corn inside her Nike and leave that note?"

Mrs. Shum shifts the car into reverse. "It must be," she says firmly. "There's a lot of local tribe people who hate that the National Park Service owns this land. They hate that we disturb the ruins, even if it's our work that preserves them." She accelerates out of the parking lot. "I wouldn't put it past someone to make Emily disappear as a way of stopping work in the ruins." Her hands tighten on the wheel. "Just wait, Paige, soon there will be rumors going around that the ruins are cursed and that Emily's disappearance is just like that Native American tribe that vanished six hundred years ago."

She turns on her blinker and glances over her shoulder at the long, empty highway. "If you ask me, I think that whole scene was staged. Someone wanted those sneakers to be found."

Mrs. Shum's theory sounds farfetched, but at least it's an alternative to believing my father is involved. I lean back in the seat and point the air-conditioning at my face. "I think so, too," I say.

She glances sideways at me, her face unreadable. We fall into a more general discussion about a Native American art show in town that I might like to see.

The Shums live in a modern stucco-and-glass house in a development called Painted Canyon. The house is larger than my father's, but smaller than Jeremy Brown's. It's filled with a variety of Southwestern art and Native American pottery and weaving. In the family room, we pause in front of an oversized oil painting of a buck with fierce brown eyes and an impressive rack of antlers. The neck is arched, proud, and his face has a regal expression. When I praise her about it, she dismisses the compliment with a wave of her hand.

"An anniversary gift for Dr. Shum," she says.

For lunch she serves me iced tea and a spinach quiche that is the first homemade meal I've had since I arrived in Arizona. When I compliment it, her eyes go soft.

"My mother always told me that a woman needed to have one good dish for company. Mine's quiche."

"My mom makes great pasta." And just like that, I miss her so much it hurts. I haven't talked to her in almost a week. I don't know what to say to her. Just thinking about it makes me sad and confused and angry.

"You'll be seeing her soon." Mrs. Shum touches my hand. "Just a few more weeks and you'll be on your way back to New Jersey, won't you?"

I take a swallow of cold sweet tea. "Yes."

"And you're a senior, right?"

"Technically a junior." She doesn't need to know about the classes I failed on purpose.

"Even better," she says, "you'll have more time to figure out what you want to do when you go to college." She wipes her mouth with a paper napkin and then sets it down on her empty plate. "Do you have any idea yet?"

I shake my head.

She nods sympathetically. "It's hard for you girls today. So many choices now. And yet, if I were to give you some advice…" She pauses. "Can I give you some advice, Paige?" She waits for my nod. "Look at who you were before you became the person you are now."

It sounds like a riddle and I don't say anything.

She taps her polished fingertips on the wooden tabletop. "What did you love doing most when you were a child?" she asks, studying me closely. "Those things tell you about yourself. They're your passion. What were you happiest doing, Paige, when you were five?"

"I don't even remember being five," I tell her.

But that's a lie. I loved sitting in the sun and carefully digging Birthday Barbie out of the ground. How happy I was burying her and finding her, burying her and finding her. Me, an archeologist? No way.

Kim O'Brien

But there was a time when it was what I wanted most in the world. It all changed when we moved to New Jersey and I saw what Dad's profession did to our family. Only now, I realize that I had things wrong.

I put my fork down. "I'll think about it."

"You do that." Mrs. Shum looks at my empty plate. "Pie? Or are you ready to see the studio?"

"The studio."

Mrs. Shum's studio is a wood and glass building behind the pool. She unlocks a thick door and switches on a light. We step into an oversized room with tall ceilings, open wooden beams, and an entire back wall covered in glass. At first, it looks like everything has been put in storage. The work tables, the easels—everything has been covered with sheets. The studio smells of paint and raw, wet clay.

Mrs. Shum begins turning over a series of canvases leaning against the wall. They're all of the cliffs that house the ruins, but from different angles. There's a close-up of the T-shaped entrance on the second level and one blackened, almost undecipherable painting of what I finally realize is one of the windows.

I compliment her, but she gives me what is becoming a familiar dismissive wave. "I really prefer working in clay," she says.

As if to prove this, she leads me past a potter's wheel with chips of dry, gray clay clinging to it to a table centered in front of the wall of windows. There's something under a sheet, and when Mrs. Shum removes this and a plastic sheet beneath, I see a sculpture of a man and a woman kissing. Their dark clay faces tilt against each other. The man has his hand supporting the woman's neck. The woman has her eyes closed, but the ecstasy is clear in both their faces.

As we circle the table, I realize there's a tiny bit of space between their mouths. Mrs. Shum has captured the moment before a kiss happens. I think of Jalen, that moment when his lips touched mine and how overwhelming it was, how that first brush of his lips took my breath away. The sculpture could be me and him, and then I realize that's the point. Anyone who's ever been in love can see himself or herself.

"It's incredible," I tell her.

"It isn't finished yet. Sometimes you have to live with a piece of art for a while before you figure out what it is."

"I think it's perfect."

She laughs. "Have you sculpted before, Paige?"

"In middle school. I made a pencil holder."

"That's not sculpting," she says, replacing the plastic cover and sheet on the sculpture of the lovers. "The grade of clay they use is terrible. What do you say? Want to give it another try?"

"I'll probably be terrible."

"No one is terrible," she chides. Walking over to the counter near the sink, she opens a cabinet drawer. With a metal tool, she scoops out a portion of clay and sets it on a table. "You'll want to wet your hands," she says, "but don't put too much water on the clay. It's already pretty moist."

I slide my hands over the cool, smooth roundness, unsure exactly what I want to make.

"Close your eyes," Mrs. Shum instructs, standing behind me. "See with your fingers. The clay will tell you what it wants to be."

She's watching me, so even though it feels kind of silly, I do exactly what she asks. I close my eyes and run my hands over the roundness of the ball and let my fingers explore the shape. I let tiny indents become eye sockets beneath the slightly rounded plane of a brow. I draw a line down what becomes the scalp and draw long, silky hair with my finger. I have never explored Jalen's face with my hands, and yet slowly, my fingers shape the shape of his lips, the slight flare of his nostril.

At some point I am aware of Mrs. Shum leaving me to lose myself in the memory of Jalen kissing me, how clichéd it seemed to think he was the other half of myself, and yet that's how it felt.

I don't know how long I work. Only that my fingers smooth and pinch and shape. I step back, narrow my gaze. Try again to capture the perfection of his face. It isn't him at all. The expression is too blank. I don't know how to capture the life in his eyes.

Mrs. Shum comes up behind me so silently I jump. "Excellent," she says. "I thought you would have a good eye, but this is even better than I expected."

I cringe at the lopsided nose and the clumsy, thick lips. "It's horrible."

Mrs. Shum's eyes stay on my sculpture. "It's Jalen, isn't it?"

I nod, a little shyly, surprised but kind of proud. "You could tell?"

"Absolutely. Would you like to see what I made?" she asks, and we walk over to her table.

The second I see her sculpture, my breath catches in my chest. For a moment a physical pain seems to explode in my stomach, and I feel dizzy, lightheaded.

The girl Mrs. Shum has sculpted is beautiful. I study her smooth clay brow, her oval eyes, and her perfectly shaped full lips. The girl's hair falls straight past her shoulders and is exquisitely detailed with fine lines.

I look up at Mrs. Shum, trying to breathe and holding back the sharp points of unshed tears. Why would she do this? Did she want to hurt me? I would never have thought her so cruel. Doesn't she think I miss her enough?

"Why did you sculpt Emily?" I finally manage. My voice is choked, raw.

Mrs. Shum blinks at me in surprise, and then her face seems to collapse in sudden understanding. "Oh, no, honey," she says, "That's not Emily—that's you. You were sculpting Jalen, so I sculpted *you,* Paige. You think I haven't noticed how the two of you look at each other?" She gives a small laugh even as I blush. "Fight for him, Paige. The only thing that really matters in life is love."

TWENTY-EIGHT

Jalen

This is what I know about love.

My grandfather owned a small tire and auto parts shop on the Navajo Nation. It had been going under for as long as my father could remember. One afternoon, Grandfather asked my father and uncle to take an order of tires to a garage in Phoenix. They had car trouble along the way, and so they arrived just a little after closing. The owner of the garage saw them, locked the door, and flipped a closed sign in the window. When my father called to him through the glass, the owner told them to come back the next morning. My father explained they had driven five hours and it would take them only fifteen minutes to unload the tires. He did not mention that they could not afford either the lost time or the cost of the gasoline, although that probably was understood by everyone.

What happened next is less clear. There was more arguing through the glass, a sour comment about reading the clock versus following the sun, and then my uncle slammed his fist through the window and turned the closed sign to open.

My father, with the stacks of tires still strapped in the bed of the pickup, drove my uncle to the nearest emergency room. There, a nurse with soft, brown eyes and hair like black silk helped pick the glass from Uncle Billy's hand. By the time my uncle's hand was ready to be stitched, my father had the nurse's telephone number and a promise to have dinner. They were married three weeks later.

He said it happened like that for his father and his father before him. The men in our family fall immediately, irrevocably in love, or not at all.

Kim O'Brien

I was not raised on the reservation. Through my mother, my father found work in construction, and they bought a small house in the suburbs. When my grandparents still lived, we used to visit them on the Nation. They lived in a one-room *hogan* and there was no running water, but it smelled of fresh, warm kneeldown bread. Before dawn, my father and grandfather would wake me, and we would walk to the top of the hill and watch the sun rise.

If you drive to the Navajo Nation, it is not uncommon to see people, mostly teenagers, hitchhiking their way out. Although the land sits on top of deposits of natural gas, uranium, and minerals, jobs are scarce. Unemployment runs high. There is little government funding. Basically, we're on our own. Alcohol factors into most of the crimes, and the high school dropout rate is high.

Despite these problems, or maybe because of them, I see myself going back there someday, living there. What I'll do is still a question in my mind. My grandfather's garage is long gone, of course, but it isn't automobiles I dream of fixing. I think, mostly, what needs fixing is me.

I don't know much about love, but I do know about wanting. About wanting a girl who isn't right for you, but not being able to help it. You try to ignore, rationalize, deny, but it's there—like a thirst that burns your throat or a dream you don't want to wake up from.

You will fall in love, but you won't help her and she's going to die. My uncle was drunk when he said those words, but how can I dismiss them? How can I hope that he was confused about the whole falling-in-love thing and Emily Linton was the doomed girl in his vision? How do I tell Paige? What if I don't? What if it's already too late?

TWENTY-NINE

Paige

Two days later, it's early evening, still burning hot, and my father and I are on the back deck assembling a new grill when the doorbell rings. We bought the Weber on the way home from the park, and although my dad said he was tired of eating microwaved dinners, I know the grill is his way of showing me that he was listening when I talked about what good fathers do. He's trying to be a better father. Just like me, keeping him company, is my way of showing him that I want to be a better daughter.

At the sound of the doorbell, my father sets down the screwdriver and glances into the house. Neither of us is expecting company, and when his gaze returns to me I see the wariness in his eyes.

"Remember, if I'm arrested, call the lawyer, the Shums, and then your mother."

After I nod, he squares his shoulders and then walks inside. I follow, bracing myself for the sight of Detective Rodriquez's round face, but it isn't the police standing on the front step. It's Jalen.

He looks freshly showered, his black hair pulled back into a sleek ponytail that still shows the lines of his comb. "Hello, Dr. Patterson," he says when my father pulls the door open. "I need to talk to your daughter."

Your daughter. Still he won't use my name. It makes me clench my jaw in frustration. He turns to me, and despite my anger, despite knowing that there's never going to be anything between us, my face heats. It doesn't seem fair that he can do this to me and I do nothing to him at all.

I will my face to blankness. "Sorry, but now isn't a good time."

My father ignores me and pulls the door open wider. "We're about to try out the new grill. There's plenty of food—why don't you stay for dinner?"

Jalen looks at me. I make my face as unwelcoming as possible, but he ignores me. "Thanks," he says and steps inside, passing so closely my face nearly touches the worn cotton of his T-shirt. I smell the clean fragrance of his soap.

"It's charcoal—not propane," my father explains, leading us through the hallway, then the kitchen, and back into the oven-like heat. "The salesperson at Home Depot thought I was crazy, but if I wanted simplicity I'd do takeout."

The grill is already almost completely together, a simple project for someone used to assembling decaying skeletons and shards of pottery. My father banters back and forth with Jalen as he finishes tightening the legs and then adds the charcoal briquettes to the basin. As soon he has a strong flame going, he excuses himself to work on the marinade, something I know needs no work as it comes out of a bottle.

The moment he's gone, Jalen says, "You're avoiding me. Why?"

I study the flames rising in a bouquet of colors from the grill. "I'm not avoiding you. I'm just busy."

He steps closer. "We need to talk about what happened."

I force myself not to back up, to hold his gaze. "What's there to discuss? Nobody understands why someone put her sneakers there, and..."

"I don't mean about Emily." He takes another step closer. My stomach knots because now he's within an arm's length of me. And his smell—that faint mix of soap, sweat and Arizona desert—moves through me. "I want to talk about us. About what happened."

He means the kiss. I glance at the back door, willing my father to appear and end this conversation. Of course he's never around when I need him. I fold my arms. "Oh, that." And then I add, so he doesn't have to, "It was no big deal."

"I hurt you. I didn't mean to. I'm sorry."

I reach for a lie like a shield. "You didn't hurt me." I force a smile. "Let's just forget about it, okay?" I'm proud of the way I deliver the line, confident that he can't see how I'm barely breathing because he's standing way too close. "So, thanks for coming, but you don't have to stay. My father is probably going to incinerate the chicken, anyway. You should save yourself."

My effort at humor falls flat. His lips tighten. "I shouldn't have kissed you, but not for the reason you think." His gaze fits mine. "It's for your own good."

I give a small, humorless laugh. "Come on, Jalen. That's just a crappy way of saying you don't like me like that—which is fine—but at least be honest."

He shakes his head. "I am."

"Okay. Message delivered. We're friends."

He doesn't move, but looks hard at me as if he's trying to tell me something he either can't, or isn't willing to say. "You don't understand."

You're right, I start to say. *I don't understand.* And then it hits me. "Oh. You have a girlfriend." I feel like an idiot. I should have realized this before.

"No." Jalen sounds a little surprised, maybe even offended. "No."

"Is it because my father is your father's boss?"

"No." He hesitates a long beat. "You'd think I was crazy if I told you."

"Try me."

He shakes his head. "You have to trust me."

My lips twist. I know a blow-off when I hear one. "Maybe *you* need to trust *me.*" When he stays silent, I know I'm right.

The reality is that we aren't going to be friends or anything at all. If there's anything I've learned from Aaron, it's that you can't be friends when one of you feels something more. The balance will always be off, the scale lopsided, the conversation awkward.

I turn away from him. "You should just leave." There's no anger left in me, only sadness, resignation.

Jalen touches my arm, no more than a brush of his fingertips, but it's enough to make me turn around, to make me look up. "I can't do that," he says softly, almost gently. "That's the one thing I can't do."

He wants me. He doesn't want me. It's like that silly game where you pull off the petals of a flower until you get to the last one. I abandon my last shred of pride and simply ask, "Why not?"

The silence stretches between us. I stare into his eyes, thinking that I could know him for a thousand years and still his thoughts would be unreadable to me. He will show me only what he wants to. I close my eyes so I am equally blank to him.

After what seems like a long moment, he says in a halting, hesitant voice, "In our culture…there are what we call holy men."

He pauses, and I open my eyes at the serious note in his voice.

"They're also called healers…or medicine men." His voice gets a little stronger. "A lot of people claim to be healers, but there are very few legitimate holy men. It's a family thing, passed down through the generations. My uncle is one of them. You saw him once—he came to the park."

The face of a fragile-looking man wearing strands of turquoise beads on his thin, hollowed chest flashes in my mind. *She has pretty eyes*, he said.

"What they do is very private. Even to discuss who they are and what they do isn't something we do. I shouldn't even be telling you this much."

I nod, afraid if I say anything he'll stop talking.

"My uncle. He is a great man, a great healer, but he's ill. And this illness he has, it affects his gift. Just how much, we don't know. Sometimes he dreams and they're just dreams, and sometimes they're more…"

I think of my dream—of Emily wandering into my room, her long pale hair eclipsing her dirt-stained face. The cloying smell of roses.

"All my life I've known that my uncle has this gift, but we don't speak of it. We try to give him privacy and respect that, despite his illness, he is a great man and the things he sees are real."

Jalen pauses, and I can see him struggling with the idea of telling me more. Without even thinking about it, I reach out and take hold of his hands. He grips mine back.

"A couple of months ago, my uncle woke me in the middle of the night. He said that a girl was in danger. She would come to me, but I would turn her away. She would die because I wouldn't help her."

"He was talking about Emily."

Jalen shakes his head. His eyes are dark and troubled. "After Emily disappeared I thought that, but it didn't make sense."

"Why not?"

He shifts his weight. Sweat beads his upper lip. "He said I would be...involved with this girl."

"Involved? What do you mean, involved?"

His cheeks flush almost imperceptibly. "You know what that means."

"No, I don't."

"He said I would have feelings for this girl. Strong feelings." He releases my hands. "I liked Emily, but I wasn't involved with her. She never came to me for help." He looks at me, and I have never seen his eyes look so sad. "But you did."

The realization is instant. "You think it was me? You think your uncle dreamed about me?"

He nods. "That's why I tried to stay away from you. I thought if we didn't get involved, the rest of the prophesy wouldn't come true."

I try to laugh it off. "You're kidding."

"If I get involved with you, you'll die. You're better off without me."

The fire in the grill has burned down slightly. My father comes to the door. He looks at me, and when I shake my head, he retreats.

"Jalen, how could your liking me get me killed?"

His lips tighten. "I knew you wouldn't believe me."

"It's not that..." But it *is* kind of that. I can't accept that walking away from me is a good thing, especially not if he has feelings for me. "It was a dream. You said yourself his dreams don't always come true."

"He said I would be responsible for your death. You don't know him. How strong his gift is." He shakes his head. "I'm not gambling with your life."

"What about what I want?"

"He *knows* things. The night Emily disappeared, before anyone knew she was gone, he was singing the death chant."

"We don't *know* she's dead."

He sighs, and it contains a world of grief. "You need my uncle's dream not to happen." He holds his hand up as I start to protest. "That's why that kiss can't mean anything. That's what I came to tell you."

Disappointment tastes bitter, like the pill you can't quite swallow. What I want is for him to want to be my boyfriend. It hurts to look at him, to see the stubborn frown and know he's made up his mind. That I'm falling for him and he's falling for me, but we still can't be together.

It's humiliating to have to plead for him to give us a chance, but I know we're only moments from him walking away. "What if it's already too late? What if whatever your uncle saw is already happening?"

I don't think he'll have a comeback, but he shakes his head. "It's not. You're still alive."

He says this flatly, without emotion, but I'm not fooled. Behind his stoic features, I feel everything he's not saying.

"Nothing is going to happen to me." I step closer to him.

"Don't," he says, but he doesn't back away.

"Don't what?" We're standing so close the tips of my sandals touch the tips of his hiking boots. The chemistry, or whatever you want to call this thing between us, instantly leaps to life. I can barely breathe.

"Don't make me want you," he says so softly that it's almost like I've imagined him saying it. His eyes look at me as if I'm everything he has always wanted and can't have.

"But you do." Even seeing him look at me this way, the sentence is more of a question than a statement.

"Of course."

"Then take a chance."

He's silent, but I can tell he's battling inside, torn between his beliefs and his feelings for me. I want to help him, but it's his decision. He has to want to be with me more than he fears losing me. My choice already is clear to him. My father appears at the door with the platter of chicken breasts in his hands. I scowl at him, and he retreats.

Jalen releases his breath slowly. "I'm sorry," he says.

My father looks puzzled when Jalen doesn't stay for dinner, but I don't explain. How could I? I know Jalen is being all noble and everything, but his leaving still hurts. I begin to wonder if my destiny is to be the girl who always gets left behind.

But being left behind isn't nearly as bad as being dead. Growing up, I heard a lot of stories about healers and medicine men and know that they are capable of doing things and knowing things that science can't explain. As much as I want to dismiss what Jalen told me, I can't.

Suddenly it feels like something has been set in motion, something that neither Jalen nor I can control. I might not have admitted it to Jalen, but I'm scared.

THIRTY

Paige

Once you start, it's hard to stop thinking about dying. When I was ten, lying in the underground cavern, my leg broken and Emily gone for help, I believed that if I fell asleep I'd die. That death sat like a person in the corner, watching me, waiting for me to close my eyes before he grabbed me.

Lying in bed, I avoid looking at the dark corners of the room and the thought that maybe you can't cheat death twice.

The air-conditioning rains down like a cold mist. I pull the covers closer. Maybe I should go back to New Jersey. On the other hand, it might not change anything. My plane could crash and I'd die running away, a coward's death. Or I could die a week later in a car crash going to the mall.

I feel sleep tugging at me, pulling me backward. As I feel myself start to doze off, I picture Emily's earnest face in the cornfield that day so long ago. *You have to face the things that scare you, Paige,* she says, *or you'll never grow up.*

I jerk myself awake. I need to be strong and do what she says.

But then, Emily's dead, isn't she?

In the morning, I'm tired, irritable. I snap at my father for leaving the dishwasher door open and the milk loosely capped, for invading my space at the table with the edge of his newspaper, for being my father.

"Since when do you drink coffee?" my dad asks, looking up from his bowl of cereal.

I raise the cup of burning, bitter liquid to my mouth. "Since now."

The drive to the park is quiet, uneventful, filled with the silence of the things I can't tell him. After the briefing, I go to his office, turn on his ancient, wheezy computer, and wait for a connection to the Internet. I guess one of the benefits of not sleeping is that it gives you plenty of time to think. It occurred to me last night that of all the places I've looked for Emily, I missed the most obvious one.

A couple of keystrokes later, I'm on the park's website. I click on the blog, but the page comes up invalid. They've pulled it. Frowning, I dig into the archives and a moment later a picture of Emily, sun-bronzed, leggy, and blonde, appears.

"Eyes of the Intern" by Emily Linton
March 12
From the moment my fingers closed around the warm metal of the first rung of the ladder, I knew my life was going to change forever. I'm getting to do something very few people get to do—climb up these 1,500-foot cliffs into the ruins of an ancient civilization that lived here a thousand years ago.

As I climbed each rung, I could feel the life I knew slipping away from me, like a snake shedding its skin. Gone were petty worries about high school, grades, the gossip of who was seeing whom. I felt the warm sky at my back—an enormous blue expanse that grew exponentially greater with each intoxicating step upward. It was here in these great limestone cliffs more than six hundred Native Americans lived—and here they disappeared. But why?

As an intern, I hope to come up with my own theory. So come with me, up these ladders, into the largest and best-preserved cliff dwellings in America. I promise to show you a world you'll never forget.

I realize I'm gripping the arms to the desk chair so tightly that my hands hurt. It's just…hard. This is Emily, and her writing is so like her:

strong and beautiful, pulling me toward her in words. Making me realize all over again just how, to her, the world was a big adventure and how unafraid she was to go after what she wanted.

I skim the responses, mostly people welcoming her to the park—*good luck with the internship; already a fan, looking forward to working with you; interesting start, looking forward to more.* There's nothing sinister or romantic-sounding so I move onto the next entry.

March 13
As I pulled myself over the edge of the cliff, I gazed up into ruins looming over me. They look kind of like a high-rise apartment building, only a burned-out, abandoned one. From the ground, you can't see the war between the cliff dwellings and time. But up close, you can see the cracks that run like scars across the face of the building and the crumbling edges of the turrets. It looks dead, lost, a place time has forgotten, but then Dr. Shum slid his finger along the ground and lifted off a layer of chalky limestone dust.

In these fragments, *he said,* there's a record—fragments of human and animal bones, remnants of plants thousands of years old. They have a story to tell us. Life amongst death.

It made me look at the ruins in a different way, and I could hardly wait to step inside the darkness of the thick masonry walls.

It feels almost as if I'm slipping into Emily's skin as I read her blog, skimming through an interview with Dr. Shum, a funny story about hiding in the shadows of the ruins and scaring a couple of structural engineers, and a trip to Topeka Well with my father to take water samples.

I flip through another couple weeks and then stop at an entry from early April.

April 1
Today as I hiked to the ruins, I glimpsed a coyote trotting through the desert. With his long legs and bushy tail, he looked a lot like a skinny German Shepherd. I watched him until he disappeared, and even then he stayed on my mind all day. He was hunting, of

course, and from his thinness not doing too well. But before you start feeling too sorry for him, I'd like to tell you the story of Coyote and the monster, an old Native American myth.

In the story, there is a monster, and it eats all of Coyote's friends. Coyote decides to get even and ties himself to the top of the tallest mountain he can find. The monster tries to blow Coyote off the mountain, but he can't. Trying a new strategy, the monster pretends to be Coyote's friend and invites him to his house. Coyote accepts, but asks if, before he goes, he can visit his friends in the monster's stomach. The monster agrees. Big mistake. Coyote cuts out the monster's heart and sets fire to his insides. Coyote frees his friends and kills the monster.

As you walk around the park, you will see a variety of plants and wildlife. To the ancient American Indians, they were such more than just birds or lizards or butterflies. Take time to look them up in the guides or on the Internet. You may be surprised at what you learn—and how relevant these myths are in our lives today. Are you the monster or Coyote? I think I'm both.

The comments on this blog are more interesting. Bone Man writes that she isn't either Coyote or a monster—she's a fox. Desert Dude likes Bone Man's comment, as do seven others. Blue Planet thanks Emily for the beautiful retelling of the myth, and King Stag says, *Nicely done. You must be reading* Earth's Song. *Good choice.*

My heart stops, and I hear myself say, *oh shit.* It's one of the books my father wrote. Is King Stag my father? I glance back at King Stag's other responses: *Already a fan; interesting perspective;* and *Well done, let's meet and discuss this some more.*

THIRTY-ONE

Paige

My head spins. I still can't believe my father and Emily were lovers, but then how do I explain the reference in the blog?

I jump at the sound of the door opening. Spinning around, I see Jalen walk into the room. I don't have time to shut down the page, but I block the screen with my body.

"Hey," he says, "they let us off early." His eyes pass over me, reading me. "Some problem with vibrations on the third level. Your father said you'd be here. What are you doing?"

He moves closer, but I keep the screen hidden from him. "Reading Emily's blog."

He nods. "Did you see anything?"

I shut down the computer as casually as I can. It's one thing for me to doubt my father, but I don't want Jalen to know about King Stag. "I don't know."

He stands so close the heat of the sun rolls off him, as if he's managed to bring some of it inside. He stays very still, and as the moment lengthens, I realize after last night's speech about staying friends that his being here is as awkward for him as it is for me. Yet he's here anyway.

"I have the rest of the day off," he says. "Want to take a ride?" He pauses. "There's this place I want to show you."

I look up. His arms are crossed and his face is as stoic as ever, but behind the shield of his dark eyes, I glimpse something. My answer means something to him. "Where?"

He shrugs. "You'll see."

After what he told me last night, I don't want any more surprises and yet I'm curious. "Why do you want me to go?"

"I think you'll like it."

A hint of a smile comes into his eyes. I don't know what he finds amusing, and then I realize he's already figured out what I am just understanding—that I'm going to go with him.

In the battered, summer-scented pickup truck, Jalen takes the highway northwest. With no air-conditioning, we ride with the windows rolled down and the wind, hot and fierce, in our faces. I don't know where we're going, but it doesn't matter. With every mile between us and the park, a feeling of lightness opens up in me. It's like we're leaving everything bad that happened there and going somewhere new to start over. I realize this chain of thought isn't fair to Emily, but I don't care.

Jalen drives with his right arm slung over the top of the wheel and his eyes steady on the shimmering black highway. We make small talk for a while, and then I kick off my sneakers, tuck my legs under me, and use my backpack as a pillow against the car door. Almost immediately, I doze off.

When I open my eyes, my neck is cramped and I'm starving. There isn't a single other car in sight, and on either side of the road, thirsty brown earth stretches for miles, dotted with bushes that look like earth's razor stubble. In the far distance, pale pink-rock mountains rise like gigantic pieces of freeform art.

Sitting up, I push a clump of loose hair behind my ear and wipe my mouth in case I've drooled. "Where are we?"

He smiles and points to a sign so far in the distance it looks half-buried in the dirt. "Almost there." The smile widens. "I was beginning to think you were going to sleep through the whole thing." The smile is something new—he's teasing me.

"I guess it's the company," I tell him and then pretend to yawn. "How long was I out?"

"A couple of hours."

A couple of hours? I feel self-conscious for being out that long. But then, I didn't sleep much last night. Having someone tell you that you're going to die is a pretty good reason for insomnia. "It felt good."

"You look better."

We drive a while farther, and just as I'm beginning to wonder where we're going, twin, beaker-shaped concrete pillars flanking a sign come closer. The sign reads, "Welcome to the Navajo Nation."

We flash past it, and I feel a rush of excitement. Even with all the restorations my father has done, we've rarely been inside land under Native American jurisdiction. Why is Jalen bringing me here? Clearly it's not a date. Probably he's trying to make up for yesterday, the whole "friends" thing. He catches me studying him.

"Don't worry," he says. "I'm not kidnapping you."

"Oh, darn," I say, as if disappointed, and then because the loose ends are driving me crazy, I pull my hair out of its elastic. I feel him watching me, although he turns his head the minute I look at him.

We pass a large, modern-looking concrete structure with a sign identifying it as a visitor's center. A colorful flag with a red, yellow, and blue rainbow hangs from a flagpole in the parking lot.

We stop for gas and sandwiches at a convenience store. A Native American woman in a black dress cinched at the waist with a silver Concho belt takes Jalen's cash. Her black eyes peer out of a weathered, round face the color of nutmeg.

Back in the car, we continue down the highway, and it's like the little convenience store never existed and we're climbing a series of mountains, giving us dazzling views of the canyons below us. Beneath us, the old truck's engine downshifts. We barely go ten miles an hour as we maneuver the turns.

We pass clusters of civilization—villages, farmlands dotted with herds of sheep or cows, and numerous mobile homes, small as metal shoeboxes tucked into the landscape.

After another twenty minutes, Jalen turns down an unpaved road. Almost immediately the underbrush and sand cover up the path. We hear them scrape the underbelly of the truck.

I almost think we've lost the road completely when I see a structure in the distance. It sits alone on a patch of sparse grassland almost invisible in the enormity of the land.

As we get closer, it takes shape, the octagonal sides and mud covering defining it as a traditional *hogan*. Jalen pulls the truck to a bumpy stop. He turns off the ignition and stares at the house.

"We're here," he says.

The place looks long abandoned. What probably once was a garden is now a patch of dry earth dotted with spindly, yellow weeds.

"Come on," Jalen urges, already at my side of the truck, pulling the creaky truck door open.

He holds my hand, but I'm not sure he's even aware of it as we step through the front door. The one-room interior smells musty and old and feels as if it's been empty for a long time. There are no windows. A stone fireplace sits in the middle of the room.

Whatever this place is, it means something to Jalen. I can see it in the way his gaze travels almost tenderly around the empty space, as if he's seeing the room not as it is, but how he remembers it.

"There was sheepskin on the floor, and they kept Pendleton blankets over there," he says, pointing. "A lantern hung on that hook and all the kitchen utensils were on that wall." His face is rapt. "And here," he points to a spot near the fireplace, "is where my grandmother made kneeldown bread." He closes his eyes, smiles. "Sometimes she made it with bacon. It was so good."

"You grew up here?"

He shakes his head. "No. My father and uncle."

It's so small it's almost impossible to imagine a family living in what is essentially smaller than my mother's garage. There's no electricity, much less a bathroom or running water.

"I came here about twice a month on the weekends," he says. "I know it doesn't look like much, but back then…" He shakes his head, as if wondering how to put it into words. "My grandmother made the best blue corn pancakes, and Grandfather… We went on long walks. The places here—the canyons and the monuments…"

I wonder if he realizes he's different here. The strong planes of his face seem to soften, and there's a look in his eyes—a sureness, maybe contentedness?

"What do you think of it?" He comes to stand next to me.

"Just that this is so different than our house in New Jersey. I can't imagine living here."

Almost instantly his mouth tightens and his eyes harden into onyx. "You don't like it."

It isn't what I mean at all. I put my hand on his forearm. "My mom's house is bigger, that's true. We have four bedrooms, three-and-a-half baths, a finished basement, and a two-car garage." I pause because it's important he gets this. "And you know what? We were all miserable there. There's no smell of blue corn pancakes, and we stopped taking long family walks when I was ten. Even before my dad left, there was this…quiet. We all pretended it wasn't there. It took me a long time to figure out it was the sound of everything falling apart. You think I wouldn't trade that for a house with the kind of memories you have?"

He looks at me a long moment, sighs, and then brushes back my overgrown bangs. "Let's eat," he says.

He spreads an orange-and-blue-striped blanket on the floor near the hearth and unpacks the sandwiches from the convenience store. He hands me a ham-and-cheese and asks about what it's like to live in New Jersey.

I tell him about life in the 'burbs—a world where everyone spends way too much money and time trying to seem totally perfect.

"There's a lot of pressure," I tell him, "to have the right look, the right clothes, the right friends." I shake my head. "People judge you all the time. Sometimes I would get so sick of that—but most of the time you try to be like everyone else so you don't get talked about."

Jalen nods. "It was important to my father that my brother and I fit in at school. He encouraged us to try out for just about every sport."

I pass him a slice of orange. "What'd you play?"

"Everything—football, baseball, basketball." He shakes his head. "It always seemed like a big waste of time."

"What did you want to do?"

He takes a long swallow of water, recaps the bottle, and gives me a guilty grin. "Study."

My brows shoot up. "Study? You're a secret nerd?"

He shrugs the way people do when they're really good at something but don't want to admit it. "I want to go to college and double major— Native American Studies and political science. After that, law school."

Law school. For a moment it's hard to picture him in a suit and a tie, but then I look into his eyes and know this is exactly right for him. He's quiet, but he misses nothing and he thinks things through. His mind works differently than mine, which takes all sorts of weird leaps and turns.

"You'll be an amazing lawyer," I tell him. "I can see you doing great things for people."

His gaze drops. "Thanks. I hope so. We'll see. How about you?"

I sigh and tell him about my childhood spent following my father around the desert, how I once dreamed of becoming an archeologist, but then saw what my dad's crazy hours and obsession with the past did to our family.

"I didn't want to be like him, but nothing else ever felt right, either." I tell him then about Stuart and my mother, and that I deliberately failed health class and tanked my SATs.

He says that what's happened isn't as important as what I do next, how I handle things now. I know he's exactly right, only it's complicated. There are so many things I don't know—how to talk to my mother about Stuart, how to go back to New Jersey and put everything behind me. And there's Jalen. How exactly does he fit into my future?

I've been quiet a long time. That's another great thing about Jalen. He never rushes you to say anything.

"I think I want to go to college and study archeology, but what if I'm not as good as my father? Everyone's going to compare us."

Jalen shakes his head. "Who cares what people think? You should go for it if that's what you want."

Like it's that simple. Like failure is a word that doesn't exist.

Lunch is over, and we gather our trash and put everything back in the paper bag. "What scares you most?" I ask as we rise to our feet.

He takes his time folding up the blanket. Finally he lifts his gaze to mine. "Wanting the wrong thing," he says.

Looking into his eyes, I know *I* am the wrong thing.

THIRTY-TWO

Paige

After lunch, we hike through the heat, dry grass, and brush to a creek near the house. It's little more than a watering hole, but reminds me of all the springs and ponds where Emily and I used to play. I kick off my sneakers and wade knee-deep into the water. The mud oozes between my toes, stirring the water into silt.

"What are you doing?"

"Cooling off." I bend over, splash some water on my arms. "It feels good." Without straightening, I watch him take a step closer until the water laps at the edge of his work boots.

I wait until he's within range, and then I grab as much water as I can and splash him. He jerks as it pelts him. Even as he shakes it free from his eyes, I scoop frantically and splatter him over and over, laughing as he steps into the creek without even pausing to take off his boots.

Bending, he throws water at me, and all at once it's war. We both launch as much water as we can at each other. We keep it up, splashing until we're out of breath, completely soaked, and laughing so hard we can barely stand.

"Enough," Jalen says, putting his hands up in a gesture of surrender.

Our eyes meet. I see the small beads of water caught in his long, black lashes and a softening of his lips. My heart beats faster, and as the moment lengthens I think he's going to kiss me, but then he lifts his arm and wipes his face.

"You're soaked," he points out.

"So are you."

"I know."

The sun is hot on my skin. His face is unsmiling, set in strong, proud lines. Nothing is going to happen between us, and it's time I accept this, stop being so obvious about what I want from him. I watch the rise and fall of his chest and will my face to a blankness that won't say anything to him. I will myself not to feel anything at all.

"We should go," he says.

We should, but I don't move. Instead, I keep my gaze locked on his.

"Why don't you ever say my name? Why don't you say, 'Let's go, Paige?'"

He blinks, and even in his still face something seems to freeze and I sense how uncomfortable I've made him. "What are you talking about?"

My hands go to my hips. "I've been thinking about this a lot. You don't speak to me unless we make eye contact. The only time you've ever said my name was the day Jeremy attacked me. Remember? You called my name. You said, 'Paige, are you okay?'"

He shakes his head and then suddenly takes great care to wring the water from the hem of his T-shirt. "So what?"

"Say my name."

He looks up, jaw tight. "We should go. It's a long ride back."

"Say, 'It's a long ride back, Paige.'"

His eyes turn dark, scornful. "I'm not a parrot."

I know I should let it drop, but I can't. "I want to hear you say my name. Friends use each other's names, Jalen."

He hesitates, muscles in his jaw clenching and unclenching. I know I'm ruining the moment, the fun we were having just moments ago, but I need to know. And so I hold his gaze and hope he can see that his answer is important to me. Finally, he sighs.

"Words have power," he says.

"Exactly. It feels impersonal when you don't use my name. It feels like you either don't know it or you've forgotten it or I'm not important enough to you to use it."

He scowls. "It's none of those things. You don't understand."

He's right—I don't.

"Okay," he says, "I'll give you an example. In the winter, we don't say the word 'bear.' To say the word is to call the bear to you."

I don't blink. "I'm not a bear."

"I know."

But to say my name might call me to him, and he doesn't want this.

Sweat rolls down my face like tears, but I'm more angry than sad. "You're never going to say my name, are you?" I can't hide the bitterness in my voice. I don't want to be the girl he simply calls "*Hey, you.*"

He shrugs, and his eyes slide away from mine.

A flash of hurt passes through me. "Fine." I walk away from him, picking my way barefoot along the water's edge, welcoming the pain of rocks and pebbles sharp as shells.

"Wait," he calls.

"Oh, were you talking to me?" The good feelings I had for him in the *hogan* and in the water are gone, replaced by hurt and anger and a selfish desire to hurt him back.

"Wait," he calls more loudly, but I keep going. I would walk all the way back to my father's house if I could.

"Wait, *Paige*," he says.

My feet stop of their own accord.

"Paige," he says again, softer now, drawing the word out, gooseflesh rising all over me, as if he has breathed the word onto me.

I turn slowly. He's standing about six feet away, an expression on his face I have never seen before. He wants me, he cares for me, yet this comes at a cost for him.

I move toward him so he doesn't have to be the one to take this next step. When our faces are inches apart, I look into his eyes.

"Paige," he says again.

He takes my face in his hands, carefully moves my hair, and then his lips close over mine. He kisses me deeply, as if everything he's been holding back has finally broken through. I taste a trace of orange and something I can't describe that belongs to him. I close my eyes, feel like I'm dissolving inside. The muscles in his back strain, and I know without a shadow of a doubt that this is real, that it isn't just a crush— that he would not be kissing me like this if it were something he could help.

When we finally stop, we hold each other for a long time. I search his eyes for a trace of regret and see, instead, amusement.

"That's why," he says gently. "Why I couldn't say your name."

I feel his heart thumping under his shirt and am suddenly aware of how tightly I'm gripping his neck. How I never want to let go of him. "Jalen," I whisper because if a name has power, I want to call him to me again and again and again.

"I've wanted to do this since I saw you," he whispers, showering my throat with kisses that leave me breathless.

"You filled my water bottle for me that day, didn't you?" I wind my fingers into the silk of his wet hair, feel the heat of his scalp.

"I saw you watching me. I wanted to do something for you."

"You didn't even look at me."

"I saw you." A shy expression forms in his eyes as he fits his gaze to mine. "I saw you, Paige." His voice is low and very serious. "I see you even when I'm not with you."

I kiss him again. I can't help it. "And the time with your uncle—you didn't introduce me…"

He shakes his head. "I wasn't sure what he'd say to you. And I kept thinking that if I kept my distance, you'd be safer."

I see the sudden shadows creep into his eyes and kiss him again. "Nothing is going to happen to me. You don't even know if I'm the girl in your uncle's dream."

He pulls back. "It's not like I have feelings for a lot of girls."

Something silvery goes through me. He cares about me. He wants to protect me. I am falling in love, and maybe he is, too. "And have there been a lot of girls?"

He smiles and his eyes are so black it must be a trick of the light. "Oh, dozens and dozens. So many I've lost count."

He's joking and I punch him lightly on the arm. "The truth."

"Just you," he says.

We kiss for a long time, and this time there's the joy of knowing that there's no one else in his mind or life but me. That all this time he's been hiding these feelings for me. He hasn't said he loves me, but I feel it.

Even after the kiss ends, we don't let go of each other. For the rest of the afternoon, as we hike the area near his grandparents' *hogan,* some part of us is always touching.

We stay until late afternoon and he says it's time to take me home. Holding hands, we walk slowly back to the truck. With its rusted paint and dented sides, it blends in perfectly with the abandoned house and garden of scraggily yellow weeds. It looks as if it belongs there, and in a crazy kind of way, it feels like now Jalen and I belong to this place, too.

On the way home, I scoot over on the bench seat and lean my head against his shoulder. He puts his arm around me, and although we don't talk much, I'm okay with that. I know he's crossed a line he never meant to cross and wouldn't have if he didn't have feelings for me. If he didn't love me. If this were not the start of something.

THIRTY-THREE

Jalen

When I get home, it's ten o'clock and Uncle Billy is waiting for me in the kitchen. He's wearing a neatly pressed button-down shirt tucked into a pair of Wranglers. His hair is neatly braided, and best of all, his eyes gaze at me without the sheen of alcohol.

"I'm ready," he says.

"Ready for what?" I drop my keys on the counter and walk to the refrigerator.

"For you to take me to Walmart," he says patiently, as if I've forgotten. "We're going to buy supplies for the yellow corn maiden."

"Uncle, I never said we'd go tonight."

"You said you'd take me."

The last thing I want to do is get back in the truck and drive to Walmart where we'll spend at least an hour as my uncle wanders around, as distractible as a child, gathering supplies.

"Another night, Uncle." I peer into the refrigerator without much interest.

Uncle Billy's finger feels skeletal as he pokes me in the back. "Maybe I should be picking up some black yarn. Maybe I should be making the blue corn maiden."

I shut the refrigerator door. "What are you talking about?" I search my uncle's eyes, twin black coins currently sparkling with humor. For a moment, I glimpse my grandfather in his broken, weathered face.

"The professor's daughter. You were with her."

"How did you know?"

He smiles. "We were talking at dinner."

A blush creeps up my neck. "What was everyone saying?"

He blinks innocently. "That you have taken an interest in her."

An interest? A rush of heat ignites in my body. I *kissed* her. And it was amazing, but what was I thinking? "We're friends."

Uncle Billy laughs. "Friends?" He teases. "Since when do you go riding around for hours with a girl? Just where did you go?"

I look away from his sharp, knowing gaze. He probably wouldn't like my answer. Wouldn't think she belonged there. "Since when is this any of your business?" I say it as if I'm teasing. My intention is not to disrespect him.

"This girl," he persists, "she reminds me of the blue corn maiden." His face realigns itself from teasing uncle into the composed features of teacher, which, when he's sober, is his favorite role. *Who else will remember if I don't pass the stories along to you?* "Do you remember the story?"

I fold my arms and lean against the edge of the tile counter. "Of course."

"The blue corn maiden," he says, completely ignoring me, "was the most beautiful of all the corn maiden daughters and the people loved her because of the delicious blue corn she gave them every year."

"Uncle, I know this."

He lifts his brows and gives me an injured look. I resign myself to the retelling— how the blue corn maiden was captured by Winter *Katsina* and brought to his house and kept there until Summer *Katsina* found her. A fierce battle between Winter and Summer—fire and ice— ensued, and then the two *katsinas* realized neither could win and they needed to make peace between themselves. They agreed to share the blue corn maiden, each getting six months of the year with her.

My uncle stops talking, and yet there's more he wants to tell me— the lesson he wants to make sure I understand, although I'm pretty sure I know where he's going with this.

"Jalen," he says, "if you get involved with her, she will divide you in half. It will be your world and her world. You cannot live like that. If you learn nothing from me, learn that."

Am I not already divided in half by blood? I bite my lip hard not to say this. And yet, if I have to choose, don't I already know which side I would take? Paige and I were happy today, but would she ever want to live on the Nation? What about her family? How would they feel about me?

"Uncle, with all respect," I say, "you don't know what you're talking about." But he does, and before he spears me with any other truths I walk out of the kitchen.

THIRTY-FOUR

Paige

Jalen arrives at six o'clock with a toolbox in his hands. A toolbox. It seems a strange thing to bring to dinner, but then I guess if I'd wanted a flowers-and-candy kind of guy, I would have stayed with Aaron Dunning.

No regrets there, especially now, looking at Jalen. His black hair is pulled tightly back and shows off his strong facial bones and his deep-set onyx eyes. His black shorts and T-shirt look freshly ironed. The care he's taken with his appearance, more than anything that shows on his face, tells me that tonight is important to him and he wants to make a good impression.

"You look nice," I say and step forward to hug him. Until now, I didn't realize how part of me expected him to change his mind about us, even after what happened in the Navajo Nation.

The hug is quick, slightly awkward, as if we're about to get caught doing something we shouldn't. Yet the pieces of what we are, what we could be to each other, are there.

"You look nice, too." His eyes linger on the red peasant blouse cinched around my waist. A happy tingle goes through me. When he lifts his gaze to mine, I feel it in my stomach.

"So what's with the toolbox? We're feeding you—not making you work." He smells of rain and soap and something that has become my favorite scent in the world.

"Your father will appreciate this more."

"Appreciate what more?" My father suddenly looms behind me. He extends his hand in greeting. "Good to see you, Jalen. Come on in."

My father was not around for the whole Aaron Dunning chapter in my life, and I really don't know what to expect from him tonight. Maybe I should have warned him. Told him that Jalen was going to tell him about us. With Aaron, I took great pride in excluding my dad from any information which would have given him the opportunity to hand out advice or approval. But most of all, I wanted my exclusion to hurt him. *Sorry, Dad, I can't talk now,* is what I'd say when he called. *I have a date.*

Jalen steps inside and immediately the entranceway shrinks. He has at least three inches over my father who, at six feet, has always seemed tall to me.

Jalen carries the toolbox into the kitchen and sets it on the counter next to a stack of archeology magazines that probably go back several years.

"Soda? Juice? Water?" my father asks, opening the cabinet and taking out one of the four glasses he owns. They're the cheap, unbreakable kind, just slightly nicer than plastic, but at least they're clean.

"Water, please," Jalen says and leans against the counter. He slouches, but his eyes are alert. "Thanks," he adds as my father hands him the glass.

"Well," my father says, opening a beer. "What project has Paige talked you into doing?"

Jalen and I exchange puzzled glances, and then I remember the toolbox. For a moment I want to laugh. Sometimes my father can be so clueless. "He's not here to work, Dad."

Jalen straightens. "I do want to work…but that's not why I'm here." He looks at me and then back to my father. "Paige and I want to see each other. Go out," he adds, and then, in the silence that follows, adds very seriously so there will be no doubt, "I would like to date your daughter."

It isn't as firm as what I'd hoped he'd say, but we'd argued a little about this earlier. I thought asking for permission was old-fashioned and silly. It was my choice, not my dad's, but Jalen said it was a way of showing respect. No matter what I said, it wouldn't change his mind. There's a depth of stubbornness to him I am just beginning to understand.

My father takes off his glasses, cleans them on the hem of his shirt almost as if he's trying to fill time while he figures out what to say. "Well," he says and holds up his glass of sweet tea. "Congratulations!" He says it loudly, as if we all have gone hard of hearing. The moment that follows is awkward, but at least the worst is over.

At dinner, we eat very well done steaks, baked potatoes, and blackened corn. We talk about progress on the restoration project, the recent sighting of a relatively rare owl by one of the park rangers, and Jalen's family. Throughout it all, Jalen answers everything, but uses as few words as humanly possible. I'm relieved when my father starts rambling on about the discovery of skeletal remains in Ethiopia that suggest early hominoids were able to climb trees as well as walk upright.

After dinner, Jalen takes out his toolbox and we start hanging pictures that have probably been resting against the wall since the day my father moved in here. We hang them more or less above the spots where they've been leaning. My mom would have known exactly where they belonged and done a much better job, but seeing them on the wall is a huge improvement.

In the dining room, Dad and Jalen space out three framed Audubon prints—a duck, a pheasant, and a turkey—that used to hang in our dining room back in New Jersey. It was a room we never used much, except on holidays. For a moment I let myself fantasize that my mom and dad will get back together, and we'll be a family again. My father will carve the Thanksgiving turkey so slowly and carefully it'll be like he's excavating bones. My mom will keep telling him to hurry before the butter peas and mashed potatoes go stone-cold, and my grandparents will laugh as if everything is funny and refill the champagne glasses.

Jalen straightens the final print. "What do you think?"

"Good," I say. "Dad?"

He nods and rubs his hand over the rough, blond stubble just beginning to cover his chin. "They're good for now," he says, "but I never really felt right about eating turkey while the damn bird was on the wall watching." He laughs, though, his first one of the night, and maybe, I think, the first real one since I've arrived.

We move to my father's office, where Jalen hammers a spring hanger into the wall for an oversized watercolor called *The Seven Navajo Bows*. My father's face lights up as he retells the story—how a maiden lived alone and one day Coyote came to visit. When they ran out of meat, the maiden used a magic horn to call spirit hunters and armed them with the seven bows and seven arrows hanging above her fireplace. The hunters brought back meat. Coyote stole the horn, but the warriors, loyal to the maiden, turned against him and Coyote had to flee.

Jalen has heard this story—only, in the version he tells us, the spirit hunters are the maiden's brothers and the magic horn is a windpipe. Coyote stole the windpipe multiple times, and ultimately, when he used it to call the spirit hunters, a swarm of bees emerged instead and stung Coyote, who ran off into the forest. The next thing I know, my father and my boyfriend are talking Native American mythology and Jalen's face has become animated, his sentences longer, his shoulders relaxed.

To illustrate a point, my father pulls his textbook, *Footsteps in the Past*, off the bookshelf behind his desk and begins flipping through the chapters.

"That's Paige," my father says, pointing at one of the photographs. "She had to be, like, six or seven in that one."

"Dad…" I try to grab the book, but Jalen lifts it out of my reach. "Stop it," I say, laughing. It feels good, though, to get the attention. I was happy back then. In the back of my brain, Mrs. Shum's voice tells me to look at who I was in order to know who I want to become. I know suddenly what that means.

The phone rings as my dad is showing Jalen a picture of a collapsed pit house. I remember my father re-laying the roof while Emily and I danced beneath, conjuring up spirits as we hopped the beams of light.

"Excuse me." With the phone pressed to his ear, my father walks out of the office.

Jalen sets my father's textbook on the shelf and pulls another book off the shelf.

"Dad likes you," I say, moving closer.

He doesn't look up, but the corners of his mouth lift. "He's cool." He reads the back cover of a book, resets it on the shelf, and then pulls out another one. "Think he'd let me borrow something?"

"Are you kidding? He'd be thrilled."

He puts the book aside and returns his attention to the shelf, running his fingers along the spines. He doesn't seem to get that we're alone. I shove his shoulder playfully. "Put the book down and talk to me."

Pushing him, however, is like trying to move an oak, and he seems completely absorbed in the book in his hands.

"Come on, Jalen," I say.

He looks up. I freeze. He's scowling deeply and his eyes are dark, almost angry. For a second I think he's mad at me, and then his gaze returns to the book. "Half of the first page is missing," he says. He holds it up. On the cover is a picture of a girl with long blonde hair tied in braids. The title reads, *The Corn Maiden and Other Nightmares.*

"So?"

"Half the first page is missing," He repeats.

A chill passes through me as it hits home that the missing page to this book might be the one we found tucked into Emily's sneaker.

"Give me that." I grab the book. He's right. The second page mentions that guy, Jude, that Master of Eyes. "You don't know that this is the same book." But we both know it is. So what's it doing on my father's shelf? I hug myself tightly to fight the feeling that I'm falling into a hole deeper and more despairing than the one Emily and I stumbled into all those years ago.

THIRTY-FIVE

Paige

Jalen turns the book over and skims the back copy. He glances up, his face unreadable. "An eleven-year-old girl with the color of corn silk gets kidnapped. Then killed. A ritual sacrifice."

I try to speak but can't. I rub my arms as if I can scrub away the layer of dread that has settled over me like a fine layer of dust. *If that page came from this book, what's it doing in my father's office?*

My heart feels like it has exploded in my chest and is now beating in a hundred places at the same time. My mind floods with terrible thoughts of Emily bleeding atop a stone tablet, begging for her life, my father's face looking coldly down at her.

"We need to tell the police."

"It could be just a coincidence," I have to push the words through the dryness of my throat and mouth.

"Or it could explain what happened to Emily."

I close my eyes, but what I really want is to cover my ears against Jalen's words, my own fears. "The police already suspect my father. If this is the book, they'll arrest him. It'll ruin him."

Jalen shakes his head as if what I'm saying makes no sense. "Your father has an alibi."

My gaze slides away from his. For the thousandth time, my mind tries to measure how long my father was gone.

Realization blooms in Jalen's dark eyes. "Shit. He wasn't with you, was he?"

I lift my chin. "Of course he was."

He looks hard into my eyes and then shakes his head. "You covered for him? All this time we've been looking for her and you couldn't tell the truth?"

"He didn't do anything wrong!"

Jalen's gaze narrows. His face is almost ugly in the anger he's not quite masking. "Then it shouldn't be a problem to tell the truth now. You owe Emily."

A hundred images of Emily flash through my mind. I see her at five, a slight gap between her teeth, smiling at me from the river bank. I see her laughing before we both jumped from the top of one tall rock to another. The images keep coming, fast-forwarding until all I see is Emily walking into my bedroom, her hair dusty and matted, her face as pale as the moon. *Have you seen my sneakers?* she asks.

I look at the book in Jalen's hand and three things occur to me. One, that it can't be the same book and we're making a huge deal out of nothing. Two, that Jalen is staring at me as if he is seeing me for the first time. And three, if I lie to him, he'll know it.

"My dad wasn't gone long enough to do anything."

"Shit." Jalen shakes his head as if he can't believe what he's heard. "Shit. Shit. Shit."

"It isn't that big a deal."

His black brows raise. "No? You broke the law. You obstructed justice. You could have ruined any chance of finding Emily. And you lied to me. You let me believe you were with him."

"Everything I told you and the police was true." My lie is by omission. "The police asked if he was with me, and he was."

"But not the whole time."

"When was I supposed to tell you? When I thought you hated me? After you told me I might be in danger? Or when you kissed me? Besides, it isn't him. I know it."

Jalen's face darkens. "From the beginning. You should have told the truth." His lips twist, and his voice rises as if he can't help it. "You lied to the police. You lied to me."

"Maybe I didn't want them to act like you're acting now. All judgmental. Jumping to conclusions."

Our gazes lock and hold. Gone is the invitation to walk into his mind, his thoughts. His eyes are as cold and hard as onyx. "If he's innocent—if this is just a page missing in a random book—then you shouldn't worry about talking to him about it."

"I don't worry about talking to him," I say tightly. "But in private. He's my father. I don't want him blindsided."

Jalen hesitates. I lay my hand on his arm, and he jumps as if I've stung him. Yesterday he wouldn't have done that, and a new kind of fear moves through me. I can probably make him do what I want, but it's going to come at a cost—maybe our relationship. "Please. You have to trust me."

Something goes flat in his eyes. "It stops tonight," he says. "If you don't tell the police by tomorrow morning, I will."

I walk him to the door, but there's no question that he's going to kiss me. His gaze doesn't find or linger on mine, and walking to his truck, his shoulders are stiff. I want to shout at his retreating back that he's a coward, that he's probably glad to have an excuse for us not to be together. At the same time, I want to run after him, to somehow make things right. He's gone before I do either.

THIRTY-SIX

Paige

After Jalen leaves, I look for my dad and nearly collide with him striding out of the kitchen. His face is pale, his lips thin and bloodless. "I've got to go out for a little while," he says.

"What's wrong?" Did he overhear Jalen and me? Does he know we found the book?

Keys jingle from his restless hands. "Nothing. I... There's just something that needs to be taken care of."

"Dad, before you go we need to talk."

He cuts me off with an impatient wave of his hand. "Later. Lock the door behind me." He starts to move around me.

"It's about Emily," I say, and he freezes. "Were you having an affair with her?"

He turns and his eyes lock onto mine. "Absolutely not," he says emphatically. "My God, she's your age."

"We found a book in your office. It has a missing page."

He starts to dismiss what I've said, and then he stops. "What?"

"We found *The Corn Maiden*."

He shakes his head impatiently. "I don't know that book. You said it's missing a page?"

"Not just any page. The first page."

He glances at his watch, frowns deeply. "We'll talk more about it when I get back." He reaches past me for the doorknob.

"Dad," I say sharply as if he's fallen asleep and I'm trying to wake him. "We need to call the police. Now."

"We will. Trust me—this is important, or I wouldn't leave you."

"Important how? Where are you going? What are doing?"

He pushes the door open. A furnace blast of heat, as if he is stepping into hell, flows through the opening. "I'll tell you everything when I get back. I'll only be an hour. Lock the door behind me," he says, and then he's gone.

But he doesn't come home in an hour and doesn't pick up when I try his cell. I'm pacing the living room when headlights slide across the blinds. My heart pounds when I pull the curtains aside and see the police car idling in our driveway. Then it drops when, moments later, Detectives Rodriquez and Torres step out of their car and give the house a long, assessing look.

At the front door, Detective Rodriquez greets me with a question. "Where's your father?" Under the porch light, the officer's heavyset features are stoic and unyielding. Next to her, tall, thin Detective Torres stands slightly hollow-eyed, as if he has seen this scene play out a thousand times and never once has it had a happy ending.

"He isn't home."

"Where is he?" Detective Rodriquez's deep-set eyes lock onto me. There's an eagerness in them I have never seen. A sick feeling spreads through my veins.

"I don't know." My heart thumps so hard it's distracting. "Why are you here?" I ask, even as the answer seems clear. Jalen must have called them right after he left. He said he'd wait, but he didn't.

"When will he be back?" Detective Rodriquez keeps her gaze locked onto mine, and I have to fight the feeling that she can read my mind.

"I don't know." Dead silence. "He didn't say."

She shakes her head as if I am her best student but I've given the wrong answer to a very basic question. "You don't have to keep doing this, Paige—lying for him." She gives me a smile that doesn't reach her eyes. "This is a search warrant," she says, and for the first time I notice the papers in her hands. "It gives us the legal ability to search your house. Please step aside."

"What are you looking for?" But I already know the answer, and it's sitting on the desk in my father's office. They move past me without answering.

I try calling my father's cell, but it just rings into voicemail. Why doesn't he pick up? Why didn't he tell me where he was going? When I can't reach him, I do the only thing I can think of—call Dr. Shum.

He's assuring me that everything will be okay when I hear Detective Rodriquez shout from my father's office, "Torres, come check this out."

I follow Lieutenant Torres into the room, where Detective Rodriquez is holding the copy of *The Corn Maiden*.

The Shums arrive just after Lieutenant Rodriquez has called in an APB for the arrest of my father, who they think has gone on the run. Stepping inside the house, Mrs. Shum hugs me as Dr. Shum demands to know what's going on.

The police answer his questions with their own. Did Dr. Shum realize my father was spending time with Emily outside the park? Did he realize they had an inappropriate relationship? Had he ever read *The Corn Maiden*?

Dr. Shum sputters in indignation. "What are you talking about? Duke is a friend of the family and is a respected member of the academic community. He would never…" His blue eyes blaze with fury. "How dare you denigrate the reputation of a world-renowned archeologist?"

Although shorter than Dr. Shum by nearly a head, Detective Rodriquez meets his gaze with a steely one of her own. "I'll ask you again. Did you ever see Dr. Patterson alone, outside the park, with Miss Linton?"

Dr. Shum looks down at her coldly. "This is a witch hunt," he says. "Any questions you want to ask me or my wife will have to be done in the presence of my attorney."

The corners of Detective Rodriquez's plump, pink lips curl up knowingly. "Consider it done," she says.

We all look up at the sound of a car door slamming. We step onto the front porch in time to see my father jogging toward the house. "Paige!" he shouts. "What's going on?"

He doesn't make it to me. The two officers intercept him. Within seconds, he is spread-eagled against the wall in the dining room. They pat him down and then cuff him. As they start to read him his rights, I feel dizzy, disoriented, as if I am here, watching this, but also apart from it.

Mrs. Shum tucks her arm around me. "Honey," she murmurs, "it's going to be okay."

But it isn't. Moments later, Detective Rodriquez charges my father with probable cause in the disappearance of Emily Linton. Detective Torres opens the back door to the squad car and puts his hand on my father's head as he gets in. For a moment, my gaze locks with my dad's. "Call your mother. Tell her to come get you." My father's voice cuts off as he loses his balance and almost stumbles into the car.

Mrs. Shum's arm tightens around me as the car backs down the driveway. She smells of paint and turpentine and something slightly sweet, like roses. "Don't worry, Paige," she murmurs. "Your father's lawyer will meet him at the police station. They'll work it out."

Dr. Shum's blue eyes rest gently on me. Under the porch light his rugged features reflect concern. "Your father is a good man," he says gruffly. "The police do this sometimes. They're under pressure to make an arrest, so they have to charge somebody."

I don't say anything, but the lump in my throat swells. I take a deep breath, and it cracks into a thousand gasping little pieces.

He doesn't know that the police have new evidence. He doesn't know about the book or that my dad no longer has an alibi. And he doesn't know that I have been betrayed by the one person I thought I could trust. In the space of a few hours, I have lost everything.

Dr. Shum's broad brow furrows, and he pats my shoulder in a gesture that's formal and yet oddly comforting. "Ah, little one," he says gently. "You've had yourself quite a night, haven't you? Are you hungry?"

Mrs. Shum brushes my hair back from my face. "We should stop at Jack In The Box," she says in the false, cheerful tone of someone who has no idea that she's saying the entirely wrong thing. "I know you girls like those black-and-white shakes."

THIRTY-SEVEN

Paige

The next morning, the sadness is still there, but something else as well—anger.

Dr. Shum can hardly drive me to the park fast enough. I barely pay attention to Mrs. Shum, who tries to distract me by talking about the ongoing construction of her exhibit. She doesn't seem to realize that I won't be in Arizona long enough to see any of it. If my mother has her way, I'll be returning to New Jersey with her and Stuart as soon as the police let me leave the state—something Stuart promised last night would happen very quickly.

In the conference room at the information center, Dr. Shum holds the morning briefing. As he announces that he will be assuming my father's responsibilities for the next few days, I scan the room, looking for Jalen.

He isn't there, so I head for the cliffs. I'm out of breath and sweating by the time I finish the long climb up the ladders. In front of me, the exterior wall of the ruins looms. Its blackened windows stare at me like empty sockets in a ruined face. In the ringing silence they seem to say, *Go away. There's nothing inside here but death.*

I slip sideways through the T-shaped entrance and into the small, dark chamber. It's noticeably cooler inside and very quiet. I don't linger in this room with its round opening to the basement chamber and memories of Jeremy Brown pinning me to the floor, shoving his slimy tongue into my mouth.

I climb the wooden ladder up the wall and through the chimney-like opening in the ceiling. More than ever, the space seems decayed and rotting, claustrophobic in the darkness. I emerge in a chamber on the third level and wind my way through the broken rooms and narrow passages. It doesn't take me long to find him.

He's standing in the small chamber where the skeletal remains of a Native American child were once found in the interior wall. Jalen's back is to me, and he's sliding his hands along the wall as if checking for cracks. His head all but touches the domed surface of the ceiling.

"Jalen," I say coldly.

He turns, wipes his forehead with his arm. His always-serious face studies me for a few seconds before he speaks. "Did you talk to him?"

I make an ugly, scoffing noise. "Like you don't know."

He shifts his weight. "Know what?"

We look at each other for a long moment. He is so physically beautiful that I want to run to him, but he betrayed me. The image of my father's face when they handcuffed him flashes through my mind. "That he was arrested. Last night."

Jalen's straight black brows pull together. "Arrested? What are you talking about?"

My hands straddle my hips. "The police showed up with a warrant two hours after you left. You told me you would give me time to talk to my dad. You lied to me. I didn't even have time to call his lawyer."

"I didn't tell anyone."

"Then how did the police know to show up?"

"I don't know."

"So it was all a bad coincidence? How stupid do you think I am?"

His jaw tightens. "You're not stupid. But you're drawing the wrong conclusions."

"How, then, did the police know to come?"

He stays silent.

I ask, "Were you ever really into me?"

I want war, but his brow unfurrows and his features go still, unreadable, as if he has been carved from mahogany. Staring at the purposeful blankness of his face, I wonder suddenly if I have fantasized everything about our relationship.

"Were you," I repeat, "ever really into me?"

His nostrils flare slightly. "What do you think?"

I clench my fists. "How long have you suspected my father?"

"What?"

"How long have you thought my father was having an affair with Emily Linton?"

He shakes his head. "It crossed my mind. But I didn't call the police."

"Liar!" My mind and heart race, trying to put all the clues together. I feel sick at the conclusion.

"It's Emily you really liked, isn't it? That's why you kept pulling back. Not because of your uncle. You were only with me to stay close to my father. To get evidence against him."

He stares at me in stunned silence. "Do you honestly believe that?"

I'm rolling down the hill now, faster and faster with the spin of a story that grows more credible by the moment. "It's a lot more believable than a story about a crazy uncle who thinks I'm going to die. What kind of illness allows someone to see the future?"

It's a fair question, made cruel by the edge of sarcasm in my voice.

His eyes turn flat and cold. "You're upset, but you don't get to talk about my uncle like that. You don't get to denigrate something you don't understand." Slowly, deliberately, he turns his back to me and resumes sliding his hands along the cracked surface of the masonry wall.

I look at the stiffness of his shoulders, the set of his head. The architecture of hurt. Yet I'm not sorry. "I never want to see you again."

For a moment, Jalen's hands stop moving. I wait for him to turn around and fight for us, to tell me I'm wrong, but then those fingers start skimming the surface of the wall. Part of me wonders what he's looking for, but mostly I feel sick with the thought that he'll never touch me again, that we'll never kiss again. I broke up with him—I told him I never wanted to see him again. Yet now that it's happened, I feel more empty and lost than I have ever felt in my entire life.

Around lunch time, my mother calls to say that she and Stuart are still at the Newark Airport. Bad storms in the Northeast have delayed and canceled flights. She thinks they might get out sometime in the next hour or so, but they're going to have connect through Chicago, which means she won't land in Phoenix until late tonight.

"But don't worry, honey," she says, "Stuart and I will be there tonight. Just try to hang in."

The soothing tone of her voice enrages me. She doesn't ask about Dad. Doesn't care that he's been arrested or if he's guilty. All she wants is to reclaim me like I'm some kind of prize. After everything that's happened, it makes me want to scream. What about how I feel or what I want? I think about how she cheated on my father and want to confront her, but long distance isn't how I want to do that.

"I love you, honey," she says.

You know nothing, I almost shout. The anger boils so hard there are no words. For the first time in my life, I hang up on her. When she calls back, I don't answer.

Walking out of my father's office, I pass Mrs. Shum in the museum section. She's supervising two workers in the process of bolting a railing to the wall. It fits perfectly with the wall-length canvases she's painted.

Mrs. Shum smiles. "What do you think?"

"I want to see my father. Will you take me?"

Her smile fades. "Why, Paige? What's happened?"

"I need to talk to him."

She studies my face. "Isn't your mother landing in a couple of hours? Why don't you wait until they get here?"

I explain about the delay, and she fingers a long silver earring. "Of course. We'll talk to Dr. Shum just as soon as I'm finished," she promises.

I can't wait that long and storm off to break my vow and make my second trip of the day to the ruins.

In the late afternoon sun, the rungs are hot, but not unbearable. The sun draws vertical lines of sweat that race each other down my back and dribble between my breasts. Higher and higher, I climb. I try not to think about Jalen, but I can't help it. Accusing him of having a thing for Emily was a long shot, but he didn't deny it. After all, he was the one who found that book in my father's office. What if he'd planted it there? What if he was the one who'd hurt her? He would be physically strong enough to move her, and his father has a key to the front gate of the park. Jalen could have borrowed it. His beauty is so strong I wonder if it's blinded me to the truth. Has anyone asked him where he was the night Emily disappeared?

The thought is so horrible that I don't notice someone else on the ladders until we meet on the ledge. Our eyes meet, and the dread fills me.

"Hello, Paige," Jeremy Brown says as if he actually *is* glad to see me.

I stare the look on his face, and it all comes back—the tang of his saliva and the bite of his fingers. "Jeremy." I have to push the word out of my suddenly dry lips.

Unless one of us retreats, we'll have to pass each other on the stone ledge between the two ladders. The thought of him sliding up against me—accidentally rubbing against me—makes my stomach roll. As far as I can see, we're alone.

I think about retreating, but then remember something else about that time in the basement chamber. The moment he realized I was scared, the more excited he got and the more he enjoyed what was happening.

"I heard about your father." Jeremy's face shines with sweat, and a lock of black hair lies lank on his face. I can't read his eyes behind his sunglasses. "I'm sorry."

"What do you know about my father?"

He shrugs. "An article in the paper. For what it's worth, Paige, I don't think he had anything to do with what happened to Emily."

I wet my lips. "Why?"

He shifts his weight. "Well, for one, he was with you, wasn't he?"

"Yes." I hold his gaze and wonder if I imagined the sarcastic note in his voice.

"So it can't be him, then," Jeremy says. "But in the meantime, do you need something? A place to stay? A ride anywhere?"

The sweat drips down the front of my tank top. Doesn't he realize he'd be the last person I'd want to stay with? "I'm staying with the Shums."

"The Shums," he repeats. "We have a guest house and a pool. You could stay with us."

"Are you crazy?"

"I'm not the creep you think I am. What happened between us was a mistake. I see that more clearly now. I'd heard you liked to play games, and I thought you were into me. I never meant to scare or hurt you."

"Who told you I liked to play games?"

He shrugs. His red shirt clings to his thin chest, but I haven't forgotten how strong he is. "Emily. She said you were fearless. That the two of you were a little wild."

I shake my head, unsure if I'm more disgusted with him or angry at Emily. Why had she been talking about me to Jeremy? And how could he possibly think I'd like what he did to me? "Liar," I say. "She never said anything, did she?"

He smiles. "Look, you want to go up the ladder; I want to go down. I'm pretty much on probation. The last thing I need is for you to go running to Dr. Shum with another story."

He takes another step and then another until he's at the halfway point. There's still time for me to retreat, but if I do, there probably won't be enough time to climb back up to the cliffs before he gets to me.

"Come on, Paige," he says. "Don't make this more than it is."

"I don't trust you." I wipe my sweaty palms on the front of my shorts, but the hands I feel are Jeremy's.

He raises his arms as if I have pointed a gun at him. "I'll take the outside. You can push me over the ledge if I try something." Twin, deep smile lines frame his mouth. "That's a joke," he adds when I don't laugh.

I take a breath and remind myself that if I want to see my father today I need to talk to Dr. Shum now. Before I can change my mind, I step forward, pressing so close to the cliffs that the rough edge scrapes my arm.

It's a mistake to do this; I know it and yet I do it anyway. I get closer and closer, and then I step into his shadow. I wait for his arm to come down—for him to trap me somehow—but then suddenly I'm past him.

When I reach the base of the third ladder, I stop and turn around. He's watching me. Grinning. "Stop it," I yell. "Stop staring at me."

"Just making sure you're safe." His voice follows me up the next two sections. "I told you, you can trust me. *I'm* not the person you need to be worried about."

It sounds like a warning and a chill goes up my spine. I pause even as I reach for the next rung. "What do you mean?"

He shrugs. Half his face is hidden by his glasses. "Read the paper. If your father wasn't having an affair with Emily, then somebody else was. And that person is still loose, isn't he?"

"If you know something, just say it." A fresh wave of heat and sweat soaks into my already wet clothing.

"I'm just trying to help you, Paige. I've always liked you. And I still do. If you ever need me, just call. Any time. Day or night. I'll help you."

He's a creep and probably just playing me. "You can help me by staying the hell away from me." I feel his gaze following me as I climb the rest of the ladder, but I don't glance down. I won't give him the satisfaction of knowing how much he scares me. When I get to the top, I hurry to the ruins and try to ignore the nagging suspicion that I am missing something—that something he said is important. As hard as I try, I can't figure out what it is.

THIRTY-EIGHT

Paige

"Would you like some salad?" Mrs. Shum pushes a hand-painted glass salad bowl toward me.

"Thank you." I put enough of the salad on my plate to be polite. In truth, the strong vinegar smell of the dressing turns my stomach.

"Is the steak all right?" Dr. Shum asks. "Not too rare?"

"It's perfect." Because he's watching, I cut off a small portion of the meat—cooked medium-well, just as I asked—put it in my mouth and chew slowly.

Dr. and Mrs. Shum exchange the anxious looks of hosts who have no idea how to please their guest. I feel bad for them. It isn't their fault that my mother's flight is delayed yet again so they're stuck with me another night. And it wasn't their fault that the detention center closed right before we got there and I wasn't able to see my father. And it isn't their fault that my heart is broken because Jalen betrayed me.

I poke the salad—a colorful creation with bits of cactus in it—and wonder if it'll stay down if I attempt to eat it.

"Your mother will be here first thing tomorrow," Mrs. Shum says brightly. "Things always have a way of looking better in the morning."

Dr. Shum winks at me. "She's disgustingly chipper in the mornings. Me, I'm a night owl. I'm almost always up, so if you want some company, I'll probably be raiding the refrigerator." He pats his flat stomach. "Looking for some of that pie. Do you like lemon chess pie, Paige?"

I nod, wondering how much longer I have to sit here, enduring this conversation. They're nice people, but they're just making things worse with their forced cheerfulness.

"I'm sorry for your situation," Mrs. Shum says, leaning forward, her green eyes sympathetic. "And I know you feel like you're imposing on us, but I want you to know that we love having you here. It isn't often that Dr. Shum and I get to have young people as our guests. For years, we tried to have children, but it didn't work out." She takes a swallow of wine and then wipes her mouth. "But we can't complain; we've had each other."

Dr. Shum raises his wine glass to his wife's. His blue eyes sparkle with mischief. "Here's to twenty years of happy marriage."

"Twenty-three," Mrs. Shum corrects.

Dr. Shum chuckles. "I know that, dear. I said twenty happy ones."

Watching them makes me wonder how many years of my parents' marriage were happy ones. Maybe none. I put my fork down and ask to be excused.

In the second-floor guest room, I walk around restlessly. It's a pretty room but not to my taste. I trail my fingers over the polished surface of an antique mahogany dresser and then finger the creamy satin on the fringed lampshade. A self-portrait of a much younger Mrs. Shum smiles at me from over the bed. Her hair is different, redder, but her green eyes are exactly the same.

Pulling back a sheer curtain, I look into the back yard. The lights give the pool water an eerie fluorescent glow. Behind the pool, Mrs. Shum's studio is dark. My gaze travels to the silver crescent of the moon.

It reminds me of the story my father told me about how Coyote and Eagle tried to steal the moon. Wanting better light to hunt in, they went to a spirit village where lightness and darkness were kept in two boxes. Coyote placed one box inside the other and then talked Eagle into letting him carry the box. When Eagle flew ahead, Coyote opened both boxes, and that created winter.

I realize now that my roots are in these stories, that this is the soil I have been raised in. That no matter what's happened, Arizona is where I belong. Even with everything that's happened, even if Jalen and I never get back together, something about this place calls me. I want to dig, explore, learn.

I'm not going back to New Jersey with my mom and Stuart.

Deciding that this feels right, I'm almost giddy with the need to tell someone, specifically Jalen. I want him to help me figure out the way to convince my parents. But then I remember the way we left things—my angry, hurtful words. Words that couldn't be true because, if they were, why haven't the police accused me of lying? Why haven't they asked for a new statement?

But if Jalen didn't tell them about my father, then who did?

I dial Jalen's cell, but he doesn't answer. I almost hang up, but then I tell him I'm sorry and ask him to call me.

Walking back to the window, I notice a light shining through the windows in the studio. Mrs. Shum was so right about looking at who I was in order to understand who I am. I want to thank her for helping me push aside everything that's gotten in the way of me finally understanding that.

It's cooler now, but still hot as I step through the kitchen door and walk barefoot along the warm flagstone patio. Above, the moon shines as brightly as the path lights that line the walkway to the studio. A lizard darts just inches from my toes and then disappears into the foliage.

The doorknob turns easily, and I step inside. Just as before, the easels are covered with white sheets and other covered canvases lean against the side walls. I smell the odor of wet paint, but I don't see Mrs. Shum anywhere.

"Mrs. Shum?" There's no answer. On the table where we sculpted sit the two heads, mine and Jalen's, tightly sealed in plastic bags. She's worked on them since I was here last, enhanced them. A small chill works up my spine at the sight of my face sealed inside plastic. The features are so uncannily real that I almost want to open the bag so I can breathe. When the air conditioner kicks on, I jump and then laugh at my nerves.

"Mrs. Shum?" I call again.

She must have just stepped away. I probably shouldn't be in here without her, but the sight of a dried clay sculpture on a worktable in the front draws me closer. It's the one Mrs. Shum showed me the last time I was here—the lovers caught in the moment before they kiss. She's finished it now, and in the lights of the studio, the skin on their clay faces seems to glow with life.

Looking closely, I see more detail. The faces have features—the man's eyes are slightly more sunken, his nose coarser, his hairline defined. My heart starts to pound. It's my father, and of course the girl is Emily.

My gaze travels to the man's strong, blunt fingers weaving themselves into the girl's hair. The detail is amazing, right down to the wedding band on his fourth finger.

Wedding band?

My gaze flies back to the man's face, noticing suddenly that it has a wider brow and the lips are fuller than my father's.

It isn't my father. The joy mixes with terror as I realize I am staring at likenesses of Dr. Shum and Emily.

Suddenly, everything seems to fall into place. I think of the portrait of the buck above the mantle in the Shums' family room. Not just a buck, I realize, but a stag. I think of Emily's blog and it all comes together.

"Oh, God," I say.

From behind me, a man's deep voice says softly, almost kindly. "It's beautiful, isn't it?"

A wave of terror shoots through me as I turn and face Dr. Shum. He's standing in the doorway holding a bottle of wine in one hand and an empty glass in the other. His rugged features sag.

My heart races. Dr. Shum is King Stag. He killed Emily, and now I'm alone with him. What do I do? Is there another way out of the studio? I search my mind, even as I smile and try to sound pleased.

"Hello, Dr. Shum," I say. "I was just admiring the sculpture of you and Mrs. Shum."

Sighing, he moves forward, one slow nightmare step at a time. "We both know that the girl in the sculpture is Emily. I do think this is Julia's best work yet. Don't you agree?"

I don't answer, but keeping my eyes on him, I back slowly away, putting the work table between us.

"I think its Julia's way of punishing me. She knows I have to look at it, that I am compelled to look at it, and she knows how it hurts me when I do." He closes his eyes and shakes his head sadly. "I loved her," he says. "I loved her so much."

I face him across the table. Somehow I have to keep him talking. "What happened to her, Dr. Shum? What happened to Emily?"

He sets down the wine, uncorks the bottle, and then pours himself a glass. "She was the yellow corn maiden. She had to die."

"What do you mean?"

He sips the wine slowly. "A necessary sacrifice." His blue eyes are red-rimmed. "What are we going to do now, Paige?"

A fresh wave of terror floods my brain because I know he's thinking about how he's going to kill me. I think about screaming, but something inside cautions me not to do anything that will set him off.

"Nothing," I say. "You aren't going to do anything with me because I think you're relieved I found out about you. You left her shoes and that note because you want to be found. How did it happen, Dr. Shum? Was it an accident? I know you loved her."

Dr. Shum drinks the contents of his glass and then pours himself another. His hands shake. "Yes. It wasn't supposed to happen, but there was nothing I could do." He extends the glass to me. "Would you like a sip?"

I shake my head, denying more than his offer of wine. For a crazy moment, I even think of trying to seduce him.

He shakes his head wearily. "You should have stayed in your room, Paige. None of this would be happening if you had."

"If you do anything to me," I say, keeping my gaze locked with his, "they'll figure it all out. They'll connect you to me and Emily."

He takes another sip of wine. "People will believe whatever story you tell them if you give them a good reason. Your best friend is missing, probably dead, and now your father has been arrested. You're a girl who isn't thinking very well right now and who's inclined to do impulsive things—like sneak out at night to see your boyfriend one last time. Sadly, hitchhiking has its risks."

"Everyone knows I'm staying with you," I say a little desperately. "You'll be the first person they suspect."

He smiles and takes another sip of wine. His blue eyes are almost kindly, the image of a professor who has to fail his favorite student. "I'm sorry, Paige." He blocks me as I make a move to run around the easel.

"Dr. Shum," I say, trying not to sound as frantic as I feel. "It's going to be obvious that you did something to me."

"It's going to look bad for me if I *don't* do something. And here's the sad truth about our legal system—it doesn't work. The burden of proof has become such a legal nightmare for the prosecution. Over and over we see that, with a good lawyer, a person can get away with just about anything."

He lunges for me, but I jump backward, out of his reach. I run around the side of the table, twisting as he grabs for me. I'm almost past him, but then his hands latch onto the cotton fabric of my tank top. It feels like he might rip it off my back as he yanks me backward.

Screaming, I strain against the harness of my shirt, but it's useless. Twisting, I kick and struggle, but it doesn't help. Even as I cry out, I realize he is much, much stronger than Jeremy Brown.

"Don't fight me. You're only making things worse for yourself."

"Let me go!" I shriek.

He bunches his grip on my shirt more tightly until it cuts into my ribs. "I'm so sorry." He pulls me against him. I smell his breath, hot and sour. "Close your eyes, little one," he whispers. "Please close your eyes."

He's crazy. I search the room for a weapon. The sheet-covered easels stand like ghosts watching us. My frantic gaze sweeps around the room again and then locks on the clay sculpture of Emily and Dr. Shum.

Dr. Shum puts his huge hand around my neck. *This isn't happening*, something inside me insists. *I'm dreaming.* Only I know I'm not.

"She talked about you," I choke out, frantic to delay what seems inevitable. "Don't you want to know what Emily said?"

His fingers tighten a fraction. "If she had talked about me, we wouldn't be standing here, would we?"

He's right, of course. I need to make up something and quickly. I try to summon up the part of myself that created the games for Emily and me all those years ago.

"She never used your name, but she'd tell me these intense dreams she had, erotic dreams about a man who loved her so much that all she had to do was think about him, and he'd call her."

The grip on my neck lessens a tiny bit. "Yes," he says. "It was like that for us. All I had to do was think her name and she called me. We had…what you call a certain synchronicity." He pauses and then, almost as if he can't help himself, adds, "What else did she say?"

I inch closer to the worktable, frantically trying to piece together a story in my mind. "That when he made love to her it was so powerful that she would weep because she didn't want it to be over."

"Yes, yes," Dr. Shum murmurs. "What else? What else did she tell you?"

"And there was another dream she had, where she would meet him in the ruins and…"

"And what?" Dr. Shum asks eagerly.

I grab the clay sculpture with both hands. "And she sent you to hell," I scream and swing the statue at him.

He ducks at the last minute, and the sculpture crashes to the ground, shattering into large chunks. Dr. Shum looks at me, his eyes wild, frantic. His fist comes up, but before he can hit me, I kick him hard between his legs. He drops to the floor with a cry of pain. I run for the door.

I hit it so hard it almost falls off the hinges. Charging into the warm night, I stub my toe on one of the stepping stones. The pain shoots up my leg, but I keep running.

I race past the rectangular pool and its neon blue water, then down the edge of the privacy fence to the gate. Coming to a panting, shaking stop, I reach for the latch. The lever lifts, but the gate remains shut. I yank it harder, more frantically, but it doesn't budge. Through the black wrought-iron bars, I see the glow of street lights on what looks like an empty street.

I rattle the gate, even as I see the padlock on the top of the bars. My heart sinks. I'm trapped. How much time before Dr. Shum finds me?

I turn to backtrack, but Mrs. Shum suddenly appears in the gap between the house and the privacy fence. Her reddish hair hangs long and loose on her shoulders, and her face shines silver-colored in the moonlight. "Paige?" she says, "what's wrong?"

I'm so relieved it's her and not Dr. Shum that I could cry. "Dr. Shum has gone crazy," I blurt out. "He killed Emily and now he's trying to kill me. We have to get out of here."

"Slow down, Paige." Her voice is infuriatingly calm. "What are you talking about?"

"There's no time to explain." I glance over her shoulder, terrified I'll see Dr. Shum. "Please. You need to trust me."

Mrs. Shum blocks my path as I try to move past her. Her thin arm grabs me with surprising strength. "Are you on drugs? Dr. Shum would never kill anyone. He's a great man. A brilliant researcher."

And a murderer. "I'm not on drugs. The painting of the stag…" My voice trails off as I realize Mrs. Shum painted the stag. She crafted the sculpture of Dr. Shum and Emily. And the book, *The Corn Maiden*— she could have planted it the day she dropped me off after I had lunch with her. She's known all along what Dr. Shum did and probably helped him cover it all up.

An eerie intensity comes into Mrs. Shum's eyes, and she smiles. "You'd better tell me exactly what happened."

"Please," I say. "Just let me go. I know you didn't have anything to do with what happened to Emily. If we go to the police together, I know they'll understand."

"Understand what?"

"That Dr. Shum killed Emily. That you were afraid of him and so you helped him cover it up."

"Is that what you think happened?" Mrs. Shum smiles, and in the moonlight, her teeth look small, white, and very sharp. "God, you girls are so stupid. You think because you're young and beautiful, you can have anything you want. You think your generation is smarter because you know all this technological crap. You even think you discovered sex." She shakes her head. "You girls don't know anything." She glances over her shoulder and yells. "Ray! Over here!"

My heart beats so loud and fast I think it will drown out my voice, but I hear myself say, "It wasn't Dr. Shum, was it? It was you, wasn't it?"

"That bitch. She had him so bewitched he thought he was in love with her—that he'd leave me for her." She shakes her head. "But I forgave him, Paige, because that's what married people have to do if they want to stay together. They forgive and forgive and forgive. Sometimes it's exhausting."

I search her eyes, but in the darkness, they're nothing more than black holes in her face. She's crazy. And she's going to kill me. The only chance I have is to get away from her. I jerk my arm from her grasp, fake right, and then go left. She snarls in rage and then something hard cracks against the side of my skull and everything goes black.

THIRTY-NINE

Jalen

We're at Walmart when my cell rings. A quick glance at the screen tells me it's Paige. I almost answer, but then, before I weaken, I let the call pass into voicemail. By now her mother has arrived and Paige Patterson is no longer my responsibility. Even if she's sorry, it doesn't change things. What illness allows someone to see the future? I still hear the scorn in her voice.

I shove my cell back into the pocket of my shorts and try not to think about her.

Next to me, my uncle pushes our shopping cart slowly down the aisle stocked with toothbrushes, toothpaste, and mouthwash. He picks up a bottle of amber-colored Listerine and swirls it around before setting it down on the shelf. He does the same with a bottle of Scope. When he moves to the generic mouthwash, I check the cell and see she's left a message. Before I can play it, Uncle Billy turns to me with a package of dental floss in his hands, and I pocket the phone again.

"This one has the best price," he says. "If you're looking for floss."

When I shake my head, he resets it on the hook and we move slowly forward. I don't bother asking him what we're doing in the dental aisle or question him when we wander into the pharmacy section. I have shopped long enough with him to know that he takes the long way to wherever he's going. To try and hurry him is like talking to a wall.

We move through sporting goods and into hardware. As Uncle Billy lingers over a pair of bolt cutters, I pull out my phone. With my back to him, I play the message.

It hurts to hear her voice, but I play it several times anyway. She's sorry. She wants me to call her. But what is she most sorry about? Calling me a liar? Ridiculing my uncle? Breaking up with me?

I pick up a flashlight, turn it over in my hands. I should be relieved that things between us are over. I don't have to choose anymore or worry about how liking her—how possibly falling in love with her—will put her in danger. Probably right now she's having dinner with her mom and they're making plans for her to go back to New Jersey. Probably by now she's remembering all the reasons she belongs there.

"What's that?" Uncle Billy peers over my shoulder. When he sees the flashlight, he nods in approval, "I liked that one, too. You'll need a battery."

"Uncle, I don't need a flashlight." I start to put it back, but he stops me.

"Maybe you do," he says. "Sometimes you don't know if you need something until it finds itself in your hands. Why don't you get it, Jalen?"

"Because it costs money?" I try and keep the sarcasm out of my voice, but my mood is dark and Uncle Billy is an easy target.

"You have to learn to trust your instincts." He takes the flashlight from my hands and puts in the cart next to the bolt cutters.

I look at him in surprise. "What do you need those for?"

Shrugging, Uncle Billy smiles, as innocent as a monk. "I don't know."

Finally we make it to the crafts aisle. While he peers closely at the two different shades of yellow yarn, I move a few steps away and pull out my cell. I'll listen to her message one more time and then delete it. However, when I unlock my screen, I dial her cell instead of my voicemail box. I start to sweat when it rings. Just what am I going to say to her? That I forgive her? That I don't want us to break up?

When the phone rings into voicemail, it turns into a non-issue. I hang up. She didn't even ask me if I called the police and turned in her father. She simply assumed I did it. If our situations were reversed, I would never have thought the same of her.

Uncle Billy holds both shades of yarn in his hands. There's so little difference between them that I can't understand why he can't just pick one. I loosen my grip on the phone. "Why don't you buy both of them?" What I really mean is hurry up.

He shakes his head, replaces them both on the shelf. "Neither is right." He pushes the cart the length of the aisle and then disappears around the corner. I follow more slowly, reminding myself to be patient. He doesn't get out of the house much, and besides, where is it I so badly want to be?

He finds a wig of blonde hair made for a doll. I pretend not to notice the tremor in his hands as he squints at it through the clear cellophane wrapping. "The hair isn't long enough, but it's better than the yarn." He places it in the cart and then spends a good amount of time picking out a bag of feathers before he ambles out of the department.

I try calling Paige again when he stops to pull a small pink sandal off a shelf of infant shoes on clearance. Once again, her cell rings a couple of times, and then her voicemail picks up. I regret immediately calling her. What's she going to think when she sees two missed calls from me?

And then I start to worry. Why isn't she answering? Before I even think about it, I take the sandal out of my uncle's hands and drop it in the shopping cart. "Come on," I tell him. "We need to get going."

"Just one more stop," he says, and my heart sinks.

We pass shelves of popcorn and peanuts and then reach the far right corner of the store. There's soda here, too, and I fake interest in a six-pack of Coke as Uncle Billy shuffles off to buy a couple of bottles of wine. It isn't his favorite drink, but it's available. I feel my shoulders sag as the real reason for this shopping trip becomes clear.

For me to watch just makes it more painful for both of us, and so I pull out my cell again. I stare at it, thinking hard what a third call will mean. It will say I forgive her and, even more than that, that I have feelings for her. Am I ready for that? My father gave up everything to be with my mother, and although I think he's happy, I wonder if I can do that.

I put the phone in my pocket, but start replaying that final scene between us. I think about how coldly I turned my back on her when she implied that there was no kind of illness that would give a man the ability to see the future. I got angry at her, but beneath it was shame. I didn't have the guts to tell her the truth. I let a lifetime of family secrets seal my lips. In protecting my uncle, I sacrificed us.

I accused her of having no faith in me, and yet I haven't really trusted her either or else I simply would have told her. *My uncle is an alcoholic.*

My heart starts to race as I call her. With each unanswered ring, my level of anxiety rises. I squeeze the phone more and more tightly, willing her to answer. I tell myself that she probably has turned it off or she's in a bad cell zone or that maybe she's figured out I'm not the guy she thought I was.

But then my gaze drops to the flashlight half-buried in the items in our cart. Of all the items in the cart, it's the only one I've chosen. And although I protested about the money, I didn't put the flashlight back, either. Or insist Uncle Billy leave the bolt cutters. *Trust your instincts,* Uncle Billy told me. Something inside is telling me that Paige needs me.

I stride over to my uncle and grab the first bottle of wine I see. "We need to go. Now."

He looks at me and then nods as if he's been expecting this all along. In the store lighting, his black eyes shine silver, like moonlight on water.

"I'm ready," he says.

FORTY

Paige

I am falling through darkness so black and deep it swallows my scream. From somewhere above me, I hear Emily call, *Paige,* and then I am on the ground. The pain radiates in my head, throbbing to the beat of my heart. I can't move. Lying here, I realize now what a mistake it was to go so deep into this underground cavern. How angry my parents are going to be.

Emily slips her arm around my waist, comforting me. She's lying behind me, cradling the length of my body with hers. *Wake up, Paige,* she says. *It's time to wake up.*

Emily's here? She isn't dead? I open my eyes to pitch darkness. "Emily?"

But I'm alone. I was dreaming, and now I'm awake. My mouth is taped shut and my wrists and ankles are bound together so tightly they have gone numb. Beneath my cheek, I feel the tight weave of carpet. I'm in the trunk of a car, racing through the darkness to a place where the Shums are going to kill me.

There's a sudden flash of light and the sound of my cell. I try to wiggle toward it, but can't get there in time. My head aches and tears of despair trickle onto my cheeks. Part of me wants to go back to sleep, to tell myself that none of this is really happening.

But it is, and I have to fight. Despite the pain in my head, I wiggle deeper in the trunk and then strike out, mermaid-style, at the corners, where the taillights might be. Every kick escalates the level of pain in my head. Worse, it doesn't work.

I'm almost relieved when the car slides to a stop. The doors bang, and then the trunk pops open. Both Shums loom into my vision, dark silhouettes against a darker backdrop.

Something wet falls onto my face as Dr. Shum bends over me, struggling to get his arms under me. He's silently crying, and in a way that makes it even worse than if he were rough with me. I try to flop my body out of his grasp, but he scoops me up. Through the duct tape, I start to sob, and immediately it feels like I'm suffocating.

"Dr. Shum is going to cut your legs loose, Paige," Mrs. Shum says. "But if you try to run away, I'll have to use this." She holds up a tire iron. A small, mean smile forms on her face. "I've gotten pretty good with it."

I look at the heavy metal bar in her hands and the light in her eyes and have no doubt she means what she says. As Dr. Shum cuts off the tape, I look around, desperately searching for a way out of this. We're in some kind of empty, unpaved parking lot. It's surrounded by trees and lit only by moonlight. In the distance, I see a mountain, rising like a great black wave.

"Stop crying," Mrs. Shum snaps as Dr. Shum straightens. "None of this would have happened if you hadn't decided to act like a hormonal teenager." She hands Dr. Shum a bungee cord and tells him to wrap it around my neck. With my hands still bound and my mouth taped, all I can do is beseech him with my eyes. He avoids my gaze and hooks it on tight.

Mrs. Shum gives my shoulder a push. "Get going."

We follow the unpaved road toward the mountain. A gate blocks us, but Dr. Shum takes out a set of keys and, with a creak and groan of rusty metal, we pass inside. The road narrows, becoming no wider than a bike path and then even that disappears into a trail so poorly visible in the moonlight that several times I step in the wrong direction. Dr. Shum pulls the bungee cord, which simultaneously stretches and tightens around my neck. Once, it gets so tight that I nearly pass out.

"Not much farther," Dr. Shum coaxes, loosening the cord.

If only I can get him alone, maybe I can talk him into letting me go. We follow the curve of the towering rock mountain rising like a shadow out of the night. It comes as almost a complete surprise when suddenly we step out of the woods and into a clearing. The path merges onto a concrete one, and all at once I recognize where we are heading.

"That's right, Paige," Mrs. Shum says as if she's read my mind. "We're going to the ruins."

I shake my head violently in denial, and the bungee cord jerks tighter. I feel my eyes bulge.

"Yes," Mrs. Shum says. "You're going to climb up there. You really don't have much choice." She taps me hard on the shoulder with the tire iron. "Dr. Shum may be a coward, but he's strong as an ox. It wouldn't be hard for me to bash in your brains and then have him carry you up the cliffs. In fact, it might be his penance, the cross he has to bear."

She looks almost pleased at the thought, and I shake my head again and make that guttural, unintelligible noise that is supposed to say, *No, don't do this.* I taste the bitter peel of chemical adhesive, but when Mrs. Shum raises the tire iron, I stop protesting and nod eagerly. Yes, I'll do what she says. I'll do anything to stay alive.

"I thought so," Mrs. Shum says. "I thought you would want to live as long as possible. If you're good, Paige, before you die, you'll see things you never imagined."

The cliffs are in front of us now, blocking everything, even the moon. The thought of climbing up there, of what is waiting there, terrifies me. My legs shake so hard it's hard to stand. But what choice do I have? If I stay alive, there's always the chance they'll mess up, and I'll escape.

Dr. Shum cuts me free. I rub the raw skin on my wrists and flex my fingers. Mrs. Shum moves ahead of me, holding the bungee cord like the leash of a dog. She puts her foot on the first rung. "You try to pull me off, and you go over with me. Understood?"

I nod, but inside I'm wondering if falling from the cliffs and taking Mrs. Shum with me is the best option I have.

We climb slowly, steadily, with me sandwiched between the Shums. I think about my mother. How upset she's going to be when she drives to the Shums' house and I'm not there. I wonder if she'll believe that I ran away. If some small part of her will be relieved that now she and

Stuart can start a new life without me. Hope stirs in me when I think about Jalen, who will not believe the Shums and start asking questions.

He'll look for me. I need to leave him clues, and so I wipe blood from my scalp and smear the sides of the cliff in places where hopefully Dr. Shum won't notice.

The moon is high and visible once again as we climb onto the lip of the cliff. As we stand on the ledge, Mrs. Shum pulls me away from the edge as if she's guessed I might take my fate into my hands and jump.

I delay again. Falling. Letting them drag me. Even pretending to faint. Dr. Shum carries me the last distance to the ruins. Cradled in his arms, I have a terrifying view of the grim set of his mouth, his broad nose, and his eyes that refuse to meet mine.

My bare shoulder scrapes rough stucco as we squeeze through the T-shaped opening. I hope I've left behind some blood or skin—something for Jalen to find. Mrs. Shum drops her backpack and extracts a flashlight. There's a *click*, and then a cone of yellow light illuminates the pitch-dark, box-like chamber.

"Down there," she says, pointing to the hole in the center of the floor.

Dread uncoils in my stomach and my legs start to tremble. There's no way I'm going down there. It's a death pit. I shake my head violently.

Mrs. Shum shrugs. "Your choice, Paige, but you're going to miss something truly special if you don't go down there. You see, when Dr. Shum did his structural analysis of the ruins, he noticed an interesting anomaly. The way the ruins sit in the cliffs, there was room for another chamber beneath the one below us. So he did some exploring... I really should let him tell the story. Would you like to, Raymond?"

Dr. Shum folds his arms and looks down at the ground. "No," he says, "I wouldn't."

There's a long, poignant pause, and then Mrs. Shum sighs. "You always leave everything to me." She draws a breath, as if she's determined not to let this relatively minor detail bother her. "To make a long story short, Paige, there's a false bottom in the *si'papu*, and underneath... well...you really need to see it to appreciate it. There's a wonderful old skeleton down there and some of the best-preserved pre-Columbian pottery that's ever been discovered. There's quite a market for it—did you know that? The Chinese can't get enough. But Ray was showing off, trying to impress the little bitch. He told her about it!" Mrs. Shum shakes her head. "I heard him! And so I hid in the ruins that night and waited. It didn't take long for your little friend to show up." She sighs. "I guess the hour for telling stories is past. Will you climb down into the basement chamber, or shall we just get on with it?"

No. No. No. I chew the gag, and to my shame, fresh tears stream down my face.

Mrs. Shum sighs. "Oh, Paige, there's no sense dragging this out."

I shake my head frantically. Through a blur of tears, I watch her take out a thick, plastic bag like the one she uses to keep clay moist. My heart sinks as I realize I've waited too long. My moment to escape isn't going to come. I'm going to die.

"You must think I'm a monster," Dr. Shum says, gripping my wrists together so tightly it feels like he's crushing my bones. "But I'm just a man. Like all men, I am flawed. Mistakes are inevitable, and fate is a cruel master. But you won't be forgotten. I'll always remember you. You and Emily. My two lovely corn maidens."

He nods. Mrs. Shum rips the tape from my mouth and slips the plastic bag over my head. Pulling it tight over my face, she peers into my eyes. "Goodnight," she says.

I suck in air, and plastic seals off my nostrils. My legs strike out. Even though I know I shouldn't, I take a deep breath. The plastic crinkles and molds to my face. I suck harder, desperate now. The plastic melts over my face, a warm, moist second skin. I can't breathe, but I can't stop trying. A thousand dancing black dots fill my vision. I'm dizzy. My mouth opens. My legs kick, but there's no strength in them. I think of Jalen, want his face to be the last thing I see, but it's the Shums who fill my blurred vision. They watch me intensely with no compassion or doubt—only a cruel sort of waiting.

The black dots connect. My lungs explode and there's nothing at all.

FORTY-ONE

Jalen

She could be anywhere. Anywhere at all. How am I going to find her?

But what if I'm overreacting? She could be at a restaurant having dinner, or even at her father's house packing her things. I'm going to look like an idiot bursting in on her with nothing to say something's wrong but the fact that she hasn't picked up her cell.

Next to me in the car, Uncle Billy has a bottle of wine in one hand and my cell in the other. He calls Paige's cell periodically and then hangs up when it rings into voicemail. Clutching the steering wheel tightly in my hands, I run a light more red than yellow. Someone leans on his horn, and Uncle Billy says mildly, "What's his problem?"

It takes us fifteen minutes to get across town and then turn into Dr. Shum's neighborhood. I'm suddenly thankful for the times I came here to help Mrs. Shum load and unload supplies so I make no wrong turns. But will I be fast enough?

I leave the truck idling and run to the house. The lights are on, but nobody comes when I ring the bell. I peer through the glass panels flanking the door. The place looks empty. Circling around, I find a side gate, but it's locked. Through the wrought-iron bars, I see the translucent glow of the pool lights, and more lights shining through the windows of a barn-like structure.

It takes me less than fifteen seconds to climb the gate and drop into the Shums' backyard. They're probably going to think I'm crazy, barging in on them like this, looking for Paige, but then Dr. Shum has always seemed like a fair man. He'll listen to me. He has to.

The door to the studio isn't fully closed, and calling out Paige's name, I push it open and step into the cool interior. The room looks empty, abandoned with its sheets draped over the easels. I'm about to leave when my gaze falls on an overturned chair. It's the only thing out of a place in a spotless room, but the sight of it draws me closer.

I walk deeper into the room, and then see what I couldn't from the back.

The cracked pieces of a sculpture lie scattered on the floor. Kneeling, I pick up one of the larger pieces and find myself staring into half the face of a girl. Emily Linton.

A sick feeling spreads through me as I sort through the fragments. A man—Dr. Patterson? No, the nose is wrong. But then I find a finger and I see the wedding band. Dr. Shum.

Fear clouds my brain, panic overriding reason. All I can think about is how the Shums must have killed Emily, and Paige must have figured it out. Now they have her. It's going to happen just like my uncle said it would. She'll die, and it'll be my fault. I kick myself for letting my pride get between us.

I have to stop them, but how? *Trust your instincts,* Uncle Billy's voice says in my head, but all my instincts scream that time is running out.

Adrenaline courses through my system, putting me in motion before I even know what I'm doing. Heart racing, I scramble over the gate and race to the truck. "Call 9-1-1," I yell at Uncle Billy, who hastily puts the wine bottle down. "Tell them Paige Patterson has been kidnapped by the Shums. Ask them to meet us at the ruins."

I don't know that she's there, but it's the only place I can think of.

Uncle Billy makes the call as I jerk the truck into reverse. The tires spin on the pavement as I accelerate onto the road. As we race through the quiet neighborhood, I hear Uncle Billy say, "I don't know. You'll have to ask my nephew that," and hands me the phone.

I know they're just doing their job, but it feels like they're idiots asking me to repeat information over and over, to explain things in such detail that I want to scream. The best I can talk them into doing is transferring me to Detective Rodriquez, and then I have to go through everything all over again. When I'm finished, there's a long period of silence. And then she seizes on the one irrelevant detail that I've told her.

"So you had a fight with your girlfriend. Is it possible that she's fine and just not speaking to you?"

"No," I shout and then slam the cell down.

I push the old truck to its limit when we hit the highway and hope that the engine won't shake itself apart before we get to the park. When we exit onto the dirt road, I'm going so fast the truck skids and I can barely hit the brakes before we crash into the long, metal arm of the gate that runs the width of the road. I careen around it, the belly of the truck scraping the ground. For a few seconds, we lean hard to the side, but then somehow we're on the road again.

The wide, open expanse of the parking lot lies ahead. It's dark, but through the moonlight and the beams of my headlights I see it's empty. Where is the Shums' car? If they haven't brought Paige here, then where is she? Jerking to a stop near the main gate, I turn to my uncle. "I thought they'd be here. But I don't see their car. What do I do?"

My uncle's hooded eyes regard me intently. "What you came here to do," he says calmly, and in his hands are the bolt cutters we bought at Walmart.

For just a second, I hesitate. Once I cut the fence, I'm vandalizing government property and there's no going back. I could go to jail. I could end up exactly like Uncle Billy.

I'm probably crazy, but I take the bolt cutters from his hands.

It takes seconds to cut through the chain link fence and slip inside the park. Uncle Billy follows. As he straightens, I turn to him. "Uncle, you need to wait here. Give me an hour, and if I'm not back, call the police."

"No," he says. "I'm going with you."

I look at his frail body, the wine bottle he clutches in his hands. "Uncle, you're not climbing the cliff."

His shoulders straighten. "You're wasting time," he says calmly. "Coyote will want to hide the blue corn maiden. We need to go. Now."

"Uncle," I say, forcing patience into my voice. "I can't save Paige *and* make sure you make it safely up the cliff. Please don't make me choose."

"You can't go up there alone."

"We don't even know she's up there."

My uncle looks at me for a long moment. "You know she's up there," he says. "And so is Coyote." He takes his bottle of wine and turns it upside-down, emptying the contents onto the packed earth. "Take this. You'll need it."

"What I need is for you to promise to stay at the bottom of the cliffs."

He nods, but his chin lifts as he thrusts the wine bottle into my hands. "Tuck it into the back of your shorts. And, Jalen," he says. "Be careful."

I scramble up the cliffs faster than I have ever climbed before. The moon has shifted, leaving the side of the mountain so dark the ladders are barely more than black scratches on the surface. It doesn't matter that I'm almost climbing blind; it's like something else has come awake in me and I give myself to it.

A faint glow of light illuminates a chamber in the ruins. The skin on the back of my neck prickles, and my heart beats faster as get nearer. Voices – a man's and a woman's drift through the darkness. It's the Shums and he's saying something about his lovely corn maiden.

My blood roars through my ears as I turn sideways, squeezing myself through the T-shaped entrance. Immediately, I see the Shums standing with their backs to me. They're blocking me from seeing something, and with a terrible certainty, I know it's Paige.

Uncle Billy's terrible prophesy flashes through my head. "*You won't help her and she's going to die.*" With a bellow of rage, I charge forward, pulling them off Paige. They scatter like rats at my attack and I drop to my knees, see the plastic bag covering Paige's head. Her eyes are closed and I can't tell if she's breathing.

I try to rip it off, but my fingers fumble with the tape and then both Shums are on me, hitting and clawing at my hands. Someone punches me hard enough to make my ear ring, and a kick to my spine makes me grunt in pain. I ignore the blows and focus on getting the bag off Paige's head.

Beside me, something falls to the ground with a low *clunk*. It's the wine bottle. The one Uncle Billy insisted I bring. I fumble for it, grab it by the neck and swing it blindly.

It connects with one of them and breaks. There's a scream of pain, and the series of blows raining on my head stop, Mrs. Shum cries, "Ray?"

"Hold on, Julia. I'm bleeding."

"What?"

"My eye! I have to make sure there's no glass in it!"

While they're distracted I grab a shard and cut the plastic bag off her head. "Paige," I say loudly, "wake up!"

She lies limp, doll-like and boneless. I shake her lightly. "Wake up!"

I know there's only a few moments before the Shums attack again. "C'mon Paige," I say and shake slightly harder. "Wake up!"

"Don't be such a baby!" Mrs. Shum snaps. "Get him!"

Paige isn't waking up. I lean closer, trying to tell if she's even breathing. There's no time to be sure. Placing the heels of my hands on her chest, I begin the compressions, pausing to blow into her mouth. *C'mon, C'mon, C'mon.* I will her to wake up. Moments pass, the panic rises in me. I push harder on her chest wanting to reach all the way into her and force her heart to start beating. *Live. Oh, shit. Please Live.*

My arms ache; salty sweat stings my eyes. I'm going to break her ribs if I push any harder, but I can't help it. I blow more air into her lungs, and then she stirs. Her whole body seems to hiccup and her eyes open wide, locking onto mine with desperation and something like surprise.

"Welcome back," I start to say, but then something hard smacks into the back of my head and the ground rushes up to meet me.

FORTY-TWO

Paige

I am nothing. There is nothing. And then suddenly, I am.

I open my eyes, try to figure out where I am and what's happening. Jalen kneels over me, hollow-eyed and breathing hard. "Welcome back," he says.

From where? My head aches, and my throat feels ringed with fire. I'm lying down as if I've been sleeping, but I'm not in my bed. And then in a flash it all comes back. Mrs. Shum's face through the plastic—her eyes catlike and cold, watching me die.

Suddenly Jalen topples forward, landing on top of me. In the dim light of a lantern, Mrs. Shum is illuminated, standing over me with the tire iron in her hand. "There," she says with satisfaction. "That ought to slow him down a little."

I instinctively close my eyes and play dead. I feel the brush of Mrs. Shum's leg as she moves closer, pulls him off me. I pray she hasn't killed him.

"She must have texted him somehow, told him how to find her." Dr. Shum says. "Check her cell."

"The damn cell," Mrs. Shum mutters. "We'll have to get rid of it." She nudges me with the toe of her shoe. "Why is it that you girls always turn out to be such colossal pains in the neck?" There's a moment of silence, and then she says, "You ought to finish him now, Ray. I don't think I hit him hard enough."

My heart races, and I know that I have to do something, but what? "Finish him?" Dr. Shum repeats. "That's your area, not mine."

"You think your hands are clean?" Mrs. Shum says. "You disgust me. You and your needs. Look what they've brought you."

As they argue, I open my eyes a crack. Jalen lies on his back next to me. Barely visible is Dr. Shum, near my feet. My head pounds. All I want to do is close my eyes and sleep.

Lie still, Paige, Emily's voice says in my head. *Don't be scared. This is just another game like the ones we played growing up. We played dead, but we always brought each other back to life, remember?*

"Don't you see," Dr. Shum says patiently, "how ridiculous this is? For Christ's sake, Julia, we're getting a body count." He sighs. "Emily was an accident, and Paige an unfortunate necessity. But Jalen? How are we going to explain it when he goes missing?"

"So we should just give ourselves up? It's a little too late for that, Ray, isn't it?"

"What other choice do we have? We have to stop. We have to stop now."

"For a man who makes his living piecing together the past, you have remarkably little imagination." Mrs. Shum says. "But I forgive you that, Ray, because that's what married people do—they forgive each other. Our faults cancel each other out in the end. You don't see it, but having young Jalen come here is actually the very thing that's going to save us."

There's a pause. "You see that broken wine bottle over there? It tells a story. Two lovers who were about to be separated and decided to meet one final time here in the ruins. They're drinking, fooling around, and things get out of hand."

"We suffocated Paige with a plastic bag, Julia," Dr. Shum says wearily. "How are you going to explain that?"

I nudge Jalen, but he doesn't move. *Wake up,* I scream at him in my head. *Wake up.*

"That's the best part," Mrs. Shum says. "It was part of a terrible game teenagers play—a sex game—where they choke themselves on purpose to heighten their experience. Only this time it went too far, and Paige died. Jalen, out of remorse, threw himself off the cliff." She pauses. "Don't you see how perfect that is, Ray? We can testify to Paige's state of mind. Even if they tie the plastic bag to us, it won't matter. Paige has been in my studio. She could have taken it herself. All we need to do is make sure Jalen's and Paige's prints are on that plastic bag."

"Julia...really?" He pauses. I can almost imagine him shaking his head. "The bump on her head...I don't think..."

"And that's the problem," Mrs. Shum snaps. "You really don't think. Do you have a better idea? I didn't think so. Hurry, Ray, get his prints on the bag. We haven't got all night."

I hear the shuffle of Dr. Shum's footsteps and then the rustle of the plastic bag. Opening my eyes a tiny slit, I can just make out Dr. Shum's dark body bent over, pressing Jalen's fingers into the plastic bag. I try to gather my strength, but my body feels like a marionette lying in a puddle of its own strings and parts.

"Maybe we should put the bag back over Paige's head just to make sure his fingerprints are in the right place." She pauses and then gives a tiny laugh. "You know, I'm beginning to frighten myself just how good I am at this. You best remember this, Ray, the next time another little girl catches your eye."

"What's left of my eye," Dr. Shum says glumly. "It stings like shit." Suddenly he gasps in surprise. "Let go. Julia, he's got my arm. I can't—"

I open my eyes as Mrs. Shum lifts the tire iron high and swings it at Jalen's head. I open my mouth and force a primitive, guttural sound to come out. It's enough to distract Mrs. Shum and the blow lands on Jalen's shoulder. He grunts and releases Dr. Shum, who begins punching him in the face.

Mrs. Shum swings the tire iron at me, but I see it coming and roll to the side. It strikes the ground near my head with a heavy *clunk*. I struggle to my knees but then a wave of dizziness hits me and I fight hard not to pass out.

To the side, I glimpse Dr. Shum and Jalen locked together into one dark shape, struggling on the ground. I hear the sickening sound of fists striking flesh, and then they knock the flashlight into the hole in the floor and the room goes dark.

Something whines. Instinctively I block my head with my arm. There's a cracking sound, like two rocks smacking together, as the tire iron connects with my forearm. Intense pain shoots up my arm, so strong it drops me to my knees. Something hot trickles down my arm. Blood.

"Will you just stay dead, you little bitch?" Mrs. Shum screams. I brace myself for another blow, but then she topples forward as Jalen tackles her from behind.

As Jalen knocks Mrs. Shum to the ground, I struggle to wrestle the tire iron from her hands, but she clings to it. Blood streams down my arm, and I use it like a weapon, letting it drip into her face, hoping it'll blind her or gross her out or do something to loosen her grip on the tire iron. . .

Suddenly Jalen grunts and releases Mrs. Shum. There are more sounds of flesh striking flesh.

Without Jalen to stop her, Mrs. Shum gathers herself into a crouching position, shifts the tire iron in her hands, and then rises to her feet. In the beam of moonlight, her hair hangs wild and loose to her shoulders. As she stands over me, she seems gigantic, stretched like a macabre shadow. I wiggle feebly away from her, my knees scraping the stone ground with every step. She follows me with the unhurried steps of someone who knows that escape is impossible.

I know a moment of hope when Dr. Shum cries out in pain. Maybe Jalen will get away. At least one of us will live.

"Jalen," Mrs. Shum says sharply. "Let Dr. Shum go before I bash in your girlfriend's head."

"Jalen," I yell, "don't! She's going to do it anyway!"

"It's over, Paige," Mrs. Shum says gently. "Just hold still for a moment. I won't miss again. I promise."

"No," Jalen yells.

I manage to move another few inches. The rock slices my skin. More blood—more evidence, I think, for the police. I feel Mrs. Shum's shadow draw closer and look around in the darkness for Jalen, for one last look.

Suddenly Dr. Shum says, "Good God."

I look around. Framed in the moonlight, a man stands in the entranceway. He's naked except for a white loin cloth wrapped around his gaunt frame. His hair is long, very straight and silver. Where his eyes should be are two black holes. He lifts his arms and says something in Navajo. He clicks on a flashlight, illuminating the room, and then opens his mouth and gives a primitive, bird-like screech.

Distracted, Mrs. Shum stares at the figure. "What the…"

She doesn't have time to finish. The *si'papu* is right behind her. I kick her as hard as I can.

She loses her balance and steps backward, tripping as her foot rolls on the broken wine bottle. She almost catches herself, but then takes one more step backward. For half a second, I see her expression change, and then she's gone, falling through the floors. I hear a muffled *thump* as she hits the ground, and then there's silence.

Dr. Shum releases Jalen and runs to the edge of the passageway. "Julia!" he shouts. "Julia!"

The man in the doorway steps forward as Jalen climbs to his feet. In the light, I recognize Jalen's uncle. He and Jalen rush over to Dr. Shum, who brushes off their grip on him. "Let go of me!" he shouts "I have to go to her! We have to help her!"

"Ray…" Mrs. Shum's voice floats out of the darkness below. "Help me."

"I'm coming," Dr. Shum says. He turns to Jalen. "Please," he says. "She's hurt. She could be dying."

"Did you help Emily when she begged for her life?"

One of Dr. Shum's eyes is blood red. The rest of his face is swollen and battered. "Julia didn't mean to hit her so hard. And then what was I to do? Emily would have been dead before we could get her off the cliffs. It would have ruined my career! All for what purpose? She was dying. I put her in the most sacred place that anyone could ever be buried in—a *si'papu.*" He glances down the hole again. "Please," he says. "Julia needs help."

The world starts to spin as a new and terrible thought occurs to me. "Emily was alive when you sealed her in the *si'papu?*"

"I told you. There was no hope for her. Now let me get to Julia!"

You're a monster, I start to tell him, but he is suddenly moving farther and farther away from me, traveling down an endless hallway. My words echo in my head, which feels so light it might detach itself and float away. The ache of my arm feels less intense, as if it's something I'm remembering rather than feeling. I'm suddenly so dizzy it's an effort to stand.

"Paige," Jalen says, but any words after that fade into the darkness.

FORTY-THREE

Paige

I open my eyes to white walls and a bank of medical equipment around me. An IV drips into my arm. There's a weird taste in my mouth and a vague memory of bright lights, the sensation of flying down a long corridor, of Jalen's face receding rapidly.

"Jalen." It comes out no louder than a whisper. Where is he? Is he okay?

I look around. My right arm is encased in a cast and hangs from a trapeze over my bed. Next to me, sitting in chairs pushed closely together, are my mother and Stuart. Jalen fills another seat near the foot of my bed. His arm is in a sling, and he's wearing a blue hospital gown. His lip is split, and one eye is swollen shut. It hurts to look at him, but it also feels awesome to know he's alive. *We're* alive.

"Hey," I say to him.

"Hey," he says back.

"Paige." My mother brushes my hair gently off my face. "You're awake. You feeling okay? Thirsty?"

When I nod, she lets me sip water through a straw, but even just a few sips are exhausting.

"You scared us, honey, but you're going to be fine," my mom says. "Your arm is broken and you lost some blood because the bone broke through, but Dr. Evanston operated and says it'll heal even stronger than it was."

With my good arm, I try to touch a very sore spot on my head, but my mother pulls my arm away. "Twelve stitches," she murmurs. "But your hair will cover the scar."

Like I care about that.

She gives me a bright smile, but there are dark circles under her eyes and her chestnut hair has the messy look of someone who hasn't looked in the mirror for a long time.

"What time is it?"

"Two in the afternoon," she says. "You were brought here early this morning. We spent most of the night looking for you." She smiles at Stuart, and a note of pride enters her voice. "Stuart found you. When we went to the Shums' house, the front door was unlocked. I almost had a heart attack when we saw the mess in the studio. We knew something was wrong. Stu called the police and then emergency rooms. Everyone tried to give us the runaround and the twenty-four-hour missing person thing, but Stu didn't let anyone push him around."

"Sometimes it helps to have a lawyer in the family. I know how the system works, Paige." Stuart winks at me. "Glad you're going to be okay."

Someone in the family—but he isn't my family, and tears prick my eyes because it isn't Stuart I want sitting next to my mother beside my bed. "Where's Dad?"

"Still in jail," my mother says. "They're processing his paperwork, but I know he'll get here as soon as he can."

"These things take time," Stuart adds.

My gaze goes back to Jalen's arm, resting in the sling. "You're hurt. How bad is it?"

He shrugs. "Not bad."

I remember the rage on Mrs. Shum's face as she swung the tire iron and know he's seriously downplaying it. "The truth."

"Collarbone's broken. They're screwing it back together later today."

"You both will have the same surgeon. Isn't that funny?" My mother gives a small, uncomfortable laugh, and Stuart reaches over to squeeze her hands. My lips feel dry and cracked, but I know they aren't nearly as bad as Jalen's. Looking at his battered face, I know several things—that he is in pain, that he will not tell anyone that he's in pain, and that he probably sat with me all night.

Fat tears pool in my eyes. How is it that I have turned out to be such a crybaby? But Jalen saved me. Even though we'd argued and broken up, he still looked for me. He climbed up those ruins in the night, he fought with the Shums, and he brought me back from the dead.

My mother lifts the cup of water to my lips, but I push it away. It's not what I need. "Mom, could you give me and Jalen a little time alone?"

Her forehead wrinkles. "You really need to rest. The police want to talk to you as well." Her gaze turns to Jalen. "You, too, Jalen. You should go back to pre-op and get ready for your surgery. Besides, if that nurse finds you here again…"

Stuart rises to his feet. "Come on, honey. Let's get a quick bite." He turns to me. His eyes are deep-set, hazel-colored, and shrewd, but looking deeper I see a warmth there I never noticed before. He winks at me, but it isn't as annoying as before.

"Stuart, she just woke up…"

"And you need to eat something," he says gently. "Fifteen minutes isn't that long."

My mother groans and rolls her eyes, but doesn't pull away when Stuart takes her hand. He smiles at her, and some of the lines in her face relax. The two of them fit together in a way that my mother hasn't fit with my father in a long time. It still hurts a little to see this, but there's no denying that she looks happier than she has in forever.

As soon as they're gone, Jalen moves to a chair by the side of the bed. He looks a little uncertain, as if he's afraid I'll break into a million pieces if he touches me. The funny thing is that I'm a little afraid to touch him, too.

"I'm so, so sorry, Jalen. I almost got you killed." The enormity of what almost happened washes through me. Hot tears fill my eyes, blurring my vision. I blink them back, trying to swallow the rapidly growing lump in my throat because there's so much I need to say to him. "I never should have said those things about your uncle or blamed you for telling the police or…"

"Shhh." He leans closer to me. "The important thing is you're okay."

"You could have died because of me."

He shakes his head. "You almost died because I didn't answer your phone call. Remember my uncle's prophesy? He said you would come to me for help, and I wouldn't give it to you. And I would watch you die."

Remembering that moment when the Shums sealed off my air sends a rush of panic through me. The doctor said that if Jalen had taken any longer, I would be dead or have irreversible brain damage. In his words, I am a very lucky girl. "But you did help me, and I didn't die. You saved me." Although nothing in his face changes, I sense the words mean something to him. "Thank you."

He shakes his head slowly. "You saved me."

We look up at each other for a long time. Even battered and bruised, his face is beautiful to me, and I want to tell him that I love him, but I don't want him to think I love him because he saved me. It's because of who he is and how I feel when I'm with him.

He reaches for my good hand, and our fingers twine together. I never want to let go of him.

"Your uncle saved us both. When he turned on the flashlight, I saw how close Mrs. Shum was to the opening of the *si'papu*." My stomach suddenly knots as I remember kicking out, Mrs. Shum stumbling backward and disappearing down the hole. "Is she alive?"

"Yes. But her back is broken. She's paralyzed."

I take it in, waiting to see if I feel guilty or pleased. Mostly I'm relieved that she isn't going to hurt anyone again. "And Emily? Did they find her?"

His features don't move, but I read the sadness in his eyes. "Yes."

I know the answer, but have to hear it anyway. "Dead?"

He nods, and a wave of sorrow passes through me. Even though I knew it was a long shot, I still hoped she'd hung on, that we'd find her alive. "If only we had found her sooner…"

He looks down at me so tenderly that I feel those weak tears prick the corners of my eyes again. "Don't blame yourself. The Shums would have gotten away with it if it weren't for you."

"For us," I tell him. "And your uncle."

"And my uncle," he agrees.

Suddenly the door to my room opens, and a tall nurse with short, spiked black hair walks into my room. She shakes her head when she sees Jalen. "Again? They're looking for you in the pre-op waiting room." Her gaze goes to the machines monitoring my vitals, and she gives a small nod. "How's your pain level?"

"It's okay."

"You want ice chips? A Popsicle?" She frowns at Jalen as if he's in the way, which he totally isn't. "What time is your surgery?"

"Four o'clock," he says.

I shake my head and exchange smiles with Jalen as the nurse adjusts my IV bag and then pulls out a handheld device and begins typing.

Jalen kisses my forehead and stands. I know he needs to go, but I still have so many questions. How did he know to come to the ruins? How did his uncle show up at just the right time? I remember Dr. Shum begging us to let him climb down into the lower chamber to be with his wife, but after that everything is blurry.

"Wait," I call out as Jalen turns to leave. "There's just one more thing I need to know."

He pauses. Even with one eye swollen shut, when he looks at me it feels like we see each other in a way that connects us, only us.

"How did I get off the cliffs?"

"I carried you down."

Beside me, the nurse stops inputting information into her computer.

"You carried me down? But your collarbone's broken."

He shrugs.

"Those ladders… How did you hold me?"

"Very carefully," he says so seriously I know he's joking.

It had to hurt. Really hurt.

Closing my eyes, I think about Jalen carrying me down the cliffs. I wish I could remember him holding me, but I don't. I wonder if his uncle tried to talk him out of it, if he said it was too risky. But then I smile, picturing how Jalen would simply fold his arms and give him that stony look—or ignore him completely.

Jalen has got to be the most stubborn person I know.

It used to drive me crazy, but now I kind of love it.

FORTY-FOUR

Paige

The next few days pass in a blur. My father is released from jail. Jalen
and I are discharged from the hospital. I go to stay with my mother and
Stuart at the Marriott near the airport. My mother and I share a room;
Stuart gets his own. I can tell they miss being together, but they're trying
to make things easier for me. I'm grateful, especially when the nightmares wake me up and my mom is there. She doesn't seem to mind
watching old movies in the middle of the night or sleeping with the
light on. I know eventually we're going to have to talk about what
happened between her and Stuart before the divorce, but I'm not ready.
Maybe I'll never be. The truth is that she's here and she loves me. For
now, that's enough.

Jalen visits me every day. My mother leaves us alone, and we spend
hours watching movies or playing board games while I'm hooked up to
the bone stimulator. We talk about everything. He tells me about his
uncle—a powerful healer, and also an alcoholic. I remember what Jalen
told me about medicine men, how the skills are passed down from one
generation to another.

"Your uncle is going to teach you to be a healer, isn't he?"

Jalen nods. I tell him I'm glad but don't ask him questions he can't
answer.

In return, I tell him about my mother's affair, how it seeped like a
poison into our house.

The stories we tell each other are ones we have never told anyone
else and probably will never repeat. But as the daughter of an archeologist, I understand the power of stories like these—how they lay bare the
bones of your family and expose the very things we've been taught

should stay hidden. How the truths in them can set the course of your life. You can either learn from the past or risk the same consequences. That is the gift of history.

The Lintons hold a funeral for Emily on the fifth day after I'm released from the hospital. The service is held in a small, nondenominational church that looks more like an auditorium than anything else. But it's bright and open with a full wall of windows.

Dr. Linton asked me to share a little bit about the friendship Emily and I had growing up—in other words, to talk about the happier times. Although Stuart objected (he honestly used that word) on the grounds that it would be too stressful for me, I overruled him.

My legs shake as I walk to the podium and look out at a pretty good-sized group of people. Jalen sits near the front and gives me an encouraging nod. There's a microphone in front of me, and as I adjust it, it makes a loud, static noise, and I feel even less worthy of talking about Emily. However, I'm here and there's no going back.

"Emily was my best friend." I hear the nervousness in my voice and take a breath. "We were five when we met. I was pretending Birthday Barbie was an Anasazi princess—only I couldn't pronounce Anasazi—I called it 'Anassie.'. Emily had to teach me."

Someone chuckles in the audience, and suddenly it's much easier to tell everyone how fearless she was. How we skinny dipped, tried to make a pet of a tarantula, and snuck out of our tent at night to look for ghosts in the ruins our fathers excavated. In the telling, I remember the best parts of her—the way she made me feel like I was the smartest, most creative person in the world, and the way she loved without holding anything back. Maybe it hadn't turned out the way it should have for her, but she'd followed her heart and that took guts.

As they take away her casket, I know I take part of her with me. That I am stronger and more appreciative of life. Thanks to her, I know who I am and, more importantly, who I want to become. She died, but I get to live. I know she would want me to see this as an opportunity, a second chance that shouldn't be wasted.

That's why, after the funeral, after I hug a weeping Mrs. Linton, I seek out my father and lead him to a quiet spot in the back of the room.

His tanned skin is paler than usual, and I can tell from the way he keeps nervously checking the knot of his tie that the service has been hard on him.

"You did a great job," he says. He lays a gentle hand on my shoulder. "I'm proud of you, Paige."

"Thanks, Dad," I say. Inside my cast, my arm itches like I have a hundred flea bites. I rub it against my dress and feel a very dull ache, but it reminds me there are worse things than broken bones. In the distance I see Jalen, talking to a group of what must be Emily's friends from school. He looks unfamiliar but handsome in a dark suit and tie. He feels my gaze and glances over, a question in his eyes. He has no clue about the conversation I'm about to have with my dad.

I look down at my new sandals, only one of the gifts my mother has been showering me with since she's arrived. The presents are her way of telling me she loves me, which makes what I have to do all the harder.

"I've been thinking, Dad." I take a deep breath. "I don't want to go back to New Jersey. I want to stay in Arizona. With you."

An expression of incredulity passes over his features. His hand goes to his head as if to readjust his cowboy hat, but then he realizes he isn't wearing one and his hand drops. A muscle works in his throat, and for once I think he's speechless.

"I want to stay here," I repeat. "Live with you."

He gives me a small smile and shakes his head. "Your mother needs you. Especially after everything that's happened."

"She has Stuart." I search his eyes, trying to read if this is the real reason he hasn't said yes. "I like it here. I like the desert, working around the old pit houses." I feel the color burning in my cheeks. "I feel like I belong here."

His expression seems to soften. "You don't know how much that means to me to hear you say that." He pauses, but I can't tell what he's thinking. "But your mom is a good parent—she loves you, Paige. It'll hurt her if you choose to stay here."

This is true, but not enough. Not anymore. My arm itches so badly I want to rip the cast off. "I'm seventeen, Dad. In six months, I'll get to decide where I live, but please don't make me wait that long. This isn't about me being angry at either of you. This is about me. What I want— what I need."

His eyes study my face, and a new light seems to burn in them. "You sure? You know I can't cook, and half the time I'm in my own world… What about your friends in New Jersey? Prom and all that."

I shrug. "I don't care about proms. New Jersey isn't right for me anymore—I think you get that. I want to help you finish restoring the ruins." I give him my best smile. "Will you let me live with you?"

"I'll have to talk to your mother," he says, but then his face softens. "But if it's up to me, it's a yes." He smiles, opens his arms, and pulls me into a hug.

It takes my parents a full day to work out a new plan for me. Even then, it's full of disclaimers—the judge has to amend the custody arrangement, I have to do well in school, I have to spend Christmas and half the summer with my mother. I think I would agree to just about anything, though, to be able to stay.

I can't wait to tell Jalen, and when he calls to invite me to have dinner with his family, I have to bite my tongue to keep from blurting it out.

He picks me up in that battered old pickup that idles like we're sitting on an earthquake. It smells of men and tools and summer, and the wind whooshes in my face as we drive down the road, ending any hope I have of arriving at his parents' house with neat, smooth hair. But it doesn't matter. I'm sitting on top of a secret so exciting I feel like I'm going to explode, and yet it's so big I don't know how to tell him.

"How are you doing?" Jalen asks as we exit my father's neighborhood and head for the highway. It's still bright, but the sun is beginning to lose the worst of the heat and the air feels like satin. I shoot him a sideways look. Today he's wearing a pair of khaki-colored shorts and a black Jimmy Eat World T-shirt.

"A little nervous," I admit. "Can we stop somewhere? I want to buy some flowers for your mother."

Jalen shoots me a sideways look. "You don't need to bring her flowers. And you don't need to worry. Everyone is going to love you."

I pick at the nubs of the worn fabric seat. "Thanks, but right now I'm the girl who almost got their son killed. I'd kind of like to change their impression of me."

"You're the girl who stopped a monster," Jalen says. "That's how they think of you."

I try to read his profile to see if he's just saying that to try to make me feel better or if he really means it. Even he doesn't, I'm glad he said it. "All the same, I'd like to bring your mom some flowers."

He smiles. "Okay."

We drive a few miles and then take an exit that turns us in the direction of the mountains. We follow a two-lane road that splits farmland on either side of us. Jalen drives a little farther, and the road narrows, becomes more rutted, and he slows down. Just as I'm about to ask where he's going, he pulls the truck to the side of the road and turns off the engine.

For a long moment, we stare out the window at clusters of orange wildflowers growing along the fence line, stretching as far as my eye can see. They look a little like marigolds, but more delicate, which seems strange considering they have to be a lot more hardy to bloom in such dry soil.

"Beautiful," Jalen says, and his eyes say that I am, too.

We turn and look at each other for a long moment. He is also beautiful, with his long dark hair framing his oval face, his skin smooth and dark, his lips so perfectly sculpted that all I think about is how much I want to kiss him.

We lean toward each other, but between the truck's gears, my broken arm, and his broken collarbone, we have to turn and shift and strain. We both laugh at the failed attempts to reach each other, how careful we have to be to line our bodies up without hurting each other. But then, his face is close to mine and his warm mouth closes over my own. We're kissing, and even though I can't hold him the way I want to, can't be as close as my body wants to be, it is amazing. I close my eyes. I belong to him and he belongs to me in a way that we can never belong to anyone else.

We pull apart for a few seconds and then start kissing again. I don't think it's ever going to be enough—I think I could kiss him forever. But then we pull back, catching our breath and grinning at each other. I love him, and I think he loves me.

"I'm staying," I say, holding his gaze. "I'm not going back to New Jersey. I'm going to live with my dad."

"Are you serious?" Jalen grabs me before I even have time to answer and hugs me so hard that I think he may have re-fractured his collarbone. "This is fantastic. Are you sure? When did you find out?"

"Today, right before you picked me up." His grin tells me he's happy, but I need to hear him say it anyway. "I don't want you to feel pressure or anything about us. If it works out with us, that's great. But if it doesn't..." I give him a small shrug.

"It's going to work out." His eyes tell me he's serious, and something inside me relaxes. We're going to be together; we're *meant* to be together. It feels scary, like I'm glimpsing something I shouldn't, but it also feels exciting and right. I know if Emily were alive, she'd be cheering me on, telling me to go for it.

They're all waiting for me when Jalen and I step through the front door to his house. I smell something delicious and glimpse an oak dining room table already set for dinner, and then a dark-haired woman with Jalen's brown eyes and smile steps forward to greet me.

She accepts the flowers as if nothing I could give her could please her more and then takes my arm, leading me into a spacious family room decorated with brown leather couches, Western artwork, and shelves of family pictures.

"Everyone," she says, "this is Paige." She smiles at a boy seated on the couch with a gaming controller in his hands. "Turn that off, Harold," she says, "and say hello to Paige."

Harold is a younger-looking version of Jalen. They have the same strong cheekbones and deep-set dark eyes, but Harold is finer-boned and the expression in his eyes is more mischievous, where Jalen's is almost always serious. "Do you want to play *Ambush IV* with me?"

"Jalen warned me not to," I admit and he laughs.

"You already know John," Jalen's mother continues, gesturing to her husband, who welcomes me with a smile.

"And my brother-in-law, Billy Yazzi."

It's the first time I've seen him since the moment he appeared framed by the moonlight in the doorway to the ruins, and I feel my palms go damp at the memory. That night he was a warrior, but right now he looks like a kindly, middle-aged man dressed in Wrangler jeans and a red button-down shirt. He's holding a plain brown bag in his lap, and as I greet him, he says, "I have something for you."

I feel myself blush with pleasure and then cross the room. Pushing aside some white tissue paper, I pull out an intricately carved wooden doll—a girl, painted yellow, with corn, seeds, and other symbols running the length of her body. I recognize her immediately—the yellow corn maiden. It reminds me of Emily—not how she died, but as she lived, holding nothing back, running fearlessly, gracefully through the corn field.

ACKNOWLEDGMENTS

This idea for this story came from a family vacation to Arizona. Among our many adventures, we visited the cliffside ruins of ancient Native Americans. The high-rise mansions were beautiful and haunting and the perfect place to set a story. It took me many drafts, and I'd like to thank my critique group–Joy Preble, Suzanne Bazemore, Bob Lamb and Dede Fox–for reading all of them. All their feedback, support, and friendship helped make the journey fun. I'd also like to thank Senior Editor Vikki Ciaffone for being the kind of editor every writer dreams about having. Thank you, Vikki, for your great editing job and for your emails that always made me smile and get excited all over again about the story. You are brilliant and kind! I'd also like to thank all the creative, talented, and totally amazing people at Spencer Hill Press who have worked on this book. Finally, I'd like to express my appreciation to Joyce Carol Oates for allowing me to use a passage from her absolutely riveting book, The Corn Maiden.

ABOUT THE AUTHOR

Kim O'Brien grew up in Bronxville, New York, in a very old Victorian house. Nightly, her mother's stories about the ghost who lived in their attic both terrified her and inspired in her a deep love of books and storytelling. She holds a bachelor's degree in psychology from Emory University, and a Master's in Fine Arts in Writing from Sarah Lawrence College. She worked for many years as a writer, editor, and speechwriter for IBM. Currently she is an adjunct professor at Lone Star College. She lives in The Woodlands, Texas, with her husband, two daughters, and four-legged friend Daisy. Kim loves to hear from readers and can be reached through her website: www.kimobrienbooks.com; Twitter: @kimobri; or her Facebook author's page.

31901056315759

CPSIA information can be obtained at www.ICGtesting.com
Printed in the USA
LVOW01s1357250315

431807LV00001B/1/P

9 781633 920026